# SENTENCED TO DEATH

# SENTENCED TO DEATH

## Betty Hechtman

**SEVERN HOUSE**

First world edition published in Great Britain and the USA in 2023
by Severn House, an imprint of Canongate Books Ltd,
14 High Street, Edinburgh EH1 1TE.

Trade paperback edition first published in Great Britain and the USA in 2023
by Severn House, an imprint of Canongate Books Ltd.

severnhouse.com

*British Library Cataloguing-in-Publication Data*
A CIP catalogue record for this title is available from the British Library.

ISBN-13: 978-0-7278-2300-7 (cased)
ISBN-13: 978-1-4483-0823-1 (trade paper)
ISBN-13: 978-1-4483-0822-4 (e-book)

*All Severn House titles are printed on acid-free paper.*

MIX
Paper from
responsible sources
FSC
www.fsc.org   FSC® C013056

Typeset by Palimpsest Book Production Ltd.,
Falkirk, Stirlingshire, Scotland.
Printed and bound in Great Britain by
TJ Books, Padstow, Cornwall.

# ONE

T hinking back, I'd expected to hear about petunias and peonies when Tizzy asked me to go with her to a meeting about a garden tour. Certainly not that it would lead to a gig that would once again put me in the middle of a death investigation. Now I wondered, if I'd known what would happen, would I have done anything differently? After just a momentary pause, I knew the answer was no.

It was a Monday evening, and I'd joined Tizzy Baxter for her evening ritual of a glass of sherry at the end of her work day. Even a few drops of anything alcoholic gave me an unpleasant feeling, so I stuck to sparkling water with a twist of lemon. We toasted the end of another day, and she mentioned having to go to a meeting.

'Come with me,' Tizzy said. 'They're a friendly group, and it's better than going home and hovering over your computer.'

I had to agree with her about that. I'd managed to fix a glaring hole in the plot of the second Derek Streeter book, and I was close to the end . . . again. But it seemed my fingers still froze when I sat down at the keyboard. The first book had been a nice success, and I worried the second one would fall flat. If I never finished it, I would never have to know. It was always a trauma when I worked on my own writing. Luckily, my fingers were a lot more active when it came to the writing I did for others. As a writer for hire, I could find the right words for any situation. I wrote whatever anybody needed, from copy for websites to celebrations of life for funerals. Even with all the emails and texts, there was still a need for love letters, which it seemed people couldn't write for themselves. I always said I would write anything, as long as it was legal.

Tizzy had started out as just a member of the writing group that met once a week in my dining room. Then we'd become friends and more. Not only had she helped me with some investigations I'd become involved with, but she was always looking for ways to help me get work as a writer for hire. Unlike me, she was a social butterfly and had lots of contacts in the neighborhood. Did I really say that? Clearly a cliché, and it had come to mind so easily. But wasn't that the point of clichés?

'Which organization is this?' I asked. Tizzy seemed to be part of every committee and group in our neighborhood on the South Side of Chicago.

'This one is called Friends of Hyde Park, and I'm just a fringe member, but I think there might be something that interests you.'

When she put it like that, how could I refuse? We finished our drinks and got ready to go. 'I'll tell Theo we're leaving,' she said.

Her husband, Theo, usually joined her for the evening sherry, though he had moved on to something a little stronger and had a martini. He'd recently joined the writing group, which I'd decided to call a workshop instead of a class, and he was in his study, working on his pages for the following night.

The sky still had some hints of pink from the sunset as we walked the few blocks. It was May, and the weather was still arguing with itself about the season. One day would have sultry heat, then the wind would change and the temperature would drop twenty degrees with an icy feel to the breeze. The barometric pressure went up and down abruptly. All those changes played havoc with people who had health issues. For the moment, though, the weather seemed to be taking a break from all the changes, and it was calm with a touch of cool.

Being so close to the campus of the University of Chicago meant there was always foot traffic and usually some student joggers. 'The meeting is in the ladies' parlor of the Unitarian Church,' Tizzy said and then chuckled. 'That's what I've always known it as, though I think the actual name is something else now. It would probably be considered sexist to call it a ladies' something.'

The church took up a whole corner with its imposing structure. The Perpendicular Gothic style of it fitted right into the Victorian Gothic of the university structures. It made for a lot of gray stone buildings heavy with decorative touches. Even though Unitarians were accepting of all beliefs, it looked very much like a traditional Christian church.

We followed the sound of voices and went into a meeting room that seemed steeped in a long-gone time. There were leaded glass windows, and the walls were paneled in dark wood. I was eyeing the moss-green carpet; being a writer made me notice details like that. I was always thinking about how I would describe something. It made life a lot more interesting.

A dozen seats were set up facing away from the window, and about the same number of people were wandering through them, finding a place to sit. I recognized some of the people, at least by appearance. Because of the university, a lot of people thought Hyde Park was like a small town within the city where people knew each other and sometimes too much of other people's business. Tizzy was busy introducing me to everyone as she led me to a pair of chairs.

I was eyeing the refreshment table off to the side. There were usually snacks with the sherry, but it turned out that those were all Theo's doing. Since he hadn't joined us, it had just been sherry for her and the lemon-flavored sparkling water for me. I'd been expecting to go home to dinner, and there was a definite gnawing in my stomach. I was considering checking out the table, hoping to nab something to quiet my hunger. But a woman went to the front and urged everyone to sit down. Some of them had little plates with piles of something covered in corn meal that smelled of cumin.

'That's Serena Lawrence,' Tizzy whispered. 'She's the president.'

I nodded with recognition as I had seen her around the neighborhood. I only hoped I would age as gracefully as the tall, slender woman. She had the advantage of a certain presence about her that captured my attention, and I forgot about the refreshment table.

'For any of you who missed it, we have decided to have a house and garden tour this year. It's all thanks to the efforts of our new member, Nicole Wentworth, who single-handedly has put together the plan.' She started to say something else, but instead introduced Nicole and said she would explain it all.

Nicole stood up and went to the front. She was much younger

than Serena – I guessed she wasn't even thirty – but she seemed confident and in charge as she took over. Her walnut-brown hair and clothes were all in perfect order, and she didn't have the end-of-the-day rumpled look the rest of us seemed to have.

'I am so excited that you've agreed to add some houses to the garden tour,' she said. 'I have a fondness for this neighborhood, having lived here for a while when I was a kid. I really longed to see the inside of houses I knew.' She seemed very comfortable talking in front of a group and being in charge. 'I wanted to let you all know where we're at. I have the houses lined up. We'll include the Malins' townhouse, the Fellowses' house, R.L. Lincoln's place, the distinctive structure that belongs to our sponsors, Roman and Ruth Scrivner, and the house of our local literary lion, Landon Donte. I talked it over with the other members, and we decided to put together a booklet with information about each house and something about the inhabitants. There will be photographs of the interior as well.'

Tizzy raised her hand and then stood up, sending a ripple through her yellow-and-blue kimono top. 'If you need someone to craft the copy, I have someone for you.' She pointed at me, and I felt an embarrassed flush as everyone turned to stare. 'Stand up,' my friend said, waving her hands.

I followed her orders, trying to will myself to stay calm and talk slowly. The two parts of my work I found hard to deal with were moments like this when I had to pitch my talents and when it came to discussing money. This was even more uncomfortable because I was interrupting. The only choice seemed to be to seize the moment. 'Of course, I'd be glad to be considered,' I said, before bringing up that I was local and reeling off some of my experience. I hesitated to mention the love letters since I had no intention of being specific about the content or who they'd been written for. I saw people nod and make acknowledging sounds when I listed several menu items at LaPorte's that I'd written descriptions of and an artist memoir I was quite proud of.

'We'll have to talk,' Nicole said, taking back control of the floor. Tizzy and I sat down, and I felt another flush of embarrassment. Nicole returned to talking about the project as a whole. 'We wouldn't be able to do this without Roman and Ruth Scrivner. Not only have they offered up their house as part of the tour, but they have donated the money to put it all together. In gratitude, we've decided to say the tour is being presented by Roman and Ruth Scrivner.'

Serena was standing on the sidelines, and I noticed her flinch when Nicole said the part about the benefactors. 'We've always listed our group as the presenter of the tour,' the president said. Before she could add anything else, Nicole took over.

'Considering how much they are doing for the tour, I decided they should have the sole listing as sponsors.' She waved for them to stand up. Roman was out of his chair and on the way to the front of the small group before Nicole had finished her gesture. He seemed to be almost dragging his wife with him.

He was a compact man with thick dark hair that showed a few strands of gray. It was hard to see his features behind the dark-rimmed glasses, other than that he had a very prominent nose. He was clearly the personality of the pair. He smiled at the group and went on about how proud he was to be part of this historic tour. 'It is an honor to be able to share our unique house, the only residence designed by Helmut Peterman. I'm sure you all recognize the name as the designer of the Riverfront Tower, among other buildings.' His gaze moved over the whole group. 'We are committed to being regarded as an important part of this community.'

I was listening and at the same time trying to work out why he looked so familiar. His wife stood next to him with a blank expression that was hard to read. Her glance kept going to the refreshment table, and I wondered if she'd missed dinner, too. They seemed to be an example of how opposites attract, in appearance at least. She was the absolute reverse of him. There was a sturdiness about his build, and there was something a little fragile about her slender frame. He had dark hair, and hers was a flaxen blond that I was sure was natural.

There was a smattering of applause as he finished and they went back to their seats.

'Thank you, again,' Nicole said to the couple. She turned her attention back to the group. 'Once we have all the material for the booklet, we're going to bring everybody together for a progressive dinner.' In case anyone didn't know what that was, she explained they would go from house to house having a

different course at each one. The Scrivners were arranging for
the catering. There was another smattering of applause that felt
automatic.

Serena took over the meeting after that and started talking
about some other business the group had to discuss. I tuned it
out as I thought of the event Nicole had talked about. Tizzy was
right to have brought me, and even though it was embarrassing,
I was glad she'd offered up my services. I was fascinated by
the different styles of the neighborhood houses, and the idea of
seeing the interiors and writing about them sounded like just
the kind of project I would enjoy. And I was curious about the
people who lived in them. Almost all the houses in the area
were old, some older than others. I thought I was perfect for
the job, but I worried that my outburst might have soured Nicole
on hiring me.

I was still lost in thought when Tizzy nudged me, and I realized the meeting had ended and everyone was heading for the
refreshment table.

Tizzy went to work the room, and I was headed back to the
refreshment table. It seemed everyone else had the same idea,
and I hung back waiting for a clear space. A man and woman
stopped next to me, and not that I meant to eavesdrop, but I
couldn't help but overhear their conversation.

'So, Landon Donte's house is on the tour. Literary lion,' the
man said, letting out a dismissive grunt. 'Everybody knows that
he bases his characters on neighborhood people. He thinks people
should be honored if they recognize themselves in his books. I
heard that some people haven't been so pleased to have dark
things about them revealed, even if he supposedly disguises their
identity. Someone confronted him about it. I heard that he keeps
a gun in his desk drawer just in case he has to defend himself.
Rumor has it that the book he's working on now is going to
ruffle feathers even more. He's even talking it up, saying this
time there are no holds barred.'

I wondered if the man realized that he had just used two
clichés. It was none of my business really, and I suppose that
speaking in clichés was different from writing them anyway. He
certainly didn't make Landon Donte sound like a nice guy. I
knew about him, but his style of writing wasn't my choice for

reading. Everything was about neurotic, unhappy people. There was enough of that in real life, and when it came to reading, I preferred something happier. It looked as if there was never going to be an opening at the refreshment table, so I decided to be like Tizzy and work the room. I introduced myself to Serena Lawrence and tried to make small talk about the house tour. She seemed most interested in talking about Landon Donte's place. 'We go way back,' she said. She had a dreamy look as she said it, and I gathered she felt differently about the writer from the man I'd overheard. As soon as I started to express my interest in working on the project, she suggested I talk to Nicole.

I excused myself and found Nicole as she was pouring herself a cup of coffee. 'I'm sorry for bursting in,' I said, 'but I'd really like to be considered for the project. I'd be happy to show you samples of my work, and you can check out my website.'

'It sounds like you are qualified, but we are still putting everything together. I just set the appointments to meet with the homeowners. The plan is that the photographer will be accompanied by me, Ruth, and Serena – and the writer if we hire one,' she said.

'That's quite an entourage. Do you really need that many people?'

She gave me a look that made me wish I hadn't said anything. 'Not that I have to explain,' she began with an edge to her voice, 'but I have to be there since I'm the one who arranged the whole thing, and it's important to make sure the interviews are handled properly and everything is smooth. Serena feels she's the representative of the organization. Roman asked that his wife be included so she feels part of the event.'

'I see,' I said, feeling I had to acknowledge what she'd said. Just a guess, but I had the feeling that she wasn't happy about having such a crew. I was curious about who she was, but I figured that if I got the job, I'd have plenty of time to find out. And if I didn't get the job, would I even care?

Tizzy had already made up a little plate for me and handed it to me when Nicole moved on to talk with someone else.

I was anxious to talk to Tizzy about the job and the group, but I didn't want to be overheard, so we made small talk while we snacked on the tidbits of food.

As we got ready to leave, I noticed that Ruth and Roman were off in a corner. Ruth had the same impassive expression she'd had when they were introduced. It was a mere guess on my part, but she looked medicated. He was helping her with her leather tote bag and appeared upset. I had left my jacket near where they were talking, and as I went to grab it, I couldn't help but eavesdrop. He was keeping his voice low, but I heard him say, 'I thought you had it under control.' He had something in his hand and put it back on the refreshment table. I tried to see what it was, but Tizzy came by, slipped her arm through mine, and pulled me to the door. I took a last glimpse back, but Roman was blocking my view.

Maybe it was because I'd written a mystery and saw plots in everything, but something with that couple was not quite right.

# TWO

'So that's why you talked me into coming,' I said as we got out to the street. Tizzy nodded.

'What's the saying, "the early bird gets the worm"?' she said, laughing, knowing that I would react to the worn-out phrase. I kept it to an eye roll, and she continued. 'I thought it would be something you'd like and . . .'

'Yes, I need the work,' I said. 'I hope I didn't blow it by seeming too eager,' I said. 'It wasn't very professional to jump up that way. You'd better give me the information on who is who.'

'I'm sure it will be fine,' Tizzy said. We were getting close to the block of 57th that had some stores and restaurants. 'The snacks were good, but just that – snacks. Want to stop for a pizza?' she asked as we neared the Mezze.

I was hungry and wanted to talk over what had just happened. As soon as I nodded, she asked if I minded if Theo joined us. 'He hates to be left out,' she said with a smile.

She obviously didn't expect me to say no, because she was already texting him as I agreed. We hung outside the restaurant until he came down the street and joined us.

'I'm surprised you didn't recognize Roman Scrivner,' Tizzy said.

'He looked very familiar, but I couldn't figure from where,' I said.

'Here's a clue,' she said and started to sing a jingle. '*Been in a crash, we're here for you. Accident at work, we're here for you . . .*' She looked at me and I picked where she had stopped.

'*Don't go Roaming, just call Roman,*' I sang before adding the phone number. I'd heard it so many times on TV that it was drilled into my mind.

'*Those other guys say they'll fight, but we say we'll win,*' we sang together.

Theo was looking at us as if we were nuts and then he nodded with understanding. 'The lawyer that advertises on television all the time. He's in that group?'

Tizzy nodded, and Theo continued. 'No wonder he's throwing money around, backing neighborhood events. He's trying to get himself a better image than a schlockmeister attorney with a cheesy catchphrase.'

'He doesn't wear the glasses in the commercial,' I said. 'That's why I didn't realize who he was,' I said. 'And don't forget how he likes to show off his satisfied clients.'

'Yes,' Tizzy said. 'Remember the one that has some guy who says he was so happy with the settlement Roman got for him that he made him best man at his wedding.' We all chuckled at the memory.

'You know who his wife is,' Tizzy said as sort of a rhetorical question.

'Other than that her name is Ruth, and she seems a little withdrawn, aloof, superior, or something else?' I said with a shrug.

'Her maiden name is Altschuler as in the Altschuler Brewery,' Tizzy said. 'I know you're not a drinker, but you must be aware that they're known as Chicago's beer lovers' favorite.'

'I have guests who drink beer,' I said. 'So, yes, I do know about Altschuler's.'

'I bet her family bankrolled his legal career,' Theo said. 'Those commercials cost a bundle. They are probably self-funding now, but it had to take deep pockets when he was starting out. He comes across as such a white knight in those ads. I wonder what the truth is.' Theo shrugged. 'If there is anything, he's done a good job of keeping those skeletons in his closet.' Theo's eyes twinkled behind his horn-rimmed glasses. 'You know me, I'm curious about everything.'

He glanced around at the brick-walled interior and tables spaced around the large area. 'You know why they call this place the Mezze?' he said. Tizzy was already rolling her eyes at her husband.

'No,' Tizzy said with an indulgent smile. 'Why don't you tell us?'

There was more twinkling of his eyes. Theo liked it even better when he was able to share his endless knowledge. 'Mezze actually means Mediterranean appetizers with a drink, which is funny since this place is known for its pizzas and burgers on black bread.' He chuckled. 'It started out as a coffee house with a few Middle Eastern dishes, and then the food offerings changed, but the name stuck.'

'I'm glad they have pizza,' I said. We decided on a large thick-crust pie with fresh tomatoes and mushrooms. Once we'd ordered, Theo went off talking about pizza.

I tried to be patient while he did a few minutes on the myth that thick-crust pizza was Chicago-style. I really wanted to see what Tizzy knew about the people I'd just met on the chance that they did hire me. 'Real Chicago pizza is called tavern pizza and is thin crust and cut into little square pieces. It was served alongside a mug of beer to working people, though it was probably just men.'

Theo sparked on the idea of beer and waved to the server. I took the opportunity to prime Tizzy for more information. 'Do you know how they chose the houses for the tour?'

'I thought they might ask to include our house,' she said. She brought up that it had been built in the late 1880s and was what she called a conjoined twin house. The two houses were mirror images of each other and shared one party wall. 'But no one asked. Nicole took care of getting the houses. There is the vintage townhouse that belongs to the Malins. She's a psychologist, and he's some kind of engineer. The Fellowses' house is a huge Victorian. He's a popular professor of sociology at the university and she . . .' Tizzy's voice faltered and she shrugged. 'I'm not sure what she does.'

The pizza came, and the server dished up a slice for each of us. Theo's beer arrived. He'd made sure to specify Altschuler's. We were occupied with our food and drink for a moment, and then Tizzy continued.

'I thought she might have gone after some of the grand houses on Woodlawn. They have ballrooms on the top floor,' Tizzy said. 'But she chose those *not conjoined* twin houses. Or at least they were twin houses when they were built. One of them belongs to R.L. Lincoln.' She paused to see if I knew who he was.

'He lives around here?' I said, surprised. He was a popular romance novelist and turned out books with amazing speed. I was sure he never sat over his keyboard trying to will the words to come.

'The other one belongs to Landon Donte,' she said.

'Ah, the neighborhood literary lion,' Theo said. 'I have used his books in my classes. I didn't realize the two authors were neighbors. I wonder if they get along. R.L. Lincoln sells a lot more books, but Landon Donte has the pedigree of being an award-winning literary genius.'

'Lastly, the Scrivners' house,' Tizzy said. 'You heard him go on about how outstanding it is. It's not hyperbole either. There isn't another house like it in the neighborhood.'

Hearing about the houses intrigued me and made me want the gig even more. I asked her about Nicole.

'She's one of those people who gets right into the middle of things. It seems like one minute she was being introduced as a new member and the next she was insisting we add houses to the garden tour and volunteering to put it together. And she did, even getting the Scrivners to finance it. I don't know much about her personally, other than that she and her family moved here recently, and her husband is doing some research at the university hospital.'

I mentioned that she'd said something about living in the neighborhood before, and Tizzy shrugged. 'With the university, there are always people coming and going. Maybe she still feels an attachment to the area. She was so determined about adding the houses to the garden tour, it was almost like she had an agenda,' Tizzy said.

As we got up to leave, Theo picked something up off the floor and opened his hand to reveal an item of red. 'Is this yours?' he asked his wife, and she shook her head and laughed.

'Theo, you may know about lots of things, but not about women's hair ties. That's something called a scrunchy, and you need longer hair than mine to use one.'

'It's mine,' I said, taking it. 'It keeps falling out of my pocket.' To demonstrate what Tizzy had said, I smoothed my shoulder-length hair back and collected it in the scrunchy. 'I use it when I want to get my hair out of the way.' I left it at that, without explaining that it was actually one of those black elastic bands that I'd crocheted over. The rows of crochet made it decorative.

I was sure that Theo would be researching the hair tie when they got home.

We parted company when we reached their street and they turned on to it. I hadn't expected to be out so late and noticed the coffee shop on the corner of my street was closing up for the night. The lighted globes on the front porch of my building were like beacons in the darkness.

How many years had I gone up the same stone stairs and into the small tiled vestibule, unlocking the glass security door and trudging up the same three flights of stairs? My whole life. A montage fluttered through my mind as I pictured myself at all different ages following the same path.

There I was, dressed for snow, holding my mother's hand as we climbed the stairs. Me as a teenager pulling up the metal cart full of groceries when it was just me and my father, and I'd taken over food shopping. And then remembering crossing the second-floor landing on a sultry summer night when I was the only resident. My father had died, and I'd inherited the condominium.

It was funny to think of the apartment as a condominium. The concept of ownership seemed more modern than the structure. The building was over a hundred years old and 'condominium' somehow seemed to refer to something more stark and modern than the solid butterscotch-colored brick building. I opened the front door and landed back in the present as I saw my black-and-white cat.

'I should call you a cat-dog,' I said as Rocky came to greet me. He certainly didn't fit the image I'd had of cats being aloof and living a parallel existence to their human companions. He was all about cuddles, came when I called his name, and usually greeted me when I arrived home.

But maybe it had to do with how he'd come to live with me. I thought back to when I'd seen him looking at me as I left the downtown pet shop. Had he actually held out his paw as if to say, *Please take me with you?* Along with my paid writing gigs, I did some freebies for the downtown pet shop to help the shelter find homes for the animals they had for adoption. I wrote up personality pieces that were supposed to tug at the heartstrings. Rocky's story had ended up tugging at mine. He was older and had been dumped by his previous family for some unknown reason. It certainly wasn't because he had any bad habits, unless bonding with his human was a negative.

I'd gone back the next day and brought him home with not one moment of regret. He seemed to feel the same.

I dropped off my jacket and sat down on the black leather couch to collect myself after my outing. Rocky jumped up and settled next to me. Only then did I pull out my smartphone. I had been so caught up in what was going on around me that I had never thought to check it for messages.

There was a text message from hours ago. It was from Ben saying he had something to tell me. There was no reason for me to feel uneasy, but I tensed up anyway.

It was complicated with Ben Monroe. He was in the writers' workshop, which made him my student; he was the brother of my downstairs neighbor, Sara Wright, who was my good friend; and he was . . . I hesitated, trying to think of the right words to describe our relationship. The best I could come up with was that we were each other's plus-one with a little more.

Relationships should be simple. I like you, you like me, done. But it never worked out that way. Even more so when you both had accumulated baggage that made you wary of getting hurt.

In my case, it had been a brief marriage when I was barely twenty. I had believed that happily-ever-after just happened after you said your vows. Not exactly. I hadn't considered that Steve would feel trapped and spend all his time hanging out anywhere but home. The divorce had been simple but left me determined not to get hurt again. I'd had some relationships since, but they had never progressed beyond casual.

Ben was divorced, too. He'd been blindsided when his wife took off. Like me, he wasn't looking to get hurt again. We were taking it slow, molasses-on-a-cold-morning slow. OK, it was almost a cliché. I'd changed *January* to *on a cold morning*. That must count for something.

He seemed ready to move ahead with things, and I was the one dragging my feet. I'd been worried about being a singleton with a cat who obsessed about clichés, but now I was beginning to think it wasn't such a bad way to be. No chance of the big hurt again. And there was the issue of him being a cop. I'd seen first-hand when I'd gone to events with him that they were like a family who understood each other. I would always feel as if I was one step outside.

I texted back asking for details and stared at the screen waiting for an answer, but there was none. I didn't take it as a slight or even a reflection on what he had to say. Ben worked in a suburban police department, and his shifts were all over the place. He could be home asleep or in the midst of a traffic stop for all I knew.

Instead of the day winding down after sherry time with Tizzy, it had revved up with the Friends of the Neighborhood meeting and the possibility of a job. I felt edgy and scattered. I considered watching a romantic comedy and went to look through my DVDs, but I couldn't settle my mind enough to pick one. There was only one solution when I felt like that.

I put on the kettle and popped a chamomile teabag in a mug. As soon as I poured the boiling water into the mug, the flowery fragrance filled the air. I took the mug of steeping tea into the living room and set it on the coffee table, then checked the big wicker sewing basket I'd bought at a yard sale. Instead of sewing supplies, it was stashed with plastic bags holding yarn and crochet hooks. I grabbed one without even checking its contents. Any one would do.

I plucked the teabag out before taking a sip of the drink known to have calming properties and looked through the bag I'd pulled out. There was a ball of pale pink yarn and just a row of chain stitches hanging off the blue metal hook. My mother had taught me how to crochet, and it had been a connection between us. Even now, decades after she was gone, just seeing crochet supplies made me re-experience how it felt to sit with her and have our hooks move almost in unison.

I'd made the usual beanies, scarves, and afghans before settling on making squares. The only thing they had in common was their size. I used a cardboard template to make sure they stayed uniform. I liked that the end was in sight when I began one, and there was no chance of me getting bored with it. They could be as simple as a plain single or double crochet, or have a complicated motif. When I collected enough of the small shapes, I sewed them together into blankets. The very first one I'd made was hanging above where I was sitting.

It had hung in my father's office at the university until . . .

My thoughts trailed off as I didn't want to relive the call I'd received one day and his sudden death. I chose to focus on how proud he'd been of my accomplishment and hung it where he could look at it.

Since I didn't always finish a square in one sitting, I left a note with the pattern along with the yarn, hook, and *work in progress* or *WIP*. There was nothing in this plastic bag, so I went with the most basic plan, which worked almost like a tranquilizer, and decided to do all half-double crochets.

The tea and repetitive movement of the hook began to work their magic, and my mind calmed. Sort of. I kept thinking back to the house tour. And a thought surfaced in my mind. I was going to do something different this time.

# THREE

Izzy came through as usual and provided the contact information for Nicole the next morning. I practiced what I was going to say a few times before I got ready to press in her phone number. It had never been my nature to go after a gig. I might pitch my abilities and show samples to someone who contacted me. But hear about a job and then actively try to get it – no. I could imagine what a mental health professional would say about it. That I feared rejection. Well, who doesn't? But this time I was going to be brave and I hoped I could do a good enough job selling myself that the feared rejection wouldn't happen.

The tour might be about houses, but the job was about people. There was a need to get along with Nicole and convince her that I could deal with the entourage that would accompany the writer, and get along with the homeowners.

I hadn't exactly taken a liking to Nicole. She wasn't particularly friendly, and there was something almost obsessive about how she had managed to push past the old guard of the group and get the houses added to the tradition of just showing off local gardens. She had secured financing and agreed to get people to open up their homes. There had to be some kind of payoff for her. I wondered what it was.

She answered with a curt hello, and I quickly explained who I was. 'I wanted to tell you that I think it was a brilliant idea to add houses to the tour and compliment you on managing to pull it off. You had to inspire the group to make a change from their tradition and you even lined up the resources to do it.'

'Thank you,' she said, sounding surprised. 'You're absolutely right; it was a job getting the group to agree to a change. I think the fact I'd already lined up Landon Donte's house made the difference. The Scrivners were glad to step up and sponsor the whole thing. They were looking to get positive attention from the neighborhood.'

I could read through what she was saying. The Scrivners wanted to be viewed as local philanthropists. Now that I had softened her up, I was ready to do my pitch.

'I just wanted to repeat how much I'd like to work with you on the writing end,' I said in my friendliest voice. I went on about my qualifications. I knew the neighborhood, my father had taught English at the university, and I appreciated the vintage quality of the houses. I ended by repeating what a wonderful idea she had come up with. I hoped I hadn't overdone it with the praise, though people never seemed to get tired of hearing how fantastic their ideas were.

'Actually, I had thought about writing the copy myself,' she said. 'How hard can it be? Just give some facts about the design of the place and a little about who lives there.'

If that was what she was thinking, there wasn't much I could say without putting down her abilities. As if that would help my cause. I attempted to end the call gracefully, but she surprised me.

'But you seem to understand what the tour is about. And it would be good to have someone focus on interviewing the residents so I could just oversee it all. You probably already know a lot about the area.' She paused for a moment. 'We have a sponsor, but that doesn't mean unlimited resources.'

She laid out what she was willing to pay, and I began to think her bit about doing it herself was just part of the negotiation. I said I would write up a proposal, and we arranged to meet to discuss the next steps.

'How about the Coffee Stop?' she said and offered a time.

'The Coffee Stop?' I repeated. 'It's been gone for years. Were you a student at UChicago?'

'Something like that,' she said in a dismissive manner.

I offered the Starbucks on 53rd, and she agreed.

I stared at the cordless phone now lying on my desk. I had done it. Even with my hesitance to go after a job, I had managed to do it and do it rather well, I thought with a certain amount of pride. It was silly, but I gave myself a high five. I'd gotten the job.

While it was fresh in my mind, I went to the computer and came up with a proposal for the job as I understood it. I had some questions about timing and such, but I was sure I could work it out when I saw her.

I had totally lost track of time and what day it was and realized with a start that it was Tuesday. The writing group would be coming over, and I needed to prepare.

Every Tuesday around seven, the group gathered around my dining-room table. They brought in work, and the rule was that someone else would read their pages out loud. That way, the writer got to hear how their work sounded read by an impartial party. They left their work for me to add my comments. The stack from last week was still waiting for me to go through.

I had been on the other side of a writing group and knew what it was like to get comments on your work – how important encouragement was, and how fragile the members were to criticism. But it was my job to help them. It was a fine line to walk, and I did my best.

I had just put the stack of their pages on the dining-room table and cleared off the placemats and fruit bowl when the doorbell went off with its croaking sound announcing the first arrivals.

I knew without looking that it was Tizzy and Theo. He had only recently joined and was super enthusiastic about his work and being in the group. I sent them back down the hall to the dining room while I waited to let the others in.

I had already decided to wait until the whole group was there before saying anything about the gig. There were some jobs I never talked about, such as when I was hired to write love letters. But there seemed to be no need for discretion with writing about neighborhood houses.

Daryl Sullivan and Ed Grimaldi arrived together, merely because they had both come into the building at the same time. They were not a couple. I inwardly laughed at the mere thought of it. Aside from the fact that Ed had a wife in a house down the street, they were light years apart. He had a graying buzz cut and wore track pants, and Daryl was probably twenty-five years younger and dressed in what passed for the latest fashion. Although, honestly, it looked as if she'd just picked the outfit with her eyes closed.

They went directly to the dining room as I closed my front

door. I was going to leave it on the latch for Ben since he always had dinner at his sister's before the group meeting.

I considered waiting by the door to catch him before he joined the others. I still hadn't had a response to my text asking for details of what he wanted to talk about, and I was curious and apprehensive about it at the same time. I was hoping for at least a hint and even looked out into the hall to see if he was on his way up from the second floor. It seemed unfair to keep the group waiting, so I left the door so he could come in and went back to my dining room.

'I guess Ben's late,' I said, taking my seat at the head of the table.

'I was just telling them about the house tour,' Tizzy said. 'Any more news on it?'

'As a matter of fact, there is,' I said, feeling my lips curving into a pleased smile. 'I got the gig. I'm giving a proposal to the woman in charge of it tomorrow.'

Tizzy was thrilled as I'd expected. 'I'm so glad I pitched you for the job.'

'I can probably help if you need to know about the heating systems or the wiring of the houses,' Ed Grimaldi said. He worked in maintenance at the university and knew how things worked. He glanced at the empty chair. 'We're not going to wait for him, are we?' he said in an impatient voice. Ben was the one who always read Ed's pages. They tended to be full of hot sex that was hard to read out loud without embarrassed giggles. Only Ben could manage it by reading it in his cop monotone voice.

'I could read them,' Theo said, holding out his hand to get the stack of papers. He glanced over the first page and began to read. '*Sven was chopping wood, his shirt thrown off to the side. Even on the November day in Juneau, the physical labor made him feel hot all over. And maybe it was thinking of the night he'd spend with Mary-Ellen.*' Theo looked up from his reading. 'Would thinking really make him warm enough to go shirtless? Maybe make it that he took off his jacket or outer shirt, but left on something like a thermal long-sleeved shirt he wore underneath.'

Ed looked at me and glowered. 'Tell him to just read and make comments at the end.' He turned back to Theo. 'Maybe you would need that long-sleeved thermal shirt, but Sven's blood runs hot,' Ed said with a touch of irritation.

It had been like that since Theo had joined the group. He was having a hard time forgetting that his day job was teaching English literature, but here he was one of the group, and I was in charge. I tried to keep it light. 'I know it's hard not to point something out,' I said to Theo. 'But I'm sure you realize that an interruption makes it hard to follow the flow of a scene.'

'Of course,' Theo said. 'It's just hard for me when I see something that seems so wrong.' I'd discovered Theo's shortcomings after a few sessions with the workshop. He seemed dedicated to facts and needed to correct things that were wrong. It wasn't the first time I'd had to smooth things out after something he'd said. We all agreed he should start again and read it straight through. After the relatively tame line about why Sven was shirtless, it went into Ed's usual throbbing, moaning, heaving, escalating thrusts and the sound of Mary-Ellen's cries of pleasure in response to Sven's sexual prowess. Theo read it through, but I could tell by his expression that it was hard for him not to question the exact logistics of what Sven was doing to make Mary-Ellen so noisy. When he brought it up at the end, Ed gave him a tired look.

'You people complained when I was too detailed about what was where.' He took a sip from his ever-present commuter mug and set it down with a thud.

I had to step in and cool things down. I could understand why it was easier to have a workshop like this made up of people writing similar types of pieces. But I had to do the best with what I had, and that was to try to keep them from commenting on the exact content.

Ed grabbed Theo's pages, trying to hide the glint in his eye. Theo was working on what he hoped would be a series of middle-grade kids' books about a superhero, Cedric Von Brainiac, who solved a situation by going off into the World of Knowledge. 'I think you'll see that I worked out how to get Cedric back and forth from his special world,' Theo said.

Ed began to read. Theo was listening, but his mouth was moving as he silently read along. It was hard not to chuckle at the difference between Ed's reading just the words on the page and Theo's interpretation of them. It was why the author didn't read their own work – they could alter the cadence or add emphasis that wasn't in the actual copy.

As soon as Ed finished, he turned to Theo with a superior air. 'The doorway you have to the other world doesn't make sense. You need to have a secret passageway that's believable. Why not have a bookcase that slides open when a certain book is pulled out? I know a bit about the structure of buildings. You could hide a walkway behind the bookcase. Just saying, since you're always so insistent on facts,' he said, tilting his head as he looked at Theo.

'And his friends could know about it,' Daryl said.

'It wouldn't be a secret passageway then, would it?' Theo said. 'Only Cedric knows about it.' He sounded adamant.

Ben slipped into his seat, and when I looked in his direction, he offered a sheepish smile and mouthed an apology before turning back to his cop demeanor.

Tizzy seemed uncomfortable and avoided looking at her husband. I wondered if she was sorry she'd let Theo join the workshop since it had changed the dynamic of the group. Theo swallowed rather loudly, which I thought indicated how hard it was for him to accept what Ed had said. Finally, he nodded. 'Thank you. I'll see what I can do.'

I heard Tizzy's breath come out in relief at Theo's comment. Her pages were next, and I noticed she gave Theo the evil eye before Ben started to read them. Theo had spoken up for his wife in the past when someone had questioned the accuracy of her description of something. She had set aside the time travel novel she'd been working on and had brought in a short story. There were just a few comments about the pacing, and Theo stayed out of it. Ben had deliberately kept to his flat cop tone when he'd read Ed's scalding hot prose since it seemed the only way to get through it without a lot of discomfort, but it didn't work as well with Tizzy's work. He'd tried to modulate his tone but always seemed to slip back into police report mode.

Ben tried to hide it, but I could tell he was tense as he handed his pages to Daryl to read. She was so wrapped up in worry about her own pages that she had a hard time reading anyone else's. Ben had brought in the last few pages of a short story he was working on. When he'd first joined the group, everything he'd brought in read like a police report – dry and just the facts given by a terse police detective – but he'd finally opened up and began to show bits of the person behind the badge.

Despite our personal relationship, we both assumed workshop mode when the group met. It did fascinate me how he seemed to don a suit of armor over his personality when he took on his cop persona. But then I suppose I changed when I was with the group and morphed into leader mode. I couldn't say *teacher* because I still felt as though I was learning myself.

I tried to listen to Ben's prose as it was read out loud, but my mind kept going back to his text from the other day and what he wanted to talk about. Was it a discussion about us? I cringed thinking about it. I wanted to leave things to work themselves out rather than talking about where we stood. Luckily, Theo rushed in to give his comments. He liked the suspense Ben was building in the scene.

Tizzy agreed to read Daryl's work and held out her hand for the pages. Daryl was the manager of a downtown store that catered to barely twenty-something women. She came from work and was always dressed in some outfit from the store. The look now seemed to be jarring and disjointed. Patterns and plaids with uneven hems and anklets with high heels. It made me glad to be past all that concern for the current style.

None of them liked criticism, but Daryl was the most thin-skinned of them all and prone to meltdowns. She also didn't take it well if she thought we were giving her unearned pats on the back. She had been writing a sweet romance with far too many details about the exact pattern of the paisley cloth napkins and how they contrasted with the ecru linen tablecloth and the white bone china dinner plate with the arrangement of butter knife, dinner knife on one side of the white bone china plate, and salad appetizer fork, salad fork, and dinner fork on the other. And then there were all the spoons.

The previous week, she'd brought in a love scene that had been limited to sweet kisses with lips brushing against each other. No surprise that Ed suggested she add some heat. We'd all held our breath when Ed made the comment, expecting an outburst, but she agreed to try.

I listened as Tizzy read. Daryl had kept to euphemisms rather than naming body parts, there were way too many details of what was where, and it seemed clinical rather than romantic, emotional, or even hot. As Tizzy handed the sheets back to Daryl, they all looked to me to do the dirty work. I tactfully suggested it might work better if she focused more on the emotion Daisy felt when Oscar wrapped his arms around her, rather than explaining what was going on with their actual body parts. I thought it had gone all right, but she suddenly pushed her chair so hard it fell backwards.

She threw up her hands and glared at us. 'There's no pleasing you people.' She was crumbling in tears as she announced she had to go. I tried to get her to stay, but she insisted she needed to be alone. It wasn't the first time this had happened, and I followed her to the door. As before, she turned back and said she'd see me the next Tuesday, so, despite the drama, we were still good.

When I came back to the dining room, the rest of them were in the process of getting ready to leave. I followed them back down the long hall to the front door and saw them off. Ben went along with the charade that he was leaving with them and went out of the door without a backward glance. He was so convincing that I wondered if he would actually come back.

# FOUR

I left the door on the latch and went about gathering up the pages they'd left for me to go over. I set them on the end of the table and put the placemats and fruit bowl back in place. All the while listening for the front door to open.

Ben had joined the workshop through a gift from his sister. She had been concerned that the only outlet he had from the stress of his job was going out and drinking with other cops, insisting they were the only ones who understood. At first, he had been what I called 'all zipped up' emotionally. It was so complete that he lacked any expression on his face and spoke only in a flat tone. His writing had been the same. What I hadn't known was that Sara was also attempting to play matchmaker.

Sara was intent on keeping her brother connected to the world that had nothing to do with law enforcement, which meant she made sure he saw a lot of her family. Ben had dinner with them before the workshop, and she had started her matchmaker moves by sending him up with a plate of food for me and requesting that he sit with me after the group while I ate it because she wanted her plate back, or she wanted to be sure I liked it, or some other excuse. It was laughable how they always seemed to have meatless leftovers that worked for me since I was a vegetarian. It got a little awkward with the rest of the group, and Ed even joked that Ben was bringing an apple for the teacher. We switched things up then, and he stopped arriving with the food. He'd leave with the others and go to his sister's, pick up the plate of dinner, and return when it was just us.

Week after week, he hung with me while I ate, but it worked, and eventually a relationship developed between us. But it was painstakingly slow. Tree sap on a cold morning moved faster. That was even less of a cliché than my molasses comment. We were both hesitant and remained at just friends. Eventually, it turned into something more, though we made sure not to tell Sara for fear she'd consider it a done deal and start planning a wedding. But it turned out to be two steps forward followed by three steps back. I think we both got scared – me more than him – by what happened when we unleashed . . . I tried to think of the right word to describe what we'd unleashed. I thought of how Ed would describe it and blushed at the thought. Finally, I settled on *unleashed the heat between us* and let it go.

There was still no sound of the door or him calling out a greeting, and I began to believe he really had left for home.

It was more than his company I enjoyed; I looked forward to the food. Sara was right that living alone wasn't conducive to a lot of elaborate cooking; her conclusion that since I was a vegetarian, I wasn't eating right, though, was wrong. I had been known to exist on peanut butter sandwiches on occasion, but I knew how to cook. I was also happy to leave it to someone else, and Sara was a great cook. My mouth was watering thinking of what she might have made.

I went to the front to drop off the group's pages in my office and was about to go back to the kitchen and see what I could find. Just as I came out into the entrance hall, the front door opened, and Ben came in holding a covered plate high on his hand, waiter-style.

'Sorry for the delays,' he said. The bland cop face was gone, and his lips curved in a crooked smile. 'I'll explain while you eat.' He looked from the living room toward the long hall that led to the back of what was described as a railroad-car-style apartment. 'Where shall I take it?'

He stared at my face. 'What's going on? You look like you're worried about something.' His manner was so nonchalant that I realized he'd forgotten about his text and maybe what he wanted to talk about, which was OK by me.

'It's the new gig I have,' I said, lightening my expression. 'You weren't here when I told the group about it.' I gestured to the living room and told him to put the dish on the coffee table. He set the plate down and took a seat on the black leather couch.

This room was my favorite room in the apartment. It was filled with things to look at, from the art on the walls to the red-toned Oriental rugs on the floor. It was a mixture of furniture and decorations that my parents had accumulated when the place was theirs, with some additions I'd made. For a moment, I thought of suggesting we sit out on the front balcony, but the wind rattled the windows, and I pictured napkins flying over the decorative wrought-iron railing and floating down to land on some unsuspecting passerby on the sidewalk.

I was about to offer him a drink when he pulled a bottle of beer out of his pocket and glanced up at me. 'It won't stay hot forever,' he said with a flourish toward the plate.

'I see it's Altschuler's,' I said, and Ben smiled.

'I thought all beer was the same to you since you don't drink it.'

'Mostly, it is, but I just happened to have met someone in the Altschuler family. She's connected to the new gig. I'm particularly proud of myself because I went after the job.' I uncovered the plate and looked over the mashed potatoes, corn, and what looked like chicken nuggets.

He noticed my concern and laughed. 'Remember, my sister has declared meatless Tuesdays. They're not real.' He suddenly sat forward. 'Sara made me promise not to tell. She wanted to be the one to give you the news. She told me over dinner that I'm going to be an uncle again.'

'Wow, that trumps the news of my gig,' I said, putting the fork with the not-chicken nugget back on the plate.

'Quentin is thrilled, but Sara's processing what it all means.'

'I imagine she is. That's a lot with Mikey still being a handful.' He noticed that I seemed to be immobilized.

'I should have waited until you finished telling me about your gig. I'm sorry for interrupting. Go on and eat, and tell me about the job.'

I tried the food – it was delicious – and described what I'd be doing for the house tour before I got to who was sponsoring it. Of course, he knew who Roman Scrivner was. You had to be dead not to have seen the commercials, but he didn't know Roman's wife was connected to his favorite beer. 'They are a strange pair,' I said as I remembered how he'd seemed to be upset with her at the end of the meeting. 'He's super outgoing, and she has a heavy sort of presence. Maybe even medicated. It's probably going to be a drag having her along on the interviews, but I gather that he's insisting on it,' I said before explaining the entourage I was going to be dealing with.

'Maybe there's something wrong with her. She could be recovering from some illness, and he's trying to get her back into the world. Or' – he paused and looked at me – 'it's some kind of mental issue.' He reeled off possibilities – she could be agoraphobic, which meant she had a fear of going places, had social anxiety, or was severely depressed, and he thought it would help if she got out. 'Any way you look at it, she's going to be a problem that comes with the job,' he said.

I finished the food, and he came back to the kitchen while I washed the plate. I'd been glad that he'd forgotten about the text, but now I was curious and brought it up.

'Oh, that,' he said with a sigh. 'I thought we needed to talk about—'

'Don't say it,' I broke in before he could get to the 'us' part.

He nodded with a knowing smile. 'You thought I was going to say talk about us, didn't you? We probably should have that conversation, but actually I was going to tell you that I'm planning to take the detective's exam.'

'Oh,' I said, feeling foolish as I handed him the plate and walked him to the door.

# FIVE

The wind had changed overnight, and I could feel the sharp air coming in under the door that led to my front balcony. At least the sky was mostly blue. I had written the proposal and had it in my peacock-blue messenger bag ready to go. Ben's empty beer bottle was still on the coffee table, and I grabbed it to take back to the kitchen. The room at the back of the apartment was flooded with the morning sun. I was sorry that I'd reacted as I had to Ben's comment about having to talk, particularly when I'd been so wrong about the subject. He'd wanted to tell me how his life would change if he became a detective. And now that I'd brought up having an 'about us' conversation, it was on his mind. I wanted to let things be without any declarations of feelings or intentions.

I let my thoughts linger on how nice it had felt to be wrapped in his arms before he rushed off the night before. Someone had called in sick, and he had to take on their night shift. I made myself snap out of it and focus on my upcoming meeting with Nicole. I hadn't particularly liked her, but if I was going to be working with her, I'd have to put that aside and try to keep things smooth. Every new gig was a challenge to me, and I wanted to give it my best effort.

The walk to 53rd gave me a chance to collect my thoughts, and I put on my pleasantest demeanor as I approached the Starbucks. Nicole was waiting at a table by a wall that was all windows, though the view of the street seemed to mean nothing to her. She was typing something into her phone and only looked up when I greeted her. She slipped her hand over the face of the phone in a move to hide what she was doing and only took it away when the screen went black.

I left my messenger bag at the table and went to get a cup of the brew of the day. I glanced back at her while I waited for my drink. The perfectly styled short dark hair and coordinated outfit gave the impression of someone who was ultra-organized and who probably achieved everything on her to-do list for the day.

When I came back to the table, she had a folder out. I got the message that there wasn't going to be a few minutes of small talk and getting to know each other, and pulled out my proposal.

'It's pretty basic,' I said, handing it to her. It said that I would interview the homeowners and include descriptions of the houses. The copy would be subject to her approval, and I listed the amount we'd agreed on. She had a pen out and was making notations. I did my best trying to read upside down, but it was impossible, and I realized I'd have to wait for her to finish to find out her changes.

She handed me back the sheet of paper and started going over her comments. 'First of all, you'll have to get the approval of the homeowners on what you write. Next, you'll be expected to work with the photographer on the layout.' She opened her folder and showed me a booklet from another tour that had the kind of layout she was thinking of. 'The opening page will list the Scrivners as sponsors of the tour and should have a photograph of them and something about them.' She let out her breath. 'Something about how important they are to the neighborhood.'

'OK,' I said, visualizing what she was describing.

'You can get what you need during the visit to their house,' she said.

'Didn't you say that Ruth Scrivner would be going on the interviews along with you, Serena, the photographer, and me?' I said. 'I could probably pick up something from her along the way.'

Nicole's face darkened, and she shook her head. 'No. I will be the only one dealing with Ruth. Roman will give you any information you need.' She caught herself, and her expression lightened. 'Ruth just wants to be in the background of the project. More like an observer.'

It was fine with me. I understood what she was trying to say. Roman Scrivner was the star of their family show. I agreed to her changes to the proposal. From there, Nicole talked about timing. She had already arranged the interviews with the home-owners and gave me a list of dates and times. It was clearly non-negotiable.

'You certainly have this all together,' I said, looking at the sheet. 'You must have done things like this before.'

Her face brightened at the compliment. 'I worked in admin at a private school before coming here,' she said. 'My husband is a researcher at the university hospital, and for now I'm looking after our girls and putting my expertise to use for things like this house tour. The group needed some fresh ideas.' She seemed to stop herself from continuing, probably realizing it wasn't a good idea to trash the group to me. I tried to make conversation and asked her about what she'd said about living in the neighborhood before.

'It's in the past and over with. I can't change what happened. Now, it's about closure.' She let out a sigh. 'How did I start talking about that?' The last comment seemed directed more at herself than me. Putting on my detective hat, I gathered that whatever she was referring to had ended badly. I was curious but also realized I should drop it.

Her phone went off, and she gave it an exasperated glance. 'I have to get to my daughter's pre-school. I'm the story reader today.'

I finally had the chance to drink my now lukewarm coffee as I read through everything she'd left for me. I was surprised to see that even though we hadn't discussed it, there was a check for part of the total amount we'd agreed on as a deposit. Maybe the way she took care of things wasn't so bad after all.

As soon as I got home, I went to my computer and started to research the houses and different styles, the names of different kinds of windows and such, so I'd be prepared to describe what I saw. One thing led to another, and I found myself researching the houses built after the Chicago fire. They had been do-it-yourself kits and called shelter cottages. There were a few still standing.

I'd gotten so lost in reading about the design elements of different styles of architecture that I was surprised to see the living room was already in shadow.

'I got worried when you didn't answer my text,' Sara said. She had Mikey with her and seemed discombobulated. Strands of her brown hair had come loose from the scrunchy holding it up. She wore an oversized T-shirt and leggings.

'Come in, come in,' I said, opening the door wider. 'I'm sorry. I was so involved with what I was doing that I didn't even notice any pings on my phone.' While they came inside, I went looking for my smartphone, wondering what else I'd missed. I stuck it in my pocket as I brought them back to the dining room. Mikey had left toys on previous visits, and I'd kept them in a box for him to play with when he came up.

'Ben said he told you,' she said, glancing down at her stomach. 'He promised he wouldn't, but I knew he would anyway. I wanted to be the one to tell you.' Her face scrunched up in upset as she started to cry, which surprised me since Sara wasn't a crier as a rule. 'Sorry.' She tried unsuccessfully to stop the tears. 'It's just – I was just thinking about Mikey going to pre-school and how I'd go back to work, and now this throws it all out the window.'

I started to offer her some of my cooking wine but then real-ized wine was off her drink list now. 'A cup of tea?' I said and looked at Mikey who was busy playing with some blocks. 'And I have some juice boxes.'

She got up and hugged me. 'I'm so sorry I didn't tell you right away. I knew you'd be my rock.'

I was a little stunned. Sara had gone through an abrupt person-ality change. Instead of being the one who was trying to organize my life and set me up with her brother, she was suddenly leaning on me. Ben and I had never announced our relationship to her, but also we weren't really hiding it anymore either. We just didn't talk about it.

I made the tea and got Mikey the juice box, and she seemed a little calmer. But to further distract her, I told her about what I was working on. I even got the list of houses and owners and showed it to her.

She pointed at one of the names. 'I didn't know he lived here,' she said in an excited voice. I looked at the name, R.L. Lincoln, and shrugged.

'He writes the best romances. They are my secret vice. It's like getting away from it all while being in the same room with Mikey and spilled oatmeal and toys everywhere.' She repeated her surprise that he was local. 'I wonder what he looks like. There's never an author picture in the books. He sure knows how to please a woman.' She laughed. 'Not in that way. The really important way, like long walks along the water, long dinners where the guy is honestly interested in what the heroine has to say. And it seems like the hero is always fabulous at giving foot massages.'

Mikey was lost in the toys, and she took her time finishing her tea before setting down the empty cup. 'Thanks for making me think of his books. That's just what I need right now. I wish Quentin was into foot massages.' She waved for Mikey to join her, and I walked them to the door.

She gave me a goodbye hug and left looking a lot brighter than when she'd arrived.

And I had something new to research.

# SIX

In preparation for the meetings, I read one of R.L. Lincoln's books. Sara was right. It was like a vacation without leaving my apartment. This one took place at a farm version of a dude ranch. City dwellers got to spend time on a farm and take part in the work. There was a cute meet between Mindy, a city type who loved designer shoes and had won the trip to the farm, and Rob, the manager of the family farm that housed guests. It was funny and cute, and when I finished the book, I had a light feeling as if the happy ending had happened to me.

In an act of fairness, I pulled out a book by Landon Donte since his house was also on the tour list. It was about a neurotic guy who had trouble with women and blamed it on his upbringing. A lot of the sentences were so convoluted that I had to read them more than once. There was some great language and social commentary, but it was depressing, and I wanted to tell the main character to quit being such a jerk. I didn't have a smile on my face when I finished that book. I also thought back to what I'd overheard and wondered if I knew the person he'd based the main character on. Then I laughed as I realized the truth. He'd probably based it on himself.

On Friday morning, I went to the first appointment that Nicole had arranged. The group of us met outside the Malins' house. Serena Lawrence touched my arm and offered me a friendly hello. Ruth Scrivner stood next to Nicole, and I hesitated to greet the sponsor of the tour. Nicole had given me the vibe that the woman was to be treated like royalty and not spoken to directly. Ignoring her seemed rude, so I nodded and smiled at her. She nodded back but her expression stayed neutral. It was hard to know how to read her reaction. Was she haughty or shy?

It was easy to figure that the man with the SLR camera slung around his neck was the photographer. I held out my hand and introduced myself, explaining that I was the writer.

'Owen Boyton, photographer if you hadn't guessed already,'

he said with a slightly tense smile. He snapped a picture of the group of us and then turned toward the Malins' townhouse and began grabbing photos of the stairway leading to the front door.

I pulled out my notebook and began to write some impressions of the exterior. There were different styles of townhouses in the neighborhood. While I was doing my research, I'd become interested in the name 'townhouse.' It implied that the owners had residences elsewhere, but here it meant a row of the same design of houses with party walls. The one we were standing outside had a flat unadorned front with an English basement – or, as some people called it, a garden level. A stairway led to the entrance, which was actually on the second floor. There were four more just like it as I glanced down the street. While they were all attached and had the same layout, the exteriors were painted in different colors. The Malins' was a moss-green with black trim around the windows, which were tall and narrow like the residence itself. The double doors matched the window trim and were also painted black.

We all went up the stairs and stopped on the landing just as a woman opened the double doors. I smiled inwardly, realizing she had the same proportions as the house. Tall and narrow.

'I didn't realize it was going to be a committee,' she said, looking askance at the group. 'I'm Christine Malin,' she said. 'Doctor Christine Malin.' As we came inside, she focused on Nicole. 'You're going to have to tell me who's who.' As Nicole went through the introductions, I looked at our host. I'd done some research on her. She was a psychologist known for a form of self-talk therapy. Nicole introduced me as the writer, Owen as the photographer, and Serena and Ruth as observers.

I was looking for something to use in the description of our host. She had a dry, distant manner. I wondered if she'd always been that way or if it was because she spent her working hours listening to people's problems. I imagined there was no way to be warm and friendly and not burn out.

'This is my husband, Jerry,' the tall woman said as a man joined us. He was slightly shorter than her and softer around the edges.

'When I heard about the tour from one of my patients, I wanted to be part of it to show off the changes we've made in our place,' the woman said. 'And I'm hoping it will put an end to people contacting me, telling me how they used to live in this house, asking if they could come by and see it again.' She pursed her lips. 'It seems that once someone has lived in a house, they feel it belongs to them forever and they should have access to it.'

'I suppose they have a lot of memories connected with it,' I said, thinking of my place and how I sometimes saw montages of the past when I sat in the living room.

'Maybe, but they need to deal with the reality that it's just a space to live in and not their personal domain forever.'

She pointed toward the staircase leading down. 'Some people have made the garden level into a separate apartment.' She glanced at her husband. 'We decided to move our kitchen down here.'

'That must have been a major job, Christine,' I said, staying next to her. She flinched at the sound of her name.

'I'd prefer it if you'd refer to me as Doctor Malin,' she said. I looked to make sure she wasn't joking. She clearly wasn't. 'So, you're the writer.' Her tone was a little condescending. It wasn't the first time I'd been treated that way and probably wouldn't be the last time either. 'What exactly are your credentials?' She eyed me with detached interest. I didn't realize I was going to have to audition for the homeowners, too. I gave a quick run-through of all that I'd done, even mentioning the love letters. Her eyebrows went up at that. 'Really, I didn't know anybody did that anymore.' She was interested to hear that I put together life celebrations for funerals. 'I don't suppose you're under any obligation not to talk about your clients the way I am. It's both legal and ethical for me. But you can probably talk all you want about the people who hire you to write love letters.' She laughed. 'They must be a sorry bunch to need your help in expressing their feelings.' She addressed the group. 'I saw the list of houses and I know all of them in passing.' She turned her gaze on Ruth. 'With the exception of you and your husband. Although I have seen his commercials.' Ruth managed a smile and added a nod of acknowledgment.

'Good luck with Landon Donte,' she said. 'I only know him socially from parties and such. He seems to think we're all fair game. You do know that he is the one who came up with calling himself the literary lion. In my judgment, he is one of those people who is either number one or a zero. He really fell off of his literary throne with that last book. He's already talking up the one he's working on, sure that it's going to be a winner. One can only hope that nobody recognizes the basis for his characters. I offered to have a look, but he insists that he doesn't need any help. For all his talking about how great he is, he's probably very fragile.'

Jerry slipped in next to her and took her arm. 'They're here to see the house, not hear about Landon Donte. They can judge for themselves when they go to his place.' He led the way down the staircase to the garden level. 'Why don't you tell them about our remodel?'

The exterior might have been 1893 but the ground-level area was completely modern. The kitchen looked out on the narrow backyard and had a six-burner stove, a center island, and an eating area by the windows. 'We call this the great room,' she said, indicating the area beyond the expansive kitchen. It morphed into a comfortable space with a sectional couch and some easy chairs with a large screen TV.

Owen was busy getting shots of the area, and I was making a note of the design of the kitchen. The others spread out and were admiring the space.

'And now for Jerry's baby,' she said as her husband opened a closet door to reveal an elevator. 'It took some doing, but then he's a structural engineer and understands that sort of thing.'

He went on for a bit about new technology and how much easier it had become to add the convenience of an elevator. 'I'm a cheer-leader for them,' he said. 'I've been offering my help to anyone interested in getting one installed.' He focused on me. 'How about giving it a try? I want to make sure you give the elevator its due when you write about our place.'

'Sure,' I said, stepping away from the group.

'It works on voice commands,' he said as we approached the door to the oval-shaped enclosure. He said something I didn't catch, and the door to the elevator slid open. Once we were inside the small space, he gave a command that I didn't understand, and the elevator went up to the second floor.

He picked up on my confusion. 'The voice command feature is very sensitive. I didn't want the elevator to start moving every time it picked up someone saying "open" or "close" in conversation, so I set it to work on French words,' he explained.

He left me to look around the living space on the main floor while he got back inside to go back down and bring the others up. 'I'm sorry Christine went on about Landon so much. He is a pretty self-centered person, and it's one of her pet peeves.'

As I'd expected, the living room was longer than it was wide. The former kitchen still had an eating area and a bar area with a sink. As I came back into the hall, the last of the group was just getting off the elevator. Dr Malin seemed ready to wrap things up. Her gaze settled on Ruth Scrivner, and she moved close to the placid woman. 'What lovely nail polish,' she said, grasping the woman's hands for a closer look. 'You must tell me the name of the shade.'

We were all stunned by Dr Malin's move. Nicole moved in as Ruth took a step back, pulling her hands away as she mumbled. 'Desert peach.'

'It's lovely,' Dr Malin said to the flaxen-haired woman. 'I'm sorry if I startled you.' As we all moved to the door, Nicole explained that they would have an option to look over and approve the copy and photographs.

'Well, then, till we meet again,' Christine Malin said, standing near the door as the group prepared to exit. I was in the rear and almost tripped on something on the floor. Jerry Malin grabbed my arm just in time and then scooped up whatever it was.

The others were already on their way down the outer staircase when I passed by Dr Malin and thanked her for her time.

'Just a thought, Veronica,' she said, touching my arm as our gazes met. 'You don't think that you might be suffering from the Cyrano effect.' I had no idea what she was talking about and gave her a blank look. 'You know – the story goes that he wrote love letters for someone else to the woman he loved and she falls in love with the letters. Maybe you're hoping or expecting the people you write those love letters for, or to, to fall in love with you?'

'That's absurd. I have a boyfriend,' I said, realizing too late that I'd answered too fast and it probably seemed as though she'd hit a sensitive spot.

'Yes, I'm sure you do.' She nodded with a knowing smile,

clearly not believing me. I wanted to give her details to prove that he was real. I felt a little desperate to erase her thinking that I was some love-starved singleton, pining for my clients or their love interests. I might be a little stuck in fussing about clichés and idioms, but what she'd said was too ridiculous.

I turned on a smile and swallowed my true feelings. 'Thank you so much for your concern,' I said.

Dr Malin gave me an approving nod. 'Good. You know half the battle is facing your problems.' She took my hand. 'I like to offer help where I see it needed.'

# SEVEN

'I hope you both got what you need,' Nicole said when I came down the stairs and rejoined the group. She looked from Owen to me.

'Less is definitely not more when it comes to photographs,' Owen said, patting his camera. 'And even more so with digital photography since there's no need to even develop film.' He said his only question was whether the Malins wanted to include photographs of more than the garden level.

'You can straighten that out when you make the visit for their approval,' Nicole said. She turned to me.

'I got more than I need,' I said, thinking of Dr Malin's comments about me. I thought about her husband and wondered if she endlessly analyzed his behavior and shared her thoughts with him. It couldn't be very pleasant.

'I thought the house was very interesting,' Serena said. 'I'm not so sure I'd like to have my kitchen on the bottom floor. Particularly since the dining room was on the upper floor.' She looked at Ruth and asked her what she thought, trying to include her.

'Lucky they have the elevator,' Ruth said in a distracted tone.

'On to the second house,' Nicole said. Since the Fellowses' house was nearby, she had grouped the two appointments together. I would have preferred some time between appointments so I could go over my notes, but Nicole was running the show. I trailed behind the others as we walked the half block, trying to add a few final notes about the Malins and their house.

We stopped outside the next house, and Owen started grabbing shots while I looked at the exterior. The Fellowses' house couldn't have been more different from the Malins'. The wood-frame house was freestanding and massive. A covered porch ran along the front, and the second floor had a turret-shaped outcropping with large windows.

Words like 'rambling' came to mind as we went up the short

staircase to the sheltered entrance. Arden Fellows was waiting for us with the outer door open. He looked every bit the professor, with a tweed jacket over jeans. I tried to find a few words to describe his looks. He had unexceptional features, which were overshadowed by an engaging smile that lit up his dark eyes.

Nicole went through our names. He introduced himself as Arden and his wife as Gena, which was a lot less formal than the Malins. There was something about his manner that made me like him instantly. His wife gave off a different, less friendly vibe. I got the feeling it was all his idea to be part of the house tour and that she wasn't pleased with our intrusion.

Arden invited us to feel free to look around while he showed Owen a good angle to photograph the living room. It was a very large room and had a lot of seating, all very comfortable looking. He explained that he often had groups of students over for events.

'We want to keep the tour to just the living room, but it's fine to include photographs of other parts of the house,' he said. 'The only way I can justify having this giant place is if I can somehow share it. The university pays me very well,' he said. His statement wasn't boastful as much as a fact. I had done a little research on him and knew that he had been an advisor to President Obama and that students actually came to the university to study with him. He never put himself on a pedestal by letting teaching assistants handle his classes, but made himself available to his students. He seemed almost too good to be true, and I wondered if he had a dark side hidden somewhere. Then I chided myself for being such a cynic.

Unlike the first stop, where Dr Malin and her husband had controlled what we saw and how we perceived it, Arden let us wander the place freely, making himself available to answer any questions.

I lost the others as I went looking for the kitchen. It was massive and had been updated with all the modern appliances. The stove had six burners. There was an additional pair of built-in ovens and a stainless steel refrigerator big enough for a restaurant. Gena caught up with me as I admired the center island with a second sink.

'It's a big place,' she said. 'Personally, I'd rather have an apartment with a view of the lake, but Arden loves to have his students over. He looks at it as more than a job,' she said, with a little disapproval in her voice. 'He never considers what it does to me.'

Just as I was thinking she might be about to disclose a dark side to him after all, I realized what she was saying was really about her. 'I suppose it must be difficult having your house overrun with students.'

She seemed to appreciate my comment. 'They all just trip over me to get to him, as if I'm nobody.' Her tone was angry rather than dejected. She let out her breath and shrugged it off before going back into tour-guide mode as she led me into the butler's pantry.

'This is all that's left from the original design,' she said. It was like the one in my place, but grander. Glass doors showed off shelves of dishes and glasses, along with serving pieces. A bistro table sat in front of a glass door leading out to the back-yard, which, like the house, was large. It was lined with old trees that gave it privacy from the neighboring house on one side and apartment building on the other. A party-size coffee pot sat on the counter, which was set up with cups along with cream and sugar. A tray of cookies was next to it. 'Help yourself,' she said and gestured toward the table.

'Arden insists we're always set up for company.' She let out a sigh as she took one of the chairs. It was pretty clear that she didn't feel the same about having a continuous open house.

'So, you're a writer,' she said, looking at me with interest. Here we go again, I thought, assuming she wanted to hear my credentials. I had only told Dr Malin about the writing I did for others – the love letters and pieces for funerals – but I went beyond that with Gena and mentioned the mystery I'd written and the writing group.

'I'm a writer, too,' she said.

'Oh,' I said as I realized her comment was meant as a conversation opener about her. I didn't know quite what to say, so I asked her what she wrote.

'I'm working on a novel,' she said. 'My teacher says it has real promise.'

'Then you're taking a class?' I asked.

'Not a class really, more like something private. He's a mentor really, rather than a teacher.' The way she spoke about 'him' made it sound as though it was more personal than a teacher or mentor. Then her tone turned, and she started talking about how great it was going to be when her book was published and the spotlight was on her. 'I wonder how Arden will feel when we go to parties and everyone pushes past him to talk to me.' Her eyes lit up at the thought.

I don't know what I was thinking, but I mentioned my writers' workshop. 'If you decide you want to try something different,' I said.

She gave me a haughty look. 'I don't think so. I'm getting help from someone famous.'

'Really?' I said surprised. 'Aren't you lucky, then! How'd you manage it?'

'It's only because he thinks my work is exceptional,' she said with a note of pride. I found that hard to believe and probably should have dropped it, but I couldn't help myself and pressed her.

'Then he's working with you gratis?' I said.

She looked down at the table and ran her finger along the handle of the cup. 'I wanted to do something for him. He's not very good with computers.' She seemed to want to leave it at that, but I couldn't let go.

'So you're his IT person?' I said.

'It was really about how great he thought my writing was, but I suppose you could put it that way.'

'Do you meet on a regular basis?' I asked.

I'd gone too far that time, and she ignored the question and pushed away from the table. 'We'd better find the others.'

Nicole gave me a pointed look when I found the group on the second floor. 'Where have you been?' she asked. I mentioned the kitchen and she scoffed at it.

'It was fine with the Malins since the placement of their kitchen seemed to be important. But I'd suggest you focus more on Arden Fellows. Be sure you take a look at his study,' she said. She glanced around her and said something about finding Ruth.

'Roman made such a deal about staying with her as if she needs a babysitter.' She went off to find the woman, and I took her suggestion and went to Arden's study. The floor was covered with a large Oriental rug, and the walls were lined with book-cases. There was a large desk and several comfortable chairs. The windows looked out on the street. It felt a little too big to be cozy, but it was definitely appealing.

Arden came in as I was looking around. 'This is my favorite room,' he said. 'Is there anything I can help you with?' he asked in a friendly tone that seemed genuine. It was easy to see why he was so well liked.

We started to make small talk, and he asked how it was going with the other homeowners. I mentioned I'd only met the Malins so far.

He was dismissive about them, and I had the feeling Arden was the kind of person who believed in the adage that if you can't say something good, say nothing. He knew the two writers, or at least *of* them. 'R.L. Lincoln manages to deliver a much-needed escape,' he said of the romance author. 'And Landon Donte is lauded for his insight into the human condition.' He let out a small chuckle. 'He may be the one who wins awards, but Lincoln brings in more money. I wonder how it works with them being such close neighbors.' His gaze met mine. 'I guess you'll find out.'

Nicole collected me after that and escorted me out with the rest of the entourage. She seemed in a hurry, and the group dispersed quickly with a reminder of our next group of appointments.

As soon as I got home, I transcribed my notes, thinking about the two houses and their inhabitants. There was no other way to put it: Dr Christine Malin had an abrasive personality and reminded me of one of those scrubby things that you used to clean pots and pans. Jerry, her husband, seemed bland in comparison. They made an interesting pair. She was focused on the inner workings of people's minds and he was all about the inner work-ings of buildings.

Arden Fellows was warm and friendly. It felt genuine, but again I thought he seemed almost too good to be true, and I had to wonder if he was. According to his wife, he had a blind spot concerning how all the attention he got affected her. Gena Fellows struck me as self-absorbed and needy. But being married to such a prestigious and well-liked person couldn't be easy either. She was probably stuck on the sidelines most of the time.

I didn't put any of my personal comments in the copy I wrote up about the two houses. I stuck to a factual description of the inhabitants and focused more on how the exteriors were from the 1880s, but the interiors had been updated with modern conveniences.

# EIGHT

Nicole was anxious to get the interviews and photographs done and had scheduled the second batch for the next day. There was a repeat of the group meeting on the sidewalk in front of the two houses. I had expected the group to be smaller, figuring that Ruth Scrivner would be bored being an observer by now and that Serena Lawrence would have realized we weren't going to do anything to reflect poorly on the Friends of Hyde Park group and she could stay home. It proved to be wishful thinking as the two women were standing with Nicole and Owen.

I had walked past these two houses countless times over the years and barely noticed them, but now I viewed them with interest. From the outside, they appeared almost to be identical twins. Both had the same shape with a three-window outcropping at one side that encompassed both the lower and upper floors. The main difference on the exterior was that one house had the Victorian touch of fish-scale siding and the other was covered in dusty blue shingles. Both front windows had a stained-glass accent at the top, and both had front porches, though one was more compact and hugged the entrance.

They both had low fences and a gate and a brick walkway to the house. The yards were just coming to life with spring flowers. I made some notes while Owen took pictures.

'Which one are we going to do first?' I asked. Nicole appeared agitated, which I imagined came from having to be Ruth's handler. The flaxen-haired benefactor didn't make it easy, and there was a heaviness about her presence. Before Nicole could answer, Ruth spoke out.

'Which one belongs to R.L. Lincoln?' she said slowly. Nicole pointed to the shingle-covered one with the smaller porch.

Ruth pulled out a paperback book from the leather tote bag she seemed to use as a purse. 'Could you get him to sign this for me?' she said, pushing the book on Nicole. I saw the cover and smiled at the fun design of a couple on a cruise ship.

'I bet it was an enjoyable read,' I said. Ruth jerked her head in my direction as if she was surprised I'd spoken to her. After a moment, she acknowledged what I'd said with a nod. She seemed to be on a different speed from the rest of us, and it occurred to me again that she might be on some mood-altering drug.

I considered sharing what my neighbor had said about his books and my own experience of reading one, calling it a guilty pleasure, but then I remembered what Arden Fellows had said, implying there was a competition between Lincoln and his neighbor, Landon Donte. I decided it was best to stay neutral and said nothing.

'We're doing R.L. Lincoln's first.' Nicole looked toward the next-door house with the blue shingles. 'Then we'll tackle Landon Donte.' She saw that Owen was still taking exterior pictures while we hung on the sidewalk.

As Owen passed close to me, I caught a whiff of a strong odor. It must have shown on my face.

'Sorry for the stench,' he said. 'I was grabbing shots of a fire. When I'm not doing this, I work for a news service.' He stopped taking pictures for a moment. 'I checked out your website.' He nodded with approval and pulled out a card. 'You do words. I do pictures. Seems like we could pass work on to each other. I do videos, too – of weddings, engagements, funerals.'

'You'd better *do* something about the smell,' Serena interrupted, making a face at Owen.

He excused himself and rushed to his car. A minute later, he came back wearing a fresh shirt.

We proceeded through the gate to the entrance of the romance writer's house.

The door was opened by a twenty-something woman who invited us inside. 'Robert told me to start things off.' She had us stop in the entrance hall. Owen took some pictures as she described how the house had a modern feel with the way the rooms flowed together. 'Robert had thought of remodeling and opening the whole first floor the way some people have done with these old Victorian houses.' She described how others had taken out all the walls that separated the rooms and used well-positioned posts to support the structure. 'But he decided the look was too jarring compared to the exterior.'

'And you are?' Serena asked.

'Sorry, my name is Ona Chapin. I'm Robert's assistant.' She had dark hair that hung loose to her shoulders and was wearing a short print dress over leggings. We all introduced ourselves, and she took us into the living room and offered us seats. 'Robert will be with you shortly.' She pointed to the room that opened off the one we were sitting in. Whatever the original intent of the room was, he used it as an office. He was sitting in an egg-shaped chair with a laptop desk pulled close. Headphones were jammed on his head, and I was instantly jealous when I saw how furiously he was typing. If only the words came that easily to me.

He continued working for a few minutes, then lifted his hands with a flourish and pulled off the headphone before he glanced toward our group and his face morphed into a smile.

'Sorry to keep you, but I had to reach my quota before I could stop,' he said as he joined us.

'You have a quota,' I said interested. 'How does that work?'

'Each day I have a set number of words I write, day in and day out, including weekends and holidays,' he said.

'What's your secret?' I asked. 'I wish I could write like that.'

'At first, it was an effort, but then it became a habit, and now if something comes up and I have to skip a day, I feel uneasy. And I owe it to my fans to keep turning out books,' he said.

'Speaking of that,' Nicole said, holding out Ruth's book to him. 'Would you sign this?'

He grabbed a pen off the table that sat amid dark gray couches and chairs that made up the seating area. 'Nicole, isn't it?' he said, looking at her.

'It's not for me,' she said and pointed at the book's owner. 'Make it out to Ruth.' He turned his attention to the tall, subdued woman.

'I hope you enjoyed it,' he said and then began writing something on the title page. She said something incoherent that I took as a yes. He handed the book to Nicole who handed it to Ruth and she slipped it into her tote bag.

The few minutes of conversation gave me a chance to take in

his appearance without being observed. I had imagined that he would either be broad-shouldered and have smoldering good looks like his heroes or be a dumpy-looking guy who wore sweatpants and had a nasal voice and complained about his food allergies. He was neither. I guessed he was somewhere in his forties, and he had an average build with neatly trimmed dark hair. He did have a stubble of a beard, which seemed calculated rather than the result of forgetting to shave. His eyes seemed dark and had an amused glint in them.

'You came here first, right?' he said, glancing out of the window toward his neighbor's house.

'As you requested,' Nicole said. 'Since you so generously offered up your place, it was the least I could do.' She turned to the rest of us and explained that she'd approached the other homeowners, but R.L. Lincoln had contacted her.

'When I heard Landon was doing it, I wanted to be part of it. I wanted you to see my place before he poisoned your minds.' His eyes went skyward, and he smiled. 'I wish him no ill will and I am not looking to badmouth him. I'm certainly in no literary competition with him. My sales speak for themselves. And I can assure you none of my books has been a disappointment like his last one was. Not that he shares with me, but he has to be worried about the one he's working on. Two disappointments might turn the literary lion into the literary alley cat.' Robert seemed to catch himself, and his face brightened. 'I didn't even know he lived next door when I got the house. Actually, my ex picked out the place, before she was my ex,' he said with a friendly shrug. 'So that we get it straight, I am not embarrassed by what I do or feel lesser than the so-called literary genius next door – no matter what he says. My writing entertains and makes my readers happy. He can't say that. His view of people is pretty bleak.' He looked at the young woman. 'Did you introduce yourself?' he asked.

'Yes,' Nicole said, answering for her. 'She said she was your assistant.'

'She sells herself short,' he said. 'She's my muse and a good friend.' He beckoned for us to follow him. 'And now to why you're here.'

He showed off his working space. The bay of three windows

looked out on a small side yard. A row of tall bushes blocked out most of the view of the apartment building. There was a wall of built-in bookcases and then a wide opening that led to the dining room. I followed him, making note of the way the rooms flowed in a circle, seeing that the doorway at the end of the dining room opened on to the entrance hall where we'd come in. Obviously, he wasn't one of those writers who wanted to be holed up in a closed-off room.

A swinging door led into the kitchen. 'I spend a lot of time in here,' he said. 'There is a lot of food and eating in my books, and I enjoy doing the research.'

'He's a great cook,' Ona said. He seemed to like the praise.

We went back into the dining room. 'I thought I'd have a display of books for the tour,' he said. 'I hope that doesn't seem too crass.'

Nicole and Serena traded glances and gave him the OK. With that, he took us back to the entrance hall.

'I could show you upstairs, but what's the point? I plan to have the stairway roped off so none of the tour people wander up there. No need for photos or a description,' he said, looking in my direction.' His lips curved in an impish smile. 'Just a hint: whatever you imagine I might have for romantic research, it's that and more.'

We drifted back into the living room, and he pointed out how the walls weren't squared off and had angles and features like the outcropping that, with windows on all sides, seemed like the perfect spot for the cart of plants with some knick-knacks in between.

'So you're the scribe behind this,' he said. 'Do you strictly write this sort of commercial copy?' he asked.

'I'm certainly not in your league,' I said, mentioning the first Derek Streeter mystery and that I was working on the second.

'I think I've heard of it,' he said in a friendly voice without a note of condescension. I felt comfortable enough to tell him about the writers' group.

'Ah, you teach and do,' he said. 'It's always a good combination.'

He was very friendly, and I took the chance to ask him if he'd be interested in stopping by the writers' workshop sometime.

'Maybe you could offer some tips and give them encouragement, an idea of what they might become.'

There was a moment of silence, and I was sure he was going to refuse and possibly chastise me for even thinking he would do something like that, but then he gave me a friendly nod. 'Sure. We can work out a time.' He looked in the direction of his neighbor's house. 'Don't ask Donte,' he said, shaking his head. 'The man has a heart of stone. He is too full of himself to want to help any aspiring writers. He's strictly quid pro quo. There has to be something in it for him.'

'I don't know if you'd call him *full of himself*. He did win that national writer's award,' Serena said. 'I didn't say anything, but I know Landon.' She fluttered her eyes and smoothed her hair. 'We've kind of lost touch, but he always includes a side character that I know is based on me. She's described as the woman with the graceful sway and the azure-blue eyes.'

Lincoln nodded with interest. 'I heard that he's known for basing some of his characters on local people.'

Nicole moved into our little circle, glanced down at my hands which were not taking notes, and gave me a pointed look. I tried to give her a nod to show I understood, but she rushed away to help Ruth who had gotten tangled up with one of the plants in the alcove with the cart.

'I'd better get to it,' I said, holding up my notebook.

'You're old school,' he said with a chuckle. 'There is nothing like pen and paper. It's the one thing my illustrious neighbor and I have in common. The only difference is I just start with it, but he sticks with it. But then you'll see when you meet him.'

There was the saying about protesting too much. For all his talk to the contrary, I thought Lincoln did have some sort of competition going on with Landon Donte.

# NINE

We regrouped outside. I took a moment to look over my notes and make sure they were legible, while Owen took pictures of the exterior of the next house. He took a break and stopped next to me, making a face as he stared at Donte's house.

'I wonder if he'll remember me.' He said it half under his breath and then turned back to me. 'I was doing some work for the neighborhood newspaper and went to get some shots for an interview. He was pretty rude and demanded to see my photos, insisting that he choose the one to use. Then he badmouthed me to the editor.' He lifted his eyebrows as he looked at me. 'Be warned. He's not a nice guy.'

He went back to grab a few more shots, and I looked to Nicole to see if it was time to go in. She seemed agitated, and I guessed that being in charge of Ruth was getting to her. Ruth seemed oblivious to everything and probably had no inkling that dealing with her got tiresome. Serena stared at Landon Donte's house with anticipation.

I moved up next to the graceful-looking woman who had lost the in-charge look of the president of the neighborhood organization and appeared almost girlish.

'I couldn't resist the chance to see him,' Serena said. 'We had a thing in the past. He wrote about it in one of his books, saying that *the brief encounter with the graceful woman with azure eyes was as hot as lightning in a summer storm*. The characters in the book end up in a mess, but in real life, I went back to my normal life with just a thought of what might have been.'

As soon as Nicole gave the word, Serena was the first one through the gate and up the stairs of the smaller front porch. I guessed that she had all kinds of expectations and I couldn't help but wonder if they would be met.

I already knew that Landon had been married three times and divorced the same number. I read a comment he'd made saying that relationships should have an expiration date stamped on them. I knew it wasn't fair since I hadn't met him, but I already didn't like him. I tried to assume a professional air and was committed to describing the author and his house in the best possible way.

'I'm Brad,' a twenty-ish man said as he invited us in. He had a self-important air as he described himself as Mr Donte's assistant. He added that he was a grad student at the university. 'Mr Donte wanted me to show you around.' I heard Serena making upset sounds.

'I thought we were going to meet with Landon,' she said.

'Don't worry, you'll get to meet him.' He stepped aside and brought us inside. The entrance hall looked identical to Lincoln's. The tiled fireplace graced one wall and the solid wood staircase was across from it.

'Mr Donte is finishing up something; in the meantime, I'll give you the grand tour.' He motioned for us to follow him. We went straight ahead into the dining room. I was expecting it to open on to a similar room to the one used by Lincoln as his writing space, but a large glass case sat where the wide doorway would have been. I even peeked behind it to see what was there and found a solid wall.

'So much for the modern look of rooms flowing together,' I said to Nicole, who seemed distressed.

'I wonder what else he did. It was such a lovely house,' she said to me before turning to see where Ruth was.

All I could think of was *different strokes for different folks*. I didn't know if it was a cliché or an idiom, but either way, it was probably tired.

Nicole suddenly grabbed my arm, seeming even more agitated. 'You have to help me out,' she said. 'Roman Scrivner put me in charge of his wife. He insisted I stay close to her and make sure she feels she has a reason to be here. I have been doing the best I can, but she's resisting. Can you give me a break – get her to stick with you? Ask her how to describe something. Just keep her with you.'

Nicole didn't give me a chance to answer but pushed me closer to the tall woman. I looped my arm with Ruth's. She looked down at our joined arms and pulled hers free.

'Sorry for grabbing you,' I said, realizing I'd overstepped. 'I was hoping you could help me with the descriptions of features.' I pointed out how the room was not squared off, but there were outcroppings with long windows. 'Why do you think the windows are like that?'

She regarded me with surprise and then glanced at the windows. I'd barely heard her speak before and was surprised by her low voice. 'If the windows looked straight out, they would give a view of the apartment building just beyond. This way, they look into the yard.'

I stepped closer to the windows and saw that she was right. 'Thank you,' I said. 'I would have missed that.' She started to wander toward a cart set up as a bar. The top was covered with bottles of different kinds of alcohol, and the lower shelf had a collection of shot glasses next to an array of other glasses. It was hardly something I intended to include in my description and guided her toward a cabinet I'd looked at before. 'He's certainly got a lot of awards,' I said. Owen was next to me, grabbing shot after shot.

'It's meant to hold dishes and such,' she said, looking more closely and then reaching to open one of the glass doors.

'No touching, please,' Brad said. 'Mr Donte is very proud of the contents of that cabinet.' He began pointing out the little statuettes and certificates explaining what each was for. It seemed to be a mixture of awards for book sales and his literary genius. 'Those are all first editions,' he said, pointing out the books lying flat on a lower shelf.

'I don't know if you care about the kitchen,' he said and led us through a swinging door. The room was large but appeared unused. We passed a door that I assumed led to the basement. 'Mr Donte said this would be perfect for the progressive dinner,' Brad said, taking us into a garden room that had been added on. The walls were all glass and had a door that led directly outside. True to its name, the furniture was wicker, and there were large potted plants and some small trees lining the clear walls.

'If you think those are glass walls, wait until you see our place,' Ruth said in a disparaging tone. I glanced around for Nicole to see if she was OK with the progressive dinner being held there, but she wasn't with us. Maybe escorting Ruth had really got to her and she'd hung back somewhere just to get a break.

Serena ran her hand along the leaf of a rubber plant and then held her skirt as she seemed to imagine dancing in the room. Brad rounded everyone up and brought us back to the front hall, just as Nicole was halfway up the stairs.

'The upper floor is off limits,' Brad said, trying to be diplomatic. He waited until Nicole came back down the stairs.

'So sorry,' she said. 'I must have misunderstood and thought you said you were going upstairs next.'

'If you come through here, Mr Donte will be with you in a few minutes.'

The living room had the same outcropping with the windows, and the shape of the room was the same as Lincoln's with the odd angle on one wall, but instead of the wide opening offering entry into the room that Lincoln used for his writing room, there was a wall with a normal door in the middle.

Brad took pride in explaining that the molded plywood lounger chair was an Eames and the bench with the leather cushion was a Mies Van Der Rohe Barcelona chair. The wooden chair would only set you back around eleven hundred dollars, but I'd seen the Mies Van Der Rohe piece selling for eleven thousand. I wanted to try out the bench-style seat, but before I could touch down, Brad got our attention.

'And now to meet him,' Brad said. It seemed a little theatrical the way he opened the door at the end of the room and held out his arm in a flourish. Classical music was playing in the background as Ruth and I walked in. Owen slipped by me and kept up his picture taking. I was glad when Nicole took over being Ruth's personal escort, so I could give all my attention to meeting Landon Donte.

Serena squeezed around me and positioned herself in the front. It seemed that all the walls were lined with bookcases. There was no fireplace as there had been in Lincoln's workspace, but the two windows were the same. It was simply furnished with a mission-style desk with a desktop computer on top. Several mission-style chairs with their wide wooden armrests and leather cushions were spaced around the room.

'Music invites my muse,' Donte said, gesturing to Brad to

turn it down. 'I hope that Brad showed you what you needed for the photographs and written copy.' He was leaning against the desk that appeared to be a long table. He seemed on the short side – maybe an inch or two taller than me. His thick, long hair was white, which contrasted with the high color in his face. He was wearing loose-cut jeans and a turtleneck sweater. He had one thumb stuck in his pocket in a half-cowboy pose, which seemed like an effort to appear nonchalant but came across as full of himself.

Serena bobbed her head, trying to get Donte's attention, but he looked over her with no reaction. Nicole handled the introductions, and when she got to Serena, he smiled at her with no recognition. I could tell she was upset as her graceful movements had become sharp and jerky.

He started talking about the tour. 'It's fine to have photographs of this room and the one next to it,' he said, 'but I must insist that the only rooms open for view are the entrance hall and the dining room.' He asked about what the other homeowners were doing. It was hard to read his reaction to the Malins or the Fellowses, but when we mentioned his neighbor, his expression darkened. 'He should be ashamed to call himself a writer with that trash he turns out. I'm not surprised he wanted to be part of the tour so he could associate himself with me.'

I saw the yellow pad on the desk and a stack of white paper and mentioned I liked writing by hand and working from hard copies. He glanced at the white pages. 'That's what I call a backup copy. Computers,' he said, shaking his head. 'Not like the old days with the poetic clack of typewriter keys dancing in time to my muse.'

At that, he looked around and, when he didn't see Brad, yelled out his name. He was letting out a second yell when the assistant rejoined us. 'You have to respond faster,' the writer said in an impatient tone. 'We're done here. Take them to the door. Then take out the trash and you can go home.' He looked at his watch. 'I'm considering you clocked out now.'

As Brad escorted us out, I could see that he was holding in his feelings, but I knew he was angry and embarrassed for being treated with so little regard in front of us. But then he did something that surprised me. He started to apologize for Landon.

'He's under a lot of pressure,' Brad began. 'He always worries about what he's working on.' He turned to look us all in the face. 'He has mood issues, too.' There was no more explanation, and we all went out of the door. I caught up with Serena and saw that she was choking back tears. I gave her arm a supportive pat, knowing she was reacting to Landon's indifference to her.

'You said it was a long time ago and that you both went back to your lives; maybe he didn't want to embarrass you,' I said, trying to calm her.

'I bet you're right,' she said, sniveling. 'Of course, that's what it was. He was just honoring my privacy.' The group was already at the sidewalk waiting for us. Serena touched my arm. 'I'm going to pull him aside at the progressive dinner when it's just the two of us. He's single now, and my husband died several years ago. There's no reason we couldn't have a new chapter.' She seemed to have regained her composure, but when we joined the others, she announced she wouldn't be accompanying us to the last house.

Even though the Donte visit had been the shortest, it was also the most exhausting. It was as if he sucked the energy from the room and kept it all for himself.

Nicole looked spent from babysitting Ruth. Only Owen seemed upbeat and was already talking about how anxious he was to see the Scrivners' house. I spent the walk there psyching myself up for the visit.

I got it. They weren't just silent benefactors, offering the backing for a short mention in the booklet we were putting together. They wanted to show off their house and their generosity to the neighborhood. I thought it was about Roman Scrivner trying to rise above the image of an attorney with a catchphrase who advertised on TV. No matter how he tried to portray himself as there to help, he was just a high-profile ambulance chaser. I wondered if *ambulance chaser* counted as a cliché. Before I had a chance to consider it further, I realized we'd reached our destination.

The Scrivners' house was near my building, and I'd walked

past it for years barely noticing it since it was set back from the street. This time I stopped and stared. Unlike any of the other houses in the neighborhood, which were built with wood or bricks, this house was almost all glass with some concrete supports. It looked like a three-story glass box and was truly one of a kind since it was the only residence designed by Helmut Peterman, whose other work had all been tall buildings.

It would have been fabulous if it was surrounded by trees or near the lake with a view of the water, but a ten-story apartment building hovered behind it, and another smaller building was ten feet to the side. I doubted that Roman Scrivner cared. It was all about owning a place that was one of a kind with a fancy pedigree.

Owen wanted to take more exterior photos, but Nicole cut him off and led us all to the door. I'm sure she was anxious to end her escort duty with Ruth. I took a deep cleansing breath and put on an upbeat expression as we stopped at the door. I was honestly curious about the house, too. We entered on the ground-floor level. An interior wall blocked the view of any living space on the bottom floor, and we went up a floating staircase, which meant slats of wood with open space all around. As soon as we got to the main level, Ruth disappeared, and I heard Nicole actually let out a sigh of relief.

'Because the house is on the historic registry, everything is the same as when it was built,' Roman said, taking us into the living room. There were floor-to-ceiling curtains on the wall of windows, which for the moment were open. This side of the place looked out on a yard with the next house as a backdrop. The whole interior was open, with the dining area and kitchen in full view. There was nothing remotely cozy about the place, and it felt very utilitarian.

Roman invited the group to sit. 'Peterman designed the furniture and had it built in.' I looked at the sitting arrangement to pick my spot. What passed as a couch and chairs were actually concrete benches with cushions on top, set around a glass coffee table with a concrete pedestal. I picked one of the chairs and noted that the cushions barely added comfort. I had started taking notes, and I felt Roman staring at me, causing me to look up.

'I know this place has been referred to as the Zender house because they were the original owners, but I want you to keep the reference to the Scrivner house. There's no reason to say anything about William Zender. It's ancient history that he was the local city politician who had a David-versus-Goliath sort of thing going with the mayor. What counts is that the house belongs to us now.'

'No problem,' I said and let him tell me about his sterling character.

'It was my idea that we have the progressive dinner so that all the homeowners on the tour could get together.'

'Then you don't know any of them?' I asked.

He hesitated and seemed to be considering how to answer. 'Not socially,' he said finally. Owen interrupted and asked for permission to wander the house and get photographs of all the rooms, but Roman insisted he stick to the area we were in. Our host stood after that and rather abruptly ended the visit. Our little group dispersed when we got outside, and I went to walk home alone. I thought over my conversation with Roman and how he'd answered when I'd asked if he knew the other homeowners. The way he'd taken his time to respond and his choice of words – *not socially* – got me thinking. Saying he didn't know them socially meant he could know them professionally. Could one of them have been a client, or had he used their professional services? The only one who had services to offer was Dr Christine Malin.

Three houses in one day, with the personalities that went with them, had left me spent. I made myself a peanut butter and jelly sandwich and a pot of strong coffee. I took the food and my notes into the dining room. Along with what I'd written about the homeowners and their abodes, I'd made some notes about things I could use in the next Derek Streeter book, if I ever finished the second one.

Mostly, it was in the form of questions. What was the connection between Serena Lawrence and Landon Donte? Was it real or in her imagination? What would happen when she confronted him? I wondered about the relationship between R.L. Lincoln and Landon Donte. For all his claims that he wasn't competitive with his neighbor, Lincoln had sounded as though he felt lesser than Donte. I'd written: *Ruth Scrivner – was she just a beer princess used to pampering and special treatment or was there a reason she needed looking after?* There were notes about Roman Scrivner and what I thought his motives were. The TV ads were meant to bring him business and make him a personality. Sponsoring the tour and ensuring his house was the star of it seemed to be about building an image of himself and his wife as a perfect example of people who used their money and power for good. I looked at what I'd written: *No one is as perfect as he was trying to appear. Was it true?*

There were notes I'd taken about the Fellowses and Malins from the previous day. Christine Malin – or Dr Malin as she insisted on being called – was the alpha in that couple, and I wondered how her husband felt about it. Arden Fellows seemed almost too good to be true. I wondered if he was oblivious to his wife's neediness, or perhaps he didn't care.

I'd even taken some notes about Nicole. There was something that didn't add up in what she'd said when she was caught going up the stairs at Landon Donte's house. She had tried to make it seem like a random mistake, but I wondered if that was true. The only one I didn't make any notes on was Owen the photographer. He seemed to be just who he claimed to be.

I was glad to leave it all for a while and go to Tizzy's for the ritual evening drinks.

'All that's left is the progressive dinner,' I said. Tizzy, Theo, and I were in their living room. She had her sherry, he had his martini, and I had sparkling water with a twist of lemon. I loved the scent of his drink, but that was as close as I got to imbibing alcohol. It had to be something with my body chemistry, but the tiniest bit of it gave me a buzz. It wasn't a pleasant feeling, either.

'Tell me about meeting Landon Donte,' Theo said. 'He's a bit of a neighborhood legend. Such a noteworthy author living in our midst. I had my class read *The Presumption of August*. It was touted as the seminal book to capture the mood of the aughts.' Theo taught English literature at Lakeside University. 'I even tried to get him to speak to my class.' The plain-looking man let out a mirthless laugh. 'I got a curt refusal from some underling.'

'I was warned about that,' I said. I explained how R.L. Lincoln had offered to talk to the writing group but warned me not to ask his next-door neighbor.

'The romance writer,' Theo said with a little chuckle. 'It might help Ed and Daryl.' He looked at his wife. 'It may even help you since your time travel book has a romantic element. But me.' He pointed at himself and shook his head. 'I can't imagine what he could offer for my Cedric Von Brainiac book.' Then he reconsidered. 'But maybe he could help all of us with the secret to being so commercially successful.'

I wondered if I should report how the session with Landon had ended and his behavior toward his assistant. I was under no obligation to protect his image, so I told them, mentioning how Brad tried to smooth things over. 'If he's under so much pressure because of what he's working on, I wonder why he even agreed to be part of the tour,' I said.

'He likes to hold court. Let them catch a glimpse of the great one. But you can be sure he won't interact with any of the people,' Theo said. 'And I'm sure he'll find a way to milk it for publicity for himself.'

'He sounds like a bore. I'm more interested in the progressive dinner,' Tizzy said. 'Do they all know each other?'

'I don't know,' I said. 'It was Roman Scrivner's idea. I suspect it was a way to get them all to come to his house so he could show it off.' I took a sip of my drink and looked around their inviting living room. 'Their house might be on the historic registry and an architectural landmark, but I wouldn't want to live there.' I told them how Roman had insisted that I only refer to it as the Scrivner house.

Theo mused about how houses in the neighborhood kept the connection to a prominent owner even after the people had moved out. He named a few, and I realized that he was right.

'Tell me how the progressive meal is going to work?' Tizzy asked, changing the subject. 'I'd like to know the mechanics in case I use it in my book.'

'Roman Scrivner arranged for the caterers at all the stops,' I said. 'The plan is that the whole group will start at the Malins' for appetizers, then move to the Fellowses' for soup. Salads will be served at R.L. Lincoln's, main course at Landon Donte's, and dessert with port wine at the Scrivners'.'

'All those personalities together,' Tizzy said, shaking her head. 'It sounds like a recipe for trouble.'

'The thought crossed my mind,' I said. 'Roman insisted that the whole group of us who made the visits come, too, so if there is trouble, I'll be in the middle of it.'

# TEN

Not only had Roman Scrivner made all the arrangements for the dinner, but he had also decided that we should all dress up for it. I took out my basic black dress that worked for any occasion and a pair of ballet flats. I made sure my hair was brushed and did the whole number on my makeup. I had all my notes in my peacock-blue messenger bag and slung it on my shoulder before I headed out.

I went to the Malins' house expecting to see the whole group. But it was only the Scrivners, Serena, and me, along with a lot of baby quiches. Roman seemed agitated, and Jerry Malin tried to distract him by showing off the elevator and offering to advise them on adding one to their place. Roman took the opportunity to bring up that their house was on a historic registry and had to remain as the famous architect had designed it. I stayed out of it and went to hang out with Serena who seemed preoccupied as I tried to make conversation.

'I'm going to do it,' the president of the neighborhood group said to me. 'As soon as I have the chance to talk to Landon alone, I'm going to tell him how I feel.'

'What are we talking about?' Dr Malin said, overhearing. The psychologist's eyebrows lifted when she heard Serena's story about being the basis for one of Donte's characters and her past relationship with him. 'I can offer a bit of professional advice. Are you sure that all your presumptions are true? You might want to think about that before you put him in a corner.'

'Then you know him?' I asked.

'Only socially. I was speaking in general terms.' She'd spoken a little too quickly, and it seemed that she was trying to distance herself from the author.

We moved on to the Fellowses' huge house. There was more of a crowd now that Nicole and Owen joined the group, but neither of the authors was there. The butternut squash soup was excellent and vegetarian.

The whole group moved on to R.L. Lincoln's place for salads. Ona was helping act as host and showed me the table of salads. It turned out she was a vegetarian, too, and we agreed that the array was a vegetarian's paradise. I was about to take a plate and help myself when Donte arrived with his assistant, Brad. The mood had seemed peaceful until now. But with the two writers in the same room, there was an uncomfortable tension, and that was before Donte noticed Ona.

Donte glared at the woman at Lincoln's side and shook his head. 'How could you?' he said with disgust. 'You had the chance to be with a literary lion and instead you chose this hack.'

Most of the others were too busy with the wine and food to notice, but Dr Malin stepped in. 'I'm sure that you don't want everyone to be privy to your personal situation. I'd be glad to act as mediator,' she said.

Donte threw the psychologist a hostile stare. 'You should talk about keeping things private,' he said in a sarcastic tone. He must have realized he might draw negative attention to himself and suddenly turned on the charm before getting the group's attention. 'Don't fill up on the rabbit food. The main course is waiting next door, and it smells delicious.' With a grand gesture, he and Brad left.

I overheard some discussion between Lincoln and Ona, and I heard him urge her to act as if nothing had happened and go next door with the group. I was super curious about Ona's relationship with Donte, but it would be awkward to ask her. I was too hyped up to eat and left my plate as Nicole got everybody to move to Donte's house.

Brad greeted us and escorted everyone to the added-on garden room. I caught up with the assistant. 'Isn't Landon joining the party?' I asked.

He seemed uncomfortable. 'I don't know. He was in a mood and went to his workroom,' he said before catching himself and lightening his tone. 'He asked me to act as the host. I'm sure he'll join the group when he's ready.'

Some tall tables had been added to the garden room. There was classical music playing in the background, and a long table was set up with trays of food, along with a selection of wine. Landon was right about the food smelling delicious.

Everyone helped themselves and milled around, eating and talking. The soup had taken the edge off my hunger, and I was more interested in checking out the details of my surroundings. I stationed myself by one of the tall tables and put my messenger bag on it, extracting my notes. I was considering whether it might be better to call the glassed-in room a conservatory or sun room when I heard something that cut through the music and din of conversation. It was a popping sound.

I wasn't the only one who heard it. The conversation stopped, and someone turned down the music as if there might be an instant replay of the sound. I heard someone say it was probably a car backfiring, and someone else mentioned firecrackers. Then I noticed Brad standing in the middle of the room with a worried look. 'It sounded like a shot to me. I have to check on Mr Donte.'

It took a moment for his words to be absorbed, and then, en masse, the group followed Brad through the kitchen, dining room, entrance hall, and around to the living room. Brad rushed to the door of Landon's workroom and tried to open it.

'It's locked,' he said in a worried tone. 'Mr Donte,' he yelled. 'Are you OK?'

When no answer came from inside, Brad looked at the rest of us. 'What should we do?'

Lincoln had the presence of mind to suggest going outside and seeing if he could peer in through the window. The group followed him outside in the darkness and gathered around the side of the house where light could be seen at the workroom windows. But even stepping back, it was impossible to see in because the windows were too high off the ground and the curtains closed.

We all followed him back inside. 'Maybe we should break in,' Lincoln said, looking at Ona for approval. When she shrugged in answer, he said he would give it a try and positioned himself to throw himself against the door. His body hit the door with a thud, but the door didn't move. He backed away, rubbing his shoulder. 'It always works in the movies,' he muttered.

'I called nine-one-one,' Dr Malin said. 'Someone had to use their head.' She gave the romance writer a disparaging shake of her head. She sent her husband to wait by the front door to let them in. Minutes later, the sound of sirens grew louder and then cut off abruptly as the first responders stopped in front of the house.

Jerry Malin brought the two uniformed officers to the living room where we were all standing by the locked door. They pounded on the door and announced who they were and called out for a response. When no answer came, they looked over the group and asked who was in charge. Brad raised his hand with an uncomfortable expression.

They asked for his permission to break into the room, and he glanced around at us for reassurance before he agreed. The cops didn't try to charge the door but used tools to pry the doorframe until it broke free and they pushed the door open.

I had positioned myself with the best view of what was going on, and when the door swung open, I saw that Landon Donte was sitting with his head down on his desk. It might have looked as though he was taking a nap except for the pool of blood.

# ELEVEN

'Ms Blackstone, we meet again,' a man's voice said. I was sitting on Donte's front stairs, leaning my head on my hands, thinking how much I wanted to go home to bed.

We'd all been hustled into the front yard by the first cops right after they broke into the room. The paramedics rushed past us with a gurney, but when they came out, the gurney was still folded up, and there was no hurry in their step. That clearly meant Landon Donte was dead. I wasn't surprised. From what I'd seen, it looked pretty final. I imagined the cops had felt the same but called the paramedics anyway, just in case.

No one had said anything, but Landon had been alone in a locked room. Could that be anything but suicide? The cops ordered us all to stay put and said that they would need statements from everybody. It was going to be a long night.

I looked up, bleary-eyed. 'Detective Jankowski,' I said in a noncommittal tone. He took me into the mobile command post that was parked in front of Donte's house. Even though it was after midnight, he was dressed in a suit, white shirt, and tie. His eyes looked tired, but then whenever I'd seen him, no matter the hour, he'd had that weary look. He'd claimed it was a four o'clock slump, but I was beginning to think it was a life slump. There had to be a long-term effect of dealing day after day with death. I was expecting him to start interrogating me about what I was doing there and maybe make some snide comment about how I always seemed to be around when a dead body showed up. At least if it was a suicide, he wouldn't decide I was a *person of interest*, which was just another way of saying *suspect*.

'Coffee?' he said as we passed a refreshment set-up. The coffee smelled as if it had been sitting on the hot plate too long, and I passed. He poured himself a cup and poured in two bags of sugar and enough cream to make it a light beige.

He led the way to one of the small rooms for 'interviews' and shut the door behind us. It was slightly claustrophobic, and I was glad for the small window.

'Now, to get down to business,' he said, opening the notebook on the small white table.

I thought of volunteering why I was there and what was going on, thinking it would get to the point and get me out of there faster, but while I was considering it, the detective said something that surprised me.

'I'm hoping you could help me,' he began. 'What can you tell me about the victim and what was going on in his life?'

'Then you acknowledge that it's a suicide,' I said.

'He was in a locked room with a gunshot wound to his head. There will be an investigation, but yes, that's what it appears to be.'

'And you want my help?' I said, trying not to sound too pleased.

He paused and seemed to measure his words. 'Yes. The writing you do seems to make you a good observer. Everyone is being tight-lipped, refusing to give more than their name and address, thanks to the lawyer among them offering his advice.'

'You mean Roman Scrivner?' I said, and he nodded.

I was flattered that he was treating me like a colleague and looking for the quickest way out of there, so I told him the purpose of the event and about the invited guests, along with a bit on Landon Donte's prestige as a writer.

'But why would he kill himself?' Jankowski asked.

'Not all writers have my sunny disposition,' I said with a tired smile. 'I know he was working on a book. Maybe it wasn't going well.'

When I started to ask him questions about the gun, he ended our talk. This time, when he said he might want to talk to me later, I didn't mind since it seemed we were both on the same side. I took it as a compliment.

Roman's requirement that we dress up turned out to be a good thing, for me at least. I had stuck to a tiny purse with essentials such as my phone and keys and worn it crossbody the whole time, which meant when we were rushed out of the house, I had it with me. No such luck for my messenger bag, which was still in the room I'd decided to call the conservatory. When I asked

Jankowski about getting it, he refused. There was yellow tape across the front door, putting the whole place off limits until the investigation was done.

He offered to have one of the uniforms drive me home. It was only a few blocks, but it was late, and I accepted.

The building had that deep quiet when everyone was asleep as I climbed the stairs to my place. I had been operating on pure adrenaline, and it wasn't until I walked inside and shut the door that the events of the evening hit me. Landon Donte was dead. We'd all been eating and talking, and he had locked himself in his workroom and shot himself in the head. It seemed incredible. I thought back to the last time I'd seen him, looking for a clue of what he was about to do. He'd had that moment with Lincoln's assistant, Ona. Did that have something to do with it?

Rocky came out of wherever he'd been sleeping and rubbed against my ankles. He followed me as I went to the black leather couch and flopped down in a heap. He cuddled next to me. I didn't know what to think or do. The ping sound coming from my purse startled me until I realized it was my phone. With all that had gone on, I'd never thought to look at it.

There was a whole series of texts from Ben. He'd known about the event and even offered to be my plus-one, but I'd said it was work and preferred to go alone. The latest text said he was worried and to call him, no matter how late.

He answered on the first ring, and I blurted out the whole story without stopping to breathe. Finally, he interrupted and ordered me to take some deep breaths. He offered to drive in and console me in person. I considered it, but I knew he had an early shift. 'Stay home and get some sleep,' I said. 'I'll be fine.'

'Are you sure?' he asked in a concerned tone. After I muttered yes, his tone lightened, and he suggested I take a shot of my cooking wine. It was meant as a joke because we both knew that while for most people some alcohol would help, it was the opposite for me.

There was just the sound of our breathing after that as neither of us was quite ready to end the call. 'Well,' I said finally, 'I'll let you get some sleep.'

'You, too.' There was silence and then he muttered an 'uh' as if he wanted to say something more but was hesitating. 'You know how I feel,' he said finally. I knew what was coming next. The most that either of us had said was that we liked each other. Hearing the other L-word was too much for me at that moment and I cut him off. 'Me, too,' I said before hanging up.

# TWELVE

Everything about the house tour ground to a halt for a few days, and then I got a call from Brad saying that Donte's house was no longer being treated as a crime scene and I could come by and pick up anything I'd left behind. I had thought it was only my messenger bag, but then I remembered I'd left my cashmere wrap as well.

Brad had offered a time to retrieve my belongings. It wasn't until I was approaching the house and saw R.L. Lincoln going inside that it occurred to me he had probably set it up for all of us to come back at the same time.

The door was open, and I went inside. Lincoln had already disappeared, and I had the entrance hall to myself. There was hammering coming from somewhere, and I assumed the door frame was being repaired. There was no one to stop me, so I followed the sound and saw that a carpenter was indeed rebuilding the door frame and the door to the workroom was open. It was the first chance I had to examine it, as much as I could with it being worked on. I was curious about the kind of lock and tried to examine the inside of the door, but the carpenter moved into the door frame and asked me to move.

Instead of backing out, I went into the bookcase-lined room. Landon's body was gone, of course, but there was still a residue of blood on the desk. Since in my mind I was almost working with Jankowski, I started to examine the rest of the table-like desk. There was a piece of cardboard that I recognized as being the back of one of the yellow legal pads I often used to write on. The pages had all been torn off. There was a paper shredder next to the desk. When I lifted the top, I saw slivers of yellow and white paper. I remembered Landon had had a stack of pages on his desk when the group had come by. He'd referred to them as his backup copy. He must have been distraught about his work in progress to destroy it. He'd shredded it all, even the handwritten stuff. I put the top back on and turned to the computer. I brushed the keyboard of his computer and the screen came on. It was clear from what Landon had said that he wasn't a fan of computers and had worked it out so he didn't have to deal with passwords or even look for a program. It went directly to what I assumed was his work in progress. The top of the screen said *The Bar by Landon Donte.* I read the paragraph below it.

> *You have to wonder why people do what they do. Or say what they say. I'd heard it all over the years of tending bar at the neighborhood hangout, where everyone from university students to locals gathered. People drank too much and then talked too much.*

There was nothing for a few lines and then: *This is drivel. I have run out of ideas. I'm done.*

That did sound like a suicide note. I was about to let it go but then began to scroll down. If that had been the end, the cursor wouldn't have moved, but instead it kept going over a blank screen until it went to the next page. I noted a 200 in the corner as if a page number had been typed in instead of formatted. It seemed like the continuation of something as I read:

> *. . . eyes changed after a few beers. Her mild exterior melted, exposing the hot hungry tigress on the prowl. When I noticed more of the bar glasses missing, I knew who had the sticky fingers. I also knew her husband would do anything to make sure no one knew about her problem. He had built himself into a celebrity with the TV ads for his used-car lot. He thought you could change a sow's ear into a silk purse, by calling it a* Second Chance Auto Emporium. *He was all about a classy image and making himself appear more than he was.*

I heard voices and hit sleep mode. The screen went dark, and I stepped away. I managed to get a look at the door as I left the room. It had been pulled loose when the cops broke in, but the remnants of the sliding bolt mechanism still hung on the inside of the door.

Brad was standing in the entrance hall with Nicole. They both glared at me as I exited the living room. 'Whatever you left is in the garden room,' Donte's assistant said. 'Nobody is supposed to be wandering around.' He directed us to follow him through the house.

I attempted to smooth things over. 'It's nice of you to still be taking care of things,' I said.

'You mean because Landon's not here to pay me?' he said, and I nodded. 'It's not altruism. His daughter hired me to stay.'

'Daughter?' I said, surprised.

'I was surprised, too. I had no idea Ona Chapin was his only child.' It took me a moment to process that Lincoln's assistant was Donte's daughter, and suddenly their confrontation made sense. The doorbell went off, and Brad went to answer it, telling me and Nicole we could go on to the garden room and get our things.

'I suppose now that Landon Donte is dead, it's going to change things,' I said to Nicole as we went through the kitchen.

She seemed agitated. 'We're going to have to sort things out.'

When we reached the garden room, it was just as we'd left it. The caterers were clearing everything away.

'I had no idea she was Donte's daughter,' I said to Nicole. 'But then her last name wasn't Donte.'

'It's probably her mother's maiden name. My guess is that they didn't get along and she was trying to establish her own identity rather than be known forever as the daughter of,' Nicole said. I would have liked to talk about it more, but she got distracted as more people arrived.

'This is the first chance I've had to get in here,' Roman Scrivner said. 'I tried to get the cops to let us clear out the dinner stuff, but they wouldn't budge.' He directed Ruth to sit in one of the wicker chairs and went to deal with the catering people.

Dr Malin cruised by Ruth without even a vague greeting – not that Ruth noticed. She seemed to be looking at the potted lemon tree and its fruit. Jerry Malin was already plucking their belongings from an array on the table.

Arden Fellows came in and greeted the group. 'I told Gena to stay home. She's fighting a migraine.' His face took on a somber expression. 'It's such a great loss and so shocking,' he said to the group as he came in. 'I suppose he suffered from severe depression.' His glance moved to Dr Malin.

'Just speaking generally,' she began, 'you never know what is going on in someone's mind. Or what pressures they're under.'

'You probably know best of all,' I said to Brad. He looked tired and overwrought, which was no surprise considering what had happened. But I also wondered if he felt some sense of relief. Landon Donte couldn't have been pleasant to work for. I'd seen first-hand how badly he had treated his assistant. I wondered if the reflected glory of working for the literary lion had made up for the abusive treatment.

'Could it have had to do with the manuscript he was working on?' I asked, thinking of the weird stuff I'd seen on the computer.

Brad put his hand over his face as if he wanted to block everything out. 'He didn't talk to me about his work, but I know his last book didn't do as well as expected, and I'm guessing he was extra worried about the one he was working on.'

'That's probably what pushed him over the edge,' Dr Malin said in her nasal voice. 'He felt desperate and couldn't perform.'

'I suppose that the manuscript he was working on will be dropped now,' Roman Scrivner said. He had left the caterers to do their work and rejoined the group.

I wondered if I should mention what I'd seen but decided not to. There was some discussion about whether someone might be brought in to finish it. 'I certainly hope so,' Serena said wistfully. 'I'd like to see that character he based on me one more time.'

'Or it will be buried with him,' Jerry Malin said as he joined his wife.

Just then Ona came in with R.L. Lincoln. He had his arm around her shoulder in support. The whole group offered their condolences. She seemed overwhelmed by it all.

'I'm here for you,' the dark-haired man said. He had the same amount of stubble on his chin that I'd seen before, cementing the idea in my mind that it was all a calculated look. 'Donte and I might have had our differences, but it seems like everything has fallen in your lap now. You're his only heir. It's a lot to deal with.'

I think the whole group collectively jumped when we heard pounding on the door at the back of the garden room. Gena Fellows was standing outside. Arden tried to race with Brad, but the assistant got to the door first and opened it.

'I thought we agreed you weren't coming,' Arden said, putting his arm around his wife. It seemed more like a hold than a sign of affection.

She appeared wild-eyed as her gaze moved across the group. 'This is a tragedy and a great loss,' she said. Then she fixated on Brad. 'You saw him every day. You should have known he was on the edge.'

Brad took on a defensive stance, but before he could speak, Dr Malin stepped in.

'We are all stressed by what happened, and being there only makes it worse. I think it's best that we all take a breath before anyone says anything they might regret.'

Arden took the opportunity to pull his wife off to the side, and I wondered about two things. She seemed over-the-top distressed. And she seemed familiar with Brad.

'Speaking of more practical matters,' Roman said, 'I hope you all took my advice and gave just your name and address and that you were in this room when it happened. The cops aren't questioning that it was a suicide – going by their guts and instinct – and are taking the expedient, easy way out,' he said in an uncomplimentary tone. 'The good news is we don't have to worry about being suspects, but my advice is never to say more than you have to.'

Owen came in and went right to the table and grabbed his camera as if it was a long-lost friend. 'I just heard the tail end of that,' the photographer said. 'He was alone in a locked room – could there be any doubt?'

'You should get a picture of all of us,' Arden Fellows suggested. Owen agreed and the group gathered together, and he began to move people around to compose the arrangement.

'Where's Nicole?' Serena said. 'We can't take the photo without her.'

Just then Nicole came into the room. Her expression was not what I expected. She had what I could best describe as a triumphant look as she cuddled her shoulder bag next to her. When she saw everyone looking at her, she changed her expression to somber. She joined the rest of us and stood next to me. 'Ladies' room,' she said by way of explanation. Something about it didn't seem right.

# THIRTEEN

A few days later, Nicole called a meeting of the Scrivners, Serena, Owen, and me to discuss the tour. We met at LaPorte's, a café and bakery on 53rd. The place was crowded when we got there, but Nicole found a table that looked out on the street and was far away from the noise. It was the kind of place where you ordered your food at a counter and someone brought it to you. We all got up to go place our orders, but Ruth didn't move and told her husband that he could take care of it for her. He seemed very protective of her, as if she was somehow fragile, and I wondered whether she was just very spoiled or there was actually something wrong with her. I'd barely managed to talk to her when the entourage toured the houses, and she remained a mystery to me.

'What's good?' Roman said to me as we approached the counter.

'Funny you should ask,' I said with a smile. 'I wrote almost all of the descriptions of the menu items. I can tell you first-hand about the vegetarian items since I tasted all of those first. With the ham sandwich and chicken salad, I had to use my imagination.' He seemed confused until I explained that I was a vegetarian.

'Not for me,' he said. 'I like my meat too much. The ham sandwich sounds good.' He laughed when he read the description out loud. '*On our homemade bread slathered with mayonnaise then layered with lettuce and thick-sliced Westphalian ham with a side of our trademark chopped-vegetable salad drenched in our homemade dressing.* Sounds good for Ruth and me.'

When we'd all ordered, we filed back to the table and made small talk until the food arrived. It took a few moments to point out who had ordered what, and then Serena asked for some pepper for her salad. The server started to point to the center of the table, but it was empty. She shrugged and said she'd bring over a set-up. Then, between bites, the discussion began.

'The tour isn't for a month and the only advertising we've done is saying that this year's garden tour includes some houses as well,' Nicole said. 'Landon's daughter is OK with us leaving it in, but I thought we might want to swap out the Donte house for another one since it's sort of infamous now.'

'I say leave it in,' Serena said as she sprinkled some of the newly arrived pepper on her Waldorf chicken salad. Mentally, I went over the description of a creamy concoction of chicken slices atop crisp apple bites, California walnuts, celery, and grapes on a bed of lettuce. I was surprised by her addition of pepper. I must have been staring because she said she liked pepper on everything. 'It was going to be the biggest draw since he is . . . well, *was* a legend in the neighborhood with all the awards he won.' She must have gone back to her dreamy memory of the author. Roman flinched at her comment.

'It's not on the historic registry, designed by a famous architect, or one of a kind, like our house is,' he said. 'And not to be boastful, but my advertisements have made me into a bit of a celebrity. I've even had people ask for my autograph.'

'I'm sure the Donte house won't outshine yours,' Nicole said. 'It seems that the easiest way to go is to just leave things as they are.' She looked around the table for agreement. They all nodded, including Roman. Nicole turned to Owen and me.

'With that settled, the two of you can go over the photos and copy and put something together. You'll need my approval first, then you'll have to show it to the homeowners to make sure they're pleased. No entourage this time.' She gave a dismissive glance at Serena and Ruth before focusing on Owen and me. 'Just you two.' We both nodded, and she asked when we could get started.

'I could start right after this,' Owen said.

'It works for me, too,' I said and offered my place. The meeting ended shortly after that and we all walked out together. The wind had changed, and it blew right through the blouse I was wearing. I started to regret not bringing a jacket and then I realized I had left it draped on the back of my chair.

I glanced at the table as I grabbed my jacket. How odd: now there were two set-ups with salt, pepper, and sugar in a metal holder.

'Too bad you don't have one of Jerry Malin's elevators,' Owen said as we trudged up to the third floor.

'I thought about that, too,' I said. 'But I can't imagine where it could be put.'

'You could ask him. I talked to him a bit, and he's an engineer. He didn't give details, but he said he had created some unusual spaces.'

I opened the door to my place, and we went inside. He stopped in the entrance hall that was big enough to have a small book-case, a telephone table left from when there was only a wired phone, and a chair that was mostly used to hang umbrellas on. He looked around at the long hall and the large living room. I knew what he was thinking. How could a writer for hire afford such a large apartment?

I didn't wait for him to comment and explained my situation of having inherited the place. 'Lucky you,' he said as he followed me down the long hall, looking into the open doorways of the bedrooms and bathroom as he went. 'Not only do I have a day job to support my photography career, but I live in a studio apartment.'

Rocky was following us down the hall, sniffing at my visitor's pant leg. 'Your cat must smell mine. I share the one-room place with Ginger. You probably figured she's an orange cat. I have photos.' He pulled out a formal picture of the cat wearing a flowered hat.

'Glad to see you have a sense of humor,' I said, handing it back to him. 'I thought we could work in here,' I suggested when we reached the dining room. The table was still clear from the writers' workshop, except for some pages I'd printed of the copy I'd written. He asked if I minded if he explored the rest of the place first. I agreed and followed along. He stopped when he reached the small bedroom and bathroom that everyone agreed had been meant as a live-in maid's room.

'This would make a nice darkroom,' he said. 'I do all the digital stuff, but I still like to use film. There's nothing like the thrill of putting a page of photo paper in a tray of chemicals and watching an image appear.'

'I'm old school, too,' I said, showing off my legal pad and pen when we got back to the dining room. I offered him a choice of drinks from coffee, tea, and cooking wine.

'Cooking wine?' he asked.

'It's actually a pretty good Merlot,' I said before giving him the rest of the story of why I only used it for cooking. 'And for serving company,' I added.

'The sign of a writer,' he said. 'Everything has a story.' He opted for a glass of sparkling water. It was different seeing him away from the group. He seemed to be about my age, nice-looking in an ordinary way, with no moles, birthmarks, or odd features. His eyes were a dark brown but lit with interest and humor as our gazes met.

'We've never really had a chance to get to know each other,' he said. 'You already know I live in a tiny place with an orange cat.'

'And you see I live in a palatial space,' I said with a flourish toward the hall.

'You probably figured that I'm single,' he said. 'It seems everyone I meet thinks I should be doing better than I am. I'm hoping the credit from doing this booklet will give me an in around here and get me more work. I would love to quit my day job and do nothing but photography.'

'I'm single, too, though there is someone,' I said. I wondered if I should go into more detail about my relationship with Ben, but it seemed too personal, so I let it be.

'Oh,' he said, sounding a little disappointed. 'Well, lucky you, then.' He sat down and put a file on the table. 'Let's get to it.'

When I took out what I'd written about Landon Donte's house, I realized I was going to have to rewrite it. In the meantime, I was curious to see the photographs of the house. I was less interested in the exteriors than the ones from the inside. There was the one of all of us with Donte, except Owen who'd taken the picture, and then some of just Donte. 'I was hoping I might get something he'd use as a publicity shot or even the cover photo of him for his next book. And that I'd get paid for it.'

The photos were excellent and really seemed to have captured Donte's personality. There was one of him sitting at his desk appearing to write that seemed particularly good. I looked at it for a long time, studying the position of everything. 'Maybe you can pitch his daughter with the picture.'

'I don't know about that. You don't have to be a detective to figure out she and her father had a difficult relationship.'

'Right,' I said. 'Not only did she change her last name so as not to be associated with him, but she was hanging out with the enemy. R.L. Lincoln and Landon Donte were at opposite ends of the literary world. It must have bothered Donte no end that his neighbor made so much more money than he did when he considered what Lincoln wrote to be aimed at instant reading pleasure rather than stirring the mind as he thought his work did.'

'It probably gave Lincoln a sense of pleasure that he had Donte's daughter working for him and whatever else is between them. He seemed to act as if he wasn't bothered by being dissed by Donte, but I bet he was,' Owen said.

'With Donte gone, he doesn't have to deal with that anymore. I wonder if it's any consolation to him that Donte was so disgusted with his own work in progress that he deleted it. And I suppose you could say he deleted himself as well, rather than face being a failure,' the photographer added.

We moved on to what I'd written about the other houses and tried to match it up to the photos. He made some suggestions for changes and we agreed on the photos we'd use.

We were just finishing up when there was a sharp rap at my door. Actually, any knock sounded sharp at the wooden door. I went to answer it while Owen gathered up his things.

Sara was standing in the doorway with Mikey hanging on to her leg. 'You didn't respond to my texts, and I could hear foot-steps coming from up here, so I knew you were home.' She had the mom look of leggings and a loose-fitting T-shirt. Her face appeared drawn and tired. 'I needed to talk to somebody. I don't know how I'm going to handle this,' she said.

Mikey let go of her leg and ran inside, going directly to the dining room where I'd accumulated some toys for him. I ushered Sara inside and was shutting the door when Owen came to the front. He smiled at Sara, and I introduced her as my neighbor. Sara's radar went up when she saw him, and he picked up on it.

'Veronica and I are working together. We're fellow freelancers who may be able to help each other.' He went to leave. 'I hope this is just the beginning of a profitable relationship for us both.'

I reiterated what Owen had said when he left and explained that we were working on a project together. I expected her to delve into it more since she had been playing matchmaker with Ben and me since day one and had even told me that she hoped I'd be her sister-in-law someday, preferably soon. But she seemed to buy my explanation and moved straight to talking about her situation.

'How am I going to do this?' she said in a weary voice. 'I feel lousy, and Mikey knows something is going on and is getting all clingy. My moods are all over the place, and I can barely look at food, let alone cook it.'

It became all about her, and I did my best to reassure her that everything would be fine and that I would help her as much as I could. But even as we were talking, I kept thinking back to Owen's visit and the photographs. He'd done such a great job with the ones of Donte, particularly the one of him sitting at his desk. And then something struck me. The photograph had reversed things, and I realized Donte's death might not have been a suicide after all.

# FOURTEEN

'Peace at last,' Ben said, coming in the door that evening. 'You were smart not joining us.' It was kind of silly that I didn't join his frequent dinners at his sister's. Although we had never told her we were seeing each other as more than friends, I was sure she knew. But with what she had going on right now, I doubted she even cared. Even so, I preferred to keep the charade going of him bringing up a plate from their dinner.

He held up a dish of square pieces of the thin-crust pizza from the Mezze. 'Sara's having a hard time with food.'

'I know. She told me. Maybe I'd better step up and bring food down to them,' I said. 'Then it'll be meatless every day.'

'Poor Quentin. He loves his meat,' Ben said with a smile. It was just small talk to ease the way of us being together. Neither of us was very smooth when it came to relationships. It was easier when we were just friends and there were no expectations. We were both divorced, and I for one was afraid of what would happen if we got too involved. It was fine to act as each other's plus-one, more for him than me. It seemed it was always the birthday of one of his colleagues, or there was a wedding or holiday party. Since he often had to work on the weekends, we didn't have a routine of going out on Saturday night. Mostly, it was like this: he'd come up after dinner at his sister's. And then there was the Tuesday-night group.

I got drinks for us, and we settled on the couch. He popped the top off his beer, took a sip, and then rolled the bottle between his hands. 'Who's this Owen guy?' he said, looking me in the eye.

'So Sara told you about him,' I said with a chuckle. 'He's the photographer on the project I'm working on. He came over so we could match up pictures with the copy I'd written.'

'Hmm,' he muttered. 'That's not the way my sister saw it.'

I thought back to the encounter. 'We're both freelancers, and he probably said something about us helping each other get business.'

He looked down at the moisture on the outside of the brown bottle. 'We really need to talk,' he said in a low voice.

I felt my stomach clench. I knew he meant about us and clarifying our relationship. We had never talked about being exclusive or dating other people, and I knew he was right, but I still didn't want to do it. So I did what I always did when things got uncomfortable. I changed the subject.

'Actually, it's because of the photographs that Owen showed me that I figured something out. I don't think Landon Donte killed himself.'

Ben smiled at me, and I thought he looked a little relieved. Maybe he didn't really want to talk about us either. I had just given him the bare details the night it had happened, but now it was all over the media about Landon Donte dying as a presumed suicide. I gathered that what I'd seen on his computer was being considered a suicide note. Speculation was that he was in despair over his writing.

I told Ben about going into the author's workroom. 'It had been released as a crime scene, but not completely cleaned up yet. The way the blood pooled, he would have had to shoot himself with his right hand, but when I saw the photograph of him using a pen, he was using his left hand.' I looked at Ben. 'I can't wait to tell Detective Jankowski.'

'You're friends with the homicide detective now,' he said, surprised. I explained how he'd almost treated me like a colleague.

'Maybe when he thought it was a suicide,' Ben said. 'But he might look at your conjecture as trying to one-up him by pointing out something he missed. And another thing – if it was a homicide, he could decide you were a suspect along with the other people there. And didn't you say the room was locked from the inside with a bolt?'

'The locked door is sort of a problem,' I said, losing my enthusiasm. 'But I'm not worried about being a suspect. By now Jankowski knows I only write about murder – in the Derek Streeter books.' Using the plural only reminded me how stuck I was in finishing the second book. I'd been at the end and then found a big hole in the plot. And now I was stalled on redoing it. It made me go back to thinking of Landon Donte and his feeling about the book he was working on.

'There were those first few lines and then the note that sounded like he felt hopeless about his work, but then it seemed he'd deleted whatever he'd written. I found a page marked two hundred, and while most of it was blank, there were a few sentences at the bottom.' I explained Landon's view of computers. 'He called a hard copy of his work his backup. Those and the handwritten pages were all shredded. I could see someone doing that who felt hopeless about their work, but what if somebody else wanted to destroy it?'

'The question is why?' Ben said. 'And I'm sure the cops checked his hand for powder burns.'

'Maybe not, since they seemed so sure it was a suicide,' I said. Ben let out his breath in a knowing sigh.

'Sometimes the old-timers get a little too reliant on their instincts. Cop gut,' he said. 'I suppose they could have skipped it. If I become a detective, that will never happen on my watch.'

'And as for why,' I said, thinking over everything I'd heard, 'he was known for basing some of his characters on local people. The book seemed to be about people at a bar talking too much. He could have revealed something that was too close to the truth.'

'Unless you can get rid of the locked room, you're spinning your wheels,' Ben said. 'Wasn't there a big advance Donte would have to pay back if he couldn't deliver the manuscript? I tried to read his previous book and couldn't get through it. Maybe the guy had just lost it. It happens. Songwriters who have written hit after hit run dry. Maybe he was desperate and chose to die rather than face failure.'

'I thought about that. I suppose he could have hidden it, but he sure didn't seem like a man on the edge. If anything, he seemed pretty cocky and full of himself. He spoke about the book as if he was confident it was good. I think he said it was going to show the desperation below the surface.'

'Sometimes things just are as they seem. Jankowski has been around a long time, and his instinct could be right. I don't think he would appreciate you questioning it either,' Ben said. We had reached an impasse and it was time to pivot again.

'Do you really think I should bring down dinner to your sister's?'

'Yes. She's in over her head,' he said, leaning against me and nuzzling my neck.

# FIFTEEN

'Hello, stranger,' Tizzy said, giving me a hug as if I was a long-lost friend when I came in the door. The sleeves of one of the colorful kimono tops that she always wore got tangled in my sweater. 'That means you never can leave,' she joked as she untangled us. It seemed like forever since I'd joined them for sherry time, and I was glad for the get-together.

Theo was waiting in the living room, and drinks and snacks were all set up. 'Mini quiches,' I said, eyeing the plate of small savory pies. 'You went all out.'

Theo waved his martini past me so I could get a good wallop of the scent. At his urging, I had finally taken a tiny sip of his drink once, expecting the taste to match the scent I loved so much. It was a sad disappointment, and even the tiny taste had given me an unpleasant buzz.

He handed me a glass of sparkling water with a slice of lime floating in it. 'OK, give us an update,' he said.

'First, you tell me what you've heard,' I said. Tizzy was always in the center of neighborhood news, and she was a member of the group that was putting on the garden and house tour.

She paused for a moment to compose her thoughts. 'What *haven't* I heard? That Landon did a whole dramatic scene before locking himself in his study.'

'A scene about what?' I said, curious.

Tizzy paused with a quizzical look. 'I assumed it was something about his book, but I didn't get details.'

'The only dramatic scenes I saw had to do with confronting his neighbor, the romance writer, and the woman with him, who turned out to be Landon's daughter. Landon talked to her as if she was somehow a traitor. She doesn't even go by his last name. It's like the opposite of riding on his coattails.' I rolled my eyes, realizing I had used a cliché, and rushed to try to cover it since I was critical of others being lazy with words. 'The trouble with

clichés is that they come to mind and roll off your tongue before
you can stop them.'

'And they get the point across quickly,' Theo said.

'So you think a father's broken heart at his daughter's rejection
pushed him over the edge?' Tizzy asked.

'There might have been another scene,' I said. 'Serena
Lawrence told me she and Landon had a relationship in the past
and that there's a character in every book based on her. Something
about a graceful woman with azure eyes. She didn't go into
detail, but I think they both might have been married when they
had their thing. She seemed to imagine that now they were both
available, they might pick up. Except . . .' I felt my shoulders
slump as I remembered when she and Landon had met again
with our entourage. 'He barely looked at her, and when he did,
he had a blank stare as if he had no idea who she was. She was
convinced it was an act and told me she was going to confront
him during the progressive dinner.'

'Did she?' Tizzy asked, wide-eyed.

'Not that I witnessed. Though I never saw Landon at all when
we were at his place. His assistant said Landon was in his workroom, and I assumed he was alone in there, but he could have
had company. I can't say for sure who was in the room where
the party was being held.' I described it and said I was trying to
decide whether to call it a conservatory or garden room.

'I'd go with conservatory,' Theo said. 'It sounds so much
more evocative.'

'I agree with Theo, but get back to Serena.'

'I don't know if the character was based on her or if it's wishful
thinking on her part. And about whatever they had – it might
have been far more important to her than it was to him.'

'In other words, he really didn't recognize her,' Theo said. 'It
happens with guys.' Tizzy looked at her husband aghast.

'Are you saying some woman from your past that you don't
remember is going to show up?'

'I said it happens with guys,' he said. 'I didn't mean me. I
promise you I remember every girlfriend I had.' He grinned
before he quickly added, 'All before I met you.'

Tizzy passed around the quiches again, and we all helped
ourselves.

'I do remember hearing that Donte bases some of his characters on real people. It doesn't seem like it would matter with the character Serena claims is based on her since she sounds lovely and is probably a background character. But most of his characters are neurotic or worse. He must do something so nobody recognizes the real person,' Theo said.

'Couldn't somebody sue him for disclosing negative things about them?' Tizzy asked.

Theo straightened his horn-rimmed glasses. 'But would they? It would be like pointing out that they did whatever the horrible person in his book did.'

'So you think Landon might have been so remorseful about something he wrote that he killed himself?' Tizzy asked.

'What if it wasn't suicide?' I said. The words hung in the air a moment before they sank in.

'Then what? Then it was murder?' Tizzy said.

'I believe it would be referred to as homicide,' Theo said. 'Until it's determined if it was unintentional or from criminal negligence.'

'He was shot in the head by somebody. It hardly seems unintentional or from negligence,' Tizzy said. 'I stand by calling it murder.' They both looked toward me.

'I have to go with Tizzy,' I said.

'You were there. You must have some insight into what happened,' Theo said.

'Yes and no. We were all in the conservatory having the main course of the progressive dinner. There was music playing and noise from the conversations. I heard a popping sound. We all thought it was the backfiring of a car or some idiot setting off firecrackers. Then Donte's assistant got concerned about him, and we all followed him when he went to check. That's when we found the door was locked – well, actually bolted on the inside.'

'That puts a chink in the idea it was murder,' Tizzy said, giving her husband a knowing look.

I nodded in agreement. Then I told them about the pool of blood pointing to a right-handed person, which it appeared he was not, and about the deleted stuff on the computer. I also explained about not telling Detective Jankowski what I thought.

'Are you going to investigate?' Tizzy asked. 'You know I'm available if you need any help.'

'Me, too,' Theo said. 'If he was murdered, the suspects are all neighborhood people, and I would be happy to use my computer to see what I can dig up.'

'I don't know if I'm going to investigate, but I am curious,' I said.

'I could see what I can find out on the grapevine,' Tizzy said, then let out a chuckle. 'You used a cliché, so I can, too.'

I laughed and thanked them both as I lifted my glass and we all made a toast to finding out the truth of what happened to Landon Donte.

The next morning, I took my coffee to the computer, pulled up the copy I'd written about Landon Donte's house, and worked on rewriting it. Owen had left me some prints of the photos for inspiration. I looked at Landon standing in front of his desk in that half-cowboy pose and studied his face for signs of any emotional turmoil. There was nothing. All I did notice was that he had his right thumb hanging from his pocket and a pen in his left hand, reinforcing that his left hand was dominant.

Finally, I let it go and went to check my emails. There was one that had come through my website. It was from someone named Amanda who was interested in love letters. She referred to them as the specialty letters I offered, but I knew that was what she meant. She'd included a phone number and I gave her a call.

I tried to get an impression of her from her voice. She sounded efficient. But we hit an obstacle when she said we would have to do everything over the phone. I wanted the work, but there was a certain responsibility that came with romantic missives. I had to make sure there was no stalking involved or anything related to domestic abuse. Women could be perpetrators of that, too.

I had to tell her that the only way I would take the job was if we met in person. 'It's not as if there are a lot of choices,' she said, sounding a little exasperated. 'But this is really important, so I'll meet with you.'

It took some back and forth before we could work out a time.

She seemed to be a busy person, and I guessed she was some kind of professional.

I was still thinking about the possibility of a new gig when I moved on to the next task of the day. I'd taken Ben's suggestion and offered to make dinner for Sara and her family. She'd been embarrassed and only accepted when I said it was the least I could do after all the dinners she'd given me.

Ben had an early shift and came to my place when he got off work. 'Since it was my idea, I wanted to help,' he said.

'We can start with shopping.' I grabbed my purse and headed to the door. I didn't have a car, so it was a pleasure to have his Wrangler instead of lugging things home in the metal shopping cart.

When we got back, he acted as my sous chef. 'Quentin will never notice the difference,' I said as I stirred the pot of chili with a plant-based meat substitute that looked almost like the real thing. It smelled delicious. He helped organize the add-ons of sour cream, corn chips, and grated cheese, and assisted in packing it all up to go downstairs.

'You really should come and eat with us,' he said. 'You made the food.'

I shook my head. I didn't even know why. And then I realized it wasn't really about Sara, but about me. It was the thing of one step forward and two steps back. I wasn't ready to present us as a couple. I laughed at myself. All the internal fussing about being a spinster (even though technically I wasn't since I had been married), who lived with a cat and her memories, and who was much too concerned about clichés, could be wiped out by admitting that Ben and I were way beyond just plus-ones for each other at events. But still I resisted. When I was totally honest, it was that I was afraid of getting in too deep, having it not work out, and being left devastated. I was protecting myself.

'Have it your way,' he said, taking the load downstairs.

While they feasted on my creation, I took a bowl of some I'd held back and read over a hard copy of the rewritten piece about Donte's house. Houses in the neighborhood were given names by the people who lived in them. If the family was notable enough, the name stuck even when they left. Surely Donte's place was going to be like that. I vaguely remembered that someone in the

Friends of Hyde Park had called the house something else, which probably referred to whoever had lived there before.

Ben came up to bring my empty pot and to tell me the meal had been a success. He saw my half-empty bowl next to a pile of notes. 'What are you working on?'

I got up to help him take everything into the kitchen and explained having to rewrite the notes about Landon Donte's house.

'Did you tell Jankowski about Donte being left-handed?' Ben asked.

'Not yet,' I said.

'He'll probably just dismiss it. He's already written it off as a suicide and is not going to investigate it as anything else based on something you said. It's not exactly a compliment to police work, but it's reality. Sorry.' He reached out to hug me. I thought it was the beginning of something and leaned into it, but he dropped his arms after a moment.

'Gotto go. Work. Someone called in sick.' It was disconcerting how he could turn off like that. It made me feel uneasy.

On Sunday morning, I felt as though I was back to old-maid mode as I set up things for my ritual special breakfast and reading the Sunday paper in the print edition. But when I started to make the waffles, I thought of Sara and ended up making a whole batch of them and taking them downstairs. I brought the French press full of smoky French-roast coffee, and we all ate together. I had no problem when Ben wasn't there.

The Sunday-night quiet set in as it got dark. It always amazed me how even with the 24/7 the world operated on now, Sunday nights still had a different feel. I always felt a dip in my mood, remembering Sunday evenings when my family was in this same spot. My mother had always made something special for Sunday-night dinner. After she was gone, I'd taken over the job of making it for my father and me, with an occasional guest. Sitting at the table alone with some leftover chili just wasn't the same.

On Monday, Owen came by again with some more photos of the Donte house. We compared them to the shots he had of R.L. Lincoln's and debated which ones to use.

'Are we pointing out that they are alike, though not exactly twin houses anymore?' he asked, laying out photos of the interior rooms that were the same, such as the entrance hall and the living room. 'Or should we show off the differences?'

'Neither,' I said. 'When I redid the copy, I deliberately didn't say anything about Landon's workroom being like a cave or having a door. I didn't want to put in anything that referred to what happened.'

We agreed on the photographs and copy. We just needed Nicole to sign off before we made the rounds of the homeowners to get their approval.

And then it was Tuesday again. I set everything else aside and focused on the group's pages. As I read over Theo's pages again, I was struck by his imagination. He had created a whole world for Cedric Von Brainiac which he accessed through a portal. When I read Ed's and Daryl's, I thought of Lincoln's offer to speak to the group and hoped the two of them would take his advice. I always agonized over Ben's pages. He'd been expressing more emotions in his main character, and I wondered how much the character reflected Ben. Tizzy's pages were the easiest. She wrote well and usually just needed minor changes.

Sara still was off cooking, though she was back to eating with a vengeance. My chili and waffles had been a big hit. But Ben had taken over and was preparing the food for their usual Tuesday-night dinner together. When I heard his menu plan, I was surprised at the complexity of the dish he was making.

'I'd like to say it was all me,' he said with a laugh. 'But they sell these meal kits with instructions at the grocery store now. I have never showed off my skills to you, but I know how to cook – the basics anyway. I promise there will be some for you. I told Quentin I was keeping to my sister's plan to have meatless Tuesdays.'

On the dot of seven, the doorbell began to do its croak sound. Tizzy and Theo were the first to arrive. She was all animated, and Theo looked a little apprehensive. 'He doesn't like to admit it, but it's hard for him to put his work out there for comments,' Tizzy said, patting his arm.

'If it's any consolation, I really liked your pages when I read them over again. They were so imaginative. The portal idea is great.'

Theo brightened. 'You know, I based it on something real that I read. There's a guy who builds armoires with false backs that lead to panic rooms.' He waited to see if I understood what a panic room was. I nodded. It seemed to be mostly the rich and famous Hollywood types or politicians who worried about being kidnapped or robbed and had a secure area in their homes.

Tizzy took him back to the dining room while I waited to let the others in. When they'd all arrived and before we got around to reading their current pages, the usual small talk moved to discussing my current project and Landon Donte's death. Tizzy, Theo, and Ben had all the details, and I told Ed and Daryl that the police were viewing it as a suicide without adding any comments.

'I bet he did himself in because he was so jealous of his neighbor,' Ed said, looking at me. 'You said he lived next door to R.L. Lincoln, right?' I nodded, and he continued, 'I've read some of his books. Just to see what's out there. I admit they are real page-turners. He's got it all in his books – romance, adventure, and some hot stuff. Personally, I'd put in more of the hot stuff.'

'It seems to be working for him,' Daryl said, giving Ed a look.

'There's no shortage of his output,' Theo said. 'But he doesn't get the kind of literary praise that Landon Donte gets. I read a review that called one of R.L. Lincoln's books "fluff and a poor man's vacation."' Theo got a puzzled look from Ed and explained. 'You know, like you can't afford to go anywhere so you read a book that takes you away from it all.'

'I bet Lincoln could care less about all the awards Donte has won. Landon Donte might get all the praise, but Lincoln gets more cash,' Ed said.

'I'm not so sure about that,' Theo said. 'I found an interview online where R.L. Lincoln was asked about Landon Donte. The interviewer asked how it was living so close to a literary genius and having his popular fiction compared to Donte's complex novels. I'm sure if I'd heard his response out loud, the tone would have been more of a joke than serious, but Lincoln said he hoped Donte would move away . . . or drop dead.'

Nobody said anything, but I'm pretty sure we were all thinking the same thing. R.L. Lincoln's wish had come true.

# SIXTEEN

Before I got started on the second round with the home-owners, I had arranged to meet Amanda Brooks, my potential love-letter client.

We had agreed to meet at LaPorte's Café. I am habitually early for appointments and got there well before the agreed time. I spend so much time alone, hovering over a computer, that it was nice to be out in the world where people were enjoying a late breakfast.

I was savoring one of their famous cinnamon rolls and a cup of light-roast coffee that had an extra punch of caffeine when I noticed Brad placing an order at the counter. He had what I'd call a professional student look. That meant that he wore a blazer over his jeans. When he turned, looking for an empty table, I waved at him.

'Join me,' I said.

'Thanks,' he said, setting down his order number and coffee on the table before he sat.

We made small talk about how good the food was and the nice atmosphere of the light-colored wood tables and so many windows looking out on the street. As I blabbered on about my favorite bakery items, it occurred to me that this was a great opportunity to get information from him about Landon Donte.

His food was delivered, and as he dove into his vegetable hash (*a hearty concoction of whatever the greengrocer brought, mixed with cubes of Yukon gold potatoes and plant-based breakfast sausage, complemented by special seasoning*), I opened up the subject.

'What happens to your job now?' I asked.

'Ona is keeping me on long-term. She's overwhelmed with dealing with everything.' He shook his head. 'She's easier to deal with than he was. People on the outside thought I was in the middle of his work, but he kept me out of it. He got real angry at me when I joked about checking out the enemy after I found a copy of R.L. Lincoln's latest book in the kitchen. He wouldn't admit to reading it, but I think he was trying to find out the secret sauce.' I gave Brad a confused look, and he explained. 'He was looking for the magic that made Lincoln's book do so well, so he could steal it.'

'Oh,' I said, surprised. 'Do you think he succeeded?'

Brad put down his fork and took a sip of his coffee. 'He never discussed his writing with me or showed me anything. My job was strictly doing household stuff and dealing with his social media.' He let out a mirthless laugh. 'It was strictly handling the mechanics. He decided what to post.'

'Did you deal with his computer?' I asked, and he shook his head.

'He would never let me near it. He had someone else helping him. Anything I did was on my laptop, on the dining-room table. Dealing with his moods was a real challenge. When he got in a bad one, he was abusive. I was really close to quitting.'

'What about the night of . . .' I hesitated, unsure how to put it. It didn't matter because Brad knew what I meant.

'He was actually in a pretty good mood. He'd had somebody in the workroom earlier, and I think he had some plans about work he was going to have done to the house. I wasn't surprised when he told me to deal with everyone for the dinner. He liked to make a grand entrance.'

'So you had no hint he was depressed or despondent?'

Brad shrugged. 'Unless something happened that I don't know about. Which is entirely possible. That's probably what happened,' he added quickly. 'That's what I told the cops.' He stabbed a hunk of potato on his fork.

'I suppose you're going to ask me about the gun. Landon kept one in his desk drawer. He was a little paranoid and thought bragging about what a great shot he was and that he had a gun would scare off anyone.' He stopped as if thinking about something. 'He was really worried about someone in your group stealing something and wanted me to have a lock put on the cabinet with his awards. He used a weird term and said there was someone with sticky fingers.'

'What about the person who helped him with his computer?'

'All I know is that he answered the door and took her to his office.' Brad took a sip of his coffee and let out a heavy sigh. 'When I first started working for him, I was excited to be so close to such an acclaimed writer. I was supposed to be happy to work for almost nothing just to be in his presence.'

He finished his coffee and got up to leave. 'Things are looking up. Ona seems grateful for my help and even gave me a raise.'

Brad left me with a lot to think about, and I even scribbled down a few notes from what he'd said. Then it was time to change gears. I took a deep breath and lightened up in preparation for my love-letter client. When I saw a dark-haired woman come in and survey the place, I held up my hand. She was wearing a dark blue suit and heels, making her stand out from the mostly casually dressed crowd.

'Veronica?' she said when she reached the table.

I nodded and smiled. 'And you must be Amanda Brooks.'

She saw me looking over her outfit. 'I just came from court,' she said. 'I'm an attorney.' She took off the jacket and draped it over the chair. 'I'll go order something. Can I get you anything?' I pointed at the leftovers of my roll and coffee, and said I was good.

She seemed direct and efficient in person, just as she had on the phone.

She'd barely gotten back to the table when her cappuccino and scrambled-egg breakfast arrived. She carefully placed a napkin in her lap and tasted the cappuccino before looking across the table at me. 'How do we do this?'

'You can begin by telling me about your situation and who the letters would be for,' I said.

'You know those dating shows, where a guy has a bunch of women to choose from. It's kind of like that. Mr X is seeing me and some others, and although it hasn't been said, I know we are in essence auditioning to be his wife. I gather we are all similar and considered well suited to be Mrs X.' She took another sip of the cappuccino and a dainty bite of the eggs. 'I have been all about my career and never thought about the domestic scene of home and hearth. But time is ticking and the thought of having a full-time companion, a couple of kids, and a country club membership sounds pretty good to me now. The whole thing. Simply put, I want him to choose me and was looking for some way to stand out from the others. I thought love letters might work. When I Googled "love letters," your website was the only one that came up.' She certainly was direct.

'Are you saying you're in love with this man?' I asked.

'I certainly like him. We would make a good team, which, in the long run, works better than something based on passion that fades.'

'It sounds like you know what you want. If I'm going to work with you, I need to know the man's identity. Ideally, I'd like to get a chance to meet him. Incognito, of course.'

'I'd rather not,' she said. 'He can't know that I hired somebody.'

I had no choice but to be honest with her. 'I have to be sure that your intentions are as you describe.'

'You mean that I'm not a stalker or have nefarious motives,' she said with a smile. 'How about this? I can't possibly let you meet him, incognito or not, but I'll tell you who he is and I'll give you an agreement stating that I'm hiring you to write letters for me and exonerating you from any responsibility for the outcome.'

She looked at me for some kind of response. She took my silence as negotiating (actually, I was thinking about eating the last bite of cinnamon roll) and upped the offer. 'As an incentive, I will promise you a bonus if we become engaged, and if it goes all the way to marriage, I will have you create the wedding invitations and write my wedding vows.'

It was more than I was usually offered, and she seemed too dispassionate to be a stalker, so I agreed. She held out her hand, and we shook on it. 'I will email the agreement to you later today. In the meantime, his name is Parker Andrews, and I'm sure you can find out whatever you want to know about him online.' She had just about finished her food. 'Now, can we talk about the letters? I want to get going on this posthaste.'

'Were you thinking actual love letters like "How do I love thee? Let me count the ways"?' I said, and she wrinkled her nose.

'I don't think that's the way to go with him. I need something that will make me stick in his mind, intrigue him, and capture his imagination. I would do it myself, but I'm an attorney, and it's not the way my mind works.'

I asked for a moment to think, and a possibility popped into my mind. 'How about we make the notes or letters anonymous but find a way to connect them with you?'

She took a moment to consider it and then brightened. 'I like it. Snag him with something intriguing. None of the others would think of that.' She picked up her cup, prepared to take a drink, and stopped. 'But he needs to know they're coming from me, without exactly knowing.'

I assured her we would come up with a way.

She was so enthused about the plan that she gave my arm a squeeze before she got up and hurried off to her next appointment.

As soon as she left, I started researching her intended on my phone. Parker Andrews was the scion of a family whose wealth came from real estate, as in they owned skyscrapers in downtown Chicago. He was doing pretty well on his own, running a private equity fund. From the many photos online of him, he appeared to be confident but on the bland side.

He had the penthouse in the most expensive building in the city, with a perfect view of Lake Michigan. She had made him sound emotionally neutral, and I had the feeling he was the kind of guy who thought about who he was with when he was on a date, but then put them out of his mind as soon as it ended. I wondered if he had an imagination that could be tickled.

# SEVENTEEN

'Here's what we have,' I said, holding out a portfolio to Nicole. Owen had left me to be the spokesperson and was standing behind me. It was hardly a good place to show off our work. Nicole had insisted we meet her outside her kids' school while she was waiting for them. I expected her to take the portfolio with her and get back to us with a list of changes, but she pulled everything out right there and looked it over. It was just a cursory glance and then she shoved it all back in the big brown envelope. 'Looks good to me,' she said just as the doors opened and a flood of kids came out.

'Wow, that was easy,' Owen said. 'It was almost like she didn't care.'

'Yes, she did seem less intense than usual. I hope the home-owners are as easy,' I said. I agreed to set up the appointments with the Malins, the Fellowses, R.L. Lincoln, and the Scrivners. 'I suppose we should show what we have to Landon's daughter.'

Setting up the appointments was easy, and I looked forward to traveling with a smaller crowd.

I did let Tizzy talk me into letting her come along on our first stop at the Malins'. She wanted to see the elevator and lower-floor kitchen. Since she was part of the organization that was arranging the tour and she'd been the one who'd helped me get the gig, I agreed.

We met the next morning on the sidewalk outside the Malins' house. 'I couldn't tell Theo I was coming with you,' Tizzy said. 'He'd be so jealous. He'd love to see that elevator and then he'd probably want one in our house.'

She had rushed over from her office on the campus of the university during her supposed coffee break. Her floral-print kimono top fluttered in the breeze. It was warm enough that the silky jacket over a collarless shirt and leggings was enough. 'Alex is very generous about letting me take extra time, but there's something I have to finish before lunch.' She let out a laugh. 'He wants to hear about the elevator, too.' I was going to tell her about my conversation with Brad, but Owen got out of a car that had just pulled to the curb.

I introduced Owen and Tizzy and watched as she did her magic. In the few minutes we stood there, she already knew where he'd gone to school, that he wanted to capture the personality of the person or place he photographed, and that was what made an artist different from someone grabbing pictures with their cell phone.

Jerry Malin answered the door and invited us in. 'Christine isn't here. She had a crisis with a patient. I'm sure I can take care of checking over the pictures and description of the house,' he said as he brought us inside.

Once I'd introduced Tizzy, and as soon as she started asking about the elevator and new kitchen, he warmed up and offered to show her everything. 'But let's take care of business first,' he said. He suggested we use their dining-room table and offered us coffee or tea.

Owen and I had laid everything out by the time Jerry brought in the drinks and a plate of cookies.

'That turned out to be some progressive dinner,' Tizzy said, looking at our host.

'It was pretty shocking,' Jerry said. 'I don't know if I agree with Christine. She thinks Donte did it when we were all there because he wanted an audience.'

'Is that a general statement?' I asked. 'Or is it personal to him?'

Jerry looked at me. 'You mean, is he a patient? As a therapist, Christine would never divulge the identity of her patients or their issues, dead or alive. She is very careful to adhere to the ethics of her profession. It's a lot easier for me. I love to talk about the elevators I've helped people in the neighborhood install. Arden Fellows wants me to help find the right place for one in their house.' He picked up the copy I'd written, reading it over. 'This is excellent. I like how you said we mixed old and new in a practical way.' He looked it over again. 'There are a few minor mistakes about the elevator.' He got a piece of paper and wrote out the corrections. I checked them over, noting that he had an odd slant to his handwriting even though it was perfectly legible.

I promised to make the corrections and put the paper in my

purse. He moved on to the photographs and seemed pleased with the ones we'd chosen.

'Did you hear the gunshot?' I asked, going back to the night of the progressive dinner. His expression faded a little.

'There was a lot of noise with the music and everyone talking,' he said with a shrug. 'It was hardly something I expected.' He picked up one of the photos of the kitchen.

'How well do you know the other people?' I asked. 'I mean, have you talked over what happened with any of the other guests there that night?'

He went on about giving the police a statement. 'I really didn't know most of them, except for Arden and Gena Fellows. Really Gena. We've been at gatherings together before. Their house is down the street.' He punctuated it with a gesture. 'Christine and Arden are always in the center of things, while Gena and I are the ones left to hold their drinks and such.' He let out a light chuckle. 'I don't mind being the support staff, but Gena is another story. She's always seemed unhappy with the background position. But everybody loves Arden. He has a way of making everyone feel comfortable. She's . . .' He searched for a word. 'Prickly. Like there's an undercurrent of anger that her husband gets all the attention. She's tried to needle me, asking if it didn't bother me that Christine is the alpha in our family.'

'Well, aren't you the talking jaybird?' Christine Malin said. None of us had noticed that she'd come home and was standing in the doorway to the dining room. The attention all turned to her as she looked over the materials on the table and then at the group.

'I thought I told you to change the time.' She focused on her husband.

'There was no reason for you to be bothered. I'm certainly capable of looking over some photographs and copy about the house.'

'But you should have told me.' She caught herself and smiled at us. 'My husband is too thoughtful.' She had a hawk-like gaze as she stopped on each of our faces and settled on Tizzy. 'You're new. I don't think we've met.' She waited while Tizzy introduced herself and gave herself the title of advisor and explained she was a member of the Friends of Hyde Park group that was putting on the garden and house tour.

'Veronica told me all about what you've done with this place, and I talked her into letting me come with her so I could see it first-hand,' Tizzy said, sounding impressed.

'I am rather proud of the work we've done.' She looked at her husband. 'Why don't you show her around while I deal with this.' She indicated the papers on the table.

'Sure,' he said, getting up. Tizzy looked back and gave me a nod.

'Let me see what you have.' She sat down, and I noticed that Jerry had left her a cup of coffee, the creamy color hinting that he'd added whatever she took in it.

'We were just talking about the other night.' My voice grew somber. 'And what happened with Landon Donte.'

She made a 'hmm' sound to acknowledge that she heard me, but her attention seemed to be on the photographs and copy.

'You're a professional, and I'm sure you would have had a different take on it from the rest of us. Did you see any hints that he was going to . . .'

'Kill himself?' she said, looking up from the photograph. 'Don't be ridiculous. I barely knew the man. I'm a psychologist, not a mind reader. I tried to step in when he had the standoff with that woman and use my professional skills to calm the situation. I didn't realize she was his daughter. I've heard since that he might have been worried about the manuscript he was working on. Something about his last book not doing well.' She peered at me. 'You're a writer, so you probably know what it's like to worry that you can't perform to your own expectations. And in his case, if he flopped again, it would all be very public.' She picked up one of the pages I'd brought and read it over.

'Of course, this is a different kind of writing. You're just presenting facts about how this place looks and who lived here and such,' she said in a dismissive manner.

I should have just let it go, but it touched a sensitive spot. It had been implied more than once that I just dropped words into a template. 'I actually do more than this sort of writing,' I said, forcing my voice to sound friendly.

'That's right, you said something about love letters before.'

Dr Malin had an amused, condescending smile. 'Tell me about the people who hire you.'

I should have let it go, but somehow I felt the need to show off what I did. I wasn't under any legal obligation to maintain confidentiality with my clients the way she was with her patients, but I still kept it very vague, describing the challenge I had with my new client. She was fascinated when I explained what the woman wanted me to do. Then she laughed. 'And I wonder what will happen when she "catches" him and he realizes she's not as fascinating as he thought.'

I was trying to think of a retort but coming up empty. I was relieved when Jerry returned with Owen and Tizzy in tow. Tizzy was looking at her watch and walking to the door. 'Thank you for the tour, but I have to get back to work,' she said.

'I think we're all finished here,' Dr Malin said, handing the photographs to Owen and the other pages to me. To make it even clearer, she got up from the table. 'I made a few corrections,' she said, looking at me.

The three of us stopped on the sidewalk outside. 'Until next time,' Owen said, putting his hand on my arm in a friendly gesture before he went on his way.

'Ben had better look out,' Tizzy said as we watched him go down the street.

'No. It's nothing like that. We're just both freelancers and simpatico.'

'Maybe you see it that way,' Tizzy said, 'but I don't think he does.'

'Whatever,' I said with a dismissive shake of my head. 'What's more important is what did you and Jerry talk about?'

She glanced down at her smartwatch as it started to vibrate on her wrist. 'I have to go. I'm late,' she said, already beginning to walk away. 'Sherry tonight at our place, and I'll tell all.' She added a little laugh. 'Aren't you always telling the group that it's good to add some suspense?'

Rocky followed me into my office when I got home. I dropped the marked-up sheets next to my computer and flopped in the chair. There were people who gave you energy and those that made you feel as though they'd sucked it all out. Dr Malin belonged to the latter. I just wanted to be done with their entry and gladly made all the corrections she had specified. I had gotten the number of burners on the stove wrong, and she didn't like that I'd called the cabinets *an antiseptic white*. I saved the file and got up to check Rocky's food bowl and make myself some lunch.

Jerry was OK – maybe even more than that – but Christine Malin rubbed me the wrong way. I'm sure she would say, in her professional opinion, it meant that she'd touched some vulnerable spots. Maybe it was true. Maybe I did feel defensive about doing the love letters, but her comments were unnecessarily cutting.

I was glad to walk over to Tizzy and Theo's for our end-of-the-day drinks. I was curious to discover whether Jerry Malin had told Tizzy anything interesting, and I could safely dump my feelings about the psychologist if I so chose. Tizzy wasn't home yet, and Theo brought me inside. He had everything set up, and we began on our drinks and snacks while we waited for her.

In the meantime, I told him about the morning visit, though mostly about how I didn't care for Christine Malin.

'You know what they say about psychologists,' he said. He didn't wait for me to answer before he continued. 'That they go into it because their own lives are a mess. What about her husband? I've heard some of them meet their spouses in therapy. The patient falls in love with the doctor.'

'She seems to dominate him, but from what he said when she wasn't there, he knows it and is OK with it,' I said.

'Did she have anything to say about what happened to Landon Donte, from a professional point of view?' Theo asked.

'She said she didn't know him and had only seen him for the few minutes when he showed up at R.L. Lincoln's.' Just then Tizzy came in and joined us.

Theo pointed to the glass of sherry waiting for her and let her settle. I restrained myself and let her have a few moments, but I was anxious to hear about what had gone on while Jerry Malin gave her a tour of the place.

She decompressed quickly and regarded me with a teasing smile. 'I think that's enough suspense,' she said. She took a moment to explain the situation to her husband before she began.

'First of all, that house is really great.' She told Theo about the elevator and they took a moment to discuss how things that used to be out of reach for all but the very rich were now available to the masses. Then she went back to my question.

'Did you notice how he tensed up when his wife walked in?' Tizzy asked.

'I must have missed it. I guess I was too intent on how they'd react to what I'd written.'

'Well, as soon as he got away from his wife, he seemed to relax again,' Tizzy said. 'I got such a different vibe from him when it was just the two of us,' she said.

'You mean he started to hit on you?' her husband said, sitting up straighter.

'No,' she laughed. 'He just talked more. He said they had considered turning the ground floor into an office where his wife could see patients since it had a separate entrance, but they were afraid it might compromise the patients' privacy. Neighbors could see who they were.' Tizzy turned to her husband. 'He said if we wanted to put in an elevator, he'd be glad to advise us on it.'

Theo got busy on his computer, which he did often, looking for information on things we were talking about. He found something about how reasonable the cost of adding an elevator was and then he went back to checking other things while Tizzy and I finished off the snacks. He suddenly sat up straight and let out an 'aha.'

'Didn't you say that Doctor Malin didn't know Landon Donte?' He looked at me, and I thought back over what I'd said and nodded.

'Maybe that's not exactly true,' he said. He turned the laptop around so that I could see the screen. He'd gone to Amazon and clicked on Landon's last book, getting a look at the beginning pages. There, in the acknowledgments, it thanked Dr Christine Malin *for her insightful feedback on his characterization of human behavior* which had confirmed his own observations. 'I wonder why she lied. I bet she knows more than she's letting on.'

It sounded right to me.

# EIGHTEEN

'What do you think it means?' I said to Ben. We were just leaving a banquet hall on the southwestern edge of the city. I had done my duty as his plus-one at a retirement party for one of the sergeants in the Weston Police Department, where Ben worked. I had just finished telling him that Christine Malin claimed not to know Landon Donte but had gotten a mention in the acknowledgments of his previous book.

'I was hoping for a different vein of conversation,' he said. He put his arm around me as we walked to his Wrangler. 'So, tell me about that meeting. Was the photographer there?'

'Yes. The point of the meeting was to show them what we had and get any corrections or requests for changes.'

'And then what?'

I was confused by what he meant. 'We took their suggestions,' I said. 'But don't you think it's strange that the psychologist said she didn't know the victim, but he thanked her for her help?'

'We'll get to that. You were going to tell me what happened after you left – with the photographer.'

'He has a name,' I said. 'Owen. And nothing happened after the meeting. I went home and I guess he did, too. And then he sent me a picture he'd taken of me and offered it for my website.' Ben stiffened, and I rolled my eyes as I suddenly understood. I was really dense. Ben was acting jealous. 'As I told Tizzy, both Owen and I are freelancers, and we might be able to help each other. That's all.'

Ben let out a sigh. 'Sorry. I just think any guy would be a fool not to be trying to get next to you.'

'Thanks,' I said. 'But I think any closeness Owen is interested in is helping him get work. But I'm flattered that you think I'm that hot.' I laughed at the word. I had never viewed myself as *hot*. It had been drummed into me as a kid that it was *pretty is as pretty does*, which was a clichéd way of saying that it was what was inside that counted, and I'd been more into who I was than how I looked. I'd never gotten caught up in manicured nails, lots of makeup, or suggestive clothes.

'Am I supposed to start listing the ways you're hot now?' he said, half joking.

'No, just tell me what you think about Doctor Malin lying about knowing the dead guy.'

He pulled into a spot in front of my building and cut the motor. 'We could discuss it upstairs,' he said. 'And maybe have that talk about where we stand with each other.' I froze at the words. It was weird. At first, he'd been the hesitant one, but now it was me. I was sure I could divert him back to the case of what really happened to Landon Donte, and I agreed.

It turned out to be a non-issue because as we passed the second floor, Sara opened the door and looked at us as if we were sailors who had just arrived at a desert island. 'Thank heaven you're here. Quentin's at work, Mikey can't sleep, and I'm falling apart.'

# NINETEEN

'Here we are again,' I said as Owen and I met up outside the Fellowses' massive house the next day. I was looking at the house, but Owen seemed to be looking at me, and I wondered if what Tizzy and Ben had said might be true. It didn't matter because I wasn't interested in him like that. I pushed away the thought and led the way to the front door.

I looked it over and compared it to what I'd written. The house was huge and sat in the middle of a sizable piece of land. I scribbled in something about the tall elm tree next to the house.

Gena Fellows answered right away. She looked over the two of us as we came inside. 'I'm glad there aren't so many of you this time. Arden isn't here. But I'm perfectly capable of handling the photographs and copy.' She took us into the spacious living room and offered us seats around a glass coffee table. She had said almost the exact same thing that Jerry Malin had said. I guess they were two betas in a pod. And that wasn't a cliché, but a modern update of one.

I watched Gena as she looked through the photographs that Owen had put on the table. She seemed dressed up for our meeting, and I recognized the simple pair of loose black pants with a violet-colored boxy top as being part of a designer collection I'd admired at Macy's – that is, until I'd seen the price. I thought back to what someone had said about Gena being prickly, and I certainly agreed.

She found a photograph that Owen had taken of her that she liked. 'You've caught the real me,' she said. 'I will definitely consider you when I'm ready for the publicity shots.'

The photographer lit up at the prospect of getting work from her. 'I can do whatever you need. Headshots or something more moody that captures your personality.' He hadn't brought his camera, but he used his phone to grab a few samples of what he could do and showed her the results. 'This should give you an idea. But using my camera and lighting will give much better results.'

'Is it something with Arden for the university?' I asked, and she bristled.

'No. This is about me and my work. I am more than Arden's wife and my kids' mother. It's bad luck to talk about things until they are settled, but I feel pretty confident.' She smiled to herself. 'Won't I surprise them all?'

She went back to looking through the pictures of the interior of the house. 'I knew I was right,' she exclaimed, holding up one of the photographs. She pointed to a row of tiny silver vases. She counted them out loud, her voice rising when she got to five. She pointed to the shelf in the living room and counted again. There were only four. 'Arden thought I was crazy when I said one was missing after the bunch of you came the first time. He insisted that I say nothing about it, that it didn't go with his reputation to accuse people of stealing doodads. He wants everybody to like him and to come across as oh-so understanding,' she said in a mocking voice. 'But there it is, clear as day. Someone in your group took one.' She turned her gaze on me in an accusatory manner.

I had to say something. The best I could come up with was an apology and promise that I would talk to Nicole since she was the one in charge of the event. 'I'm sure we'll work something out.'

Trying to move on, I handed her the copy I'd written about the place. She started to read it over and then pulled out a pencil and started making markings. 'I'm sure you'll see that the changes I have made improve the piece.'

Owen got a look at the sheets as she handed them to me, and his eyes went skyward. I glanced down at the paper and saw she had made a change in just about every line and written arrows to show altering the order of the paragraphs. My immediate response was to dismiss her changes, but then I wondered what my obligation was: please her or produce the best piece? 'I'll certainly take your suggestions into consideration,' I said, trying to be diplomatic. 'This was really about having you check the facts rather than being concerned with the style. Writing this sort of copy is my business,' I said. When I noticed Gena bristling at my comment, I tried to defuse the situation. 'But I'll show your suggestions to Nicole since she's the one in charge.'

'Who is she, anyway?' Gena peered at me for an answer. She had excluded Owen from the conversation, and he seemed relieved.

'I don't really know a lot about her,' I said. 'I heard she and her husband are new to the area, and it was her idea to add the houses to the usual garden tour. She's the one responsible for putting it together.'

'Are they taking the Donte house out of the tour?' she asked. Owen swallowed loudly in the background.

'The organizers considered it but decided to keep it in,' I said. Her demeanor changed after that, and it seemed as if she let down her defenses.

'I'm still in shock about what happened. If only Landon would have said something.' She sounded a little dazed. 'I just can't imagine him killing himself. He should never have had that gun.'

'Then you knew him?' I said.

'Yes,' she said. I waited for her to elaborate, but that was all she said before she stood up, making it clear we were done.

Owen offered his sympathies before we went our separate ways. I went home and took some time to recover from the meeting. I had been expecting it to be easy. Maybe if Arden Fellows had been there, it would have been. He was charming and friendly and agreeable. When I'd met Gena before, his personality had dominated. Dealing with her was hardly pleasant and left me in a bad mood. I started getting indignant all over again at her extreme editing of my copy. Who did she think she was? And then it came back to me. Hadn't she said something about being a writer the first time we'd met?

My thoughts were interrupted by a knock at my door. A bedraggled-looking Sara, with Mikey clinging to her leg, was in the doorway. I invited them in right away.

'I'm hoping it's just going to be like this for the first three months,' she said. 'One day I can't look at food and the next I'm ravenous. And I'm so tired.' She stuck her head in and gave a longing look at my couch.

'I'm sure you're right about the three months. And then it'll get better,' I said, trying to be reassuring. Rocky took one look at the toddler and disappeared to a hiding place. I brought them back to the dining room, and Sara collapsed on the couch while Mikey went right for the toy box.

It was a ravenous day, and I made them grilled cheese sandwiches with some fruit on the side. Sara ate two sandwiches and the leftover crust of Mikey's. I knew Sara wasn't herself because she never even asked where her brother and I had been the other night. I was so used to her trying to boost a relationship between us that it seemed strange for her to not care.

When they left, I looked over all of Gena's markings on my work again and cringed at her audacity. And then there was her fuss about the missing vase. As far as I was concerned, it was all on Nicole, or Serena since she was the president of the group. I tried calling both of them but only got voicemail. It was still bothering me when I went to Tizzy's for sherry time.

After hearing about my encounter with Gena Fellows, Theo held out the cocktail glass holding his martini. 'I think you need more than a whiff of the fragrance.' I thanked him but said no, remembering how the taste didn't match the smell.

'I'm turning it all over to a third party,' I said, mentioning that I'd left word for Nicole and Serena.

Theo looked up from the computer. 'Look what I found about Gena Fellows?' he said and turned the screen so we could all see it. There was a page announcing that a website was under construction.

As we were talking, I remembered something else about that first encounter with Gena. 'She went on about having a famous mentor. I didn't think much about who it was, but she seemed so distraught about Landon,' I said, looking at my drinking buddies. 'I wonder if he was her supposed mentor? It's hard to imagine him taking a student, but then I'm not sure how much of a mentor he was,' I said, remembering the way she'd responded when I asked how often they got together. I told them how she had simply not answered. I said. 'She talked about needing publicity shots and having something in the offing that she thought was going to surprise everyone. If you put it all together, I would guess that she'd written something and thinks it's going to get published,' I said. 'She certainly has a very high opinion of her abilities.' I'd brought with me the marked-up page and showed it to them.

'Why didn't she just say that Donte was helping her?' Theo asked.

'That's a good point,' I said. 'But thinking over my two encounters with her, it seems pretty clear that she's unhappy being in anyone's shadow. The point she seemed to make was that a famous writer recognized her talent.'

'Did she seem surprised about the suicide?' Theo asked.

'Yes, but she seemed to accept that was what it was,' I said.

'With the room bolted shut and all, maybe it was,' Theo said. 'Landon could have been one of those people who don't accept their left-handedness and taught himself to be ambidextrous.'

I shook my head. 'Even if that was true, it seems unlikely in the heat of wanting to end things that he'd go with his non-dominant hand. I think someone killed him. I just have to figure out how they bolted the door from the inside and managed to escape.'

When I got home and checked my landline, I saw there was nothing from Nicole, but Serena had returned my call. I dropped my jacket on the couch and sat down to return her call. It was a relief when she answered and the game of phone tag ended.

I explained the marked-up copy after we went through our greeting. 'I'd rather ignore her changes, but it's really outside my authority,' I said. Serena let out a sound of displeasure.

'I'm sorry that Gena Fellows is being so difficult. But she's married to a highly regarded professor, which gives her a certain amount of reflected clout. I would suggest you just swallow it and go along with her changes, but really it's up to Nicole since this tour was her idea and she's the one in charge.'

Just then Rocky jumped on the couch and butted his head against my side as if to remind me that I'd been gone a lot and he needed some attention. When I didn't respond right away, he jumped on to the coffee table and started knocking things over. As he pushed over a tiny silver metal vase with some beaded flowers in it and it rolled toward me, I remembered something.

'There's another problem,' I said, wondering how I could have forgotten about it. I told her about the missing vase.

'That's not good. Not good at all,' Serena said with a groan. 'I can't imagine what happened to it, but we can't have her broadcasting that someone in our group stole something.' I thought she was going to say something about handling it, but instead she said that she regretted ever agreeing to adding houses to the tour. 'First there was Landon's death in the middle of the progressive dinner and now this. It's too late to do anything about that now. If you don't hear from Nicole, let me know, and I'll talk to her. She has to figure out a way to cover it up.'

When I got off the phone, I was struck by how different Serena seemed from the way she'd been when she'd told me about her desire to reconnect with Landon Donte. She'd seemed starry-eyed as she'd told me about their past and how she thought he'd honored it by making her a character in his books. Now she sounded more like a mob boss looking to snuff out problems.

Nicole called me a few minutes later. Although she didn't say anything, I was sure she'd had a call from Serena.

She sounded annoyed, and I was just able to give her the basics that there was a problem with the Fellowses. 'I can't deal with this now. I'm just putting my kids to bed. Can't you just handle it?' she said.

'No. You are the boss of this project.' I couldn't believe that she was trying to dump it on me.

She huffed and puffed but finally agreed to meet in person. The time we agreed on coincided with my meeting with my romance client to go over my first missive, which I reminded myself I still had to create.

As soon as I got off the phone, I gave Rocky a lot of snuggles to make up for my absences, while my mind wandered to Amanda Brooks. What could I possibly come up with that would intrigue a financial tycoon enough that he would choose her from his stable of women?

This, on top of the situation with Gena Fellows, was too much, and I began to have a panicky feeling that I'd agreed to something I wouldn't be able to deliver. Finally, I turned to chamomile tea and crochet to calm myself so I could fall asleep, hoping the new day would bring inspiration.

# TWENTY

It didn't. The next morning, after spending too much time staring at a blank screen, I pushed away from my desk. 'I need to get out of here for a while,' I said out loud. Rocky was asleep on the burgundy wing chair in my office and opened his eyes for a moment and then closed them again. When I checked the front windows, the sun was shining and the sky was a hazy blue. The weather could be turbulent at this time of year. A change of the wind, and a cold front could move in and create thunderstorms. I was determined to seize the moment and take advantage of the peaceful sky and go out. I'd been sitting too much anyway and needed a walk to stretch my legs and clear my mind.

I considered checking in on Sara, but it was quiet as I passed her door on the second floor. Maybe she and Mikey were both catching a nap. I was surprised at how warm and moist the air felt when I got outside and took off my hoodie and tied it around my waist, glad to be out in the world and away from my computer.

I turned on 57th and headed east toward the lakefront. A group of joggers went past me with the same idea. There was something about walking along the shore that always refreshed me and, I hoped, would inspire me. The 57th Street Beach was deserted for now, but in another month the lifeguards would be back, the sand would be sprinkled with beach towels, and the sound of the waves would be mixed with the squeals of kids playing in the water. I couldn't pass the beach without thinking back to how my mother had taken me there on summer mornings. How excited I'd been to take off my shoes and run through the sand. The water would feel cold at first until the first dunk, which always left me breathless, and then I'd be used to it and splash around until my mother got me out and wrapped me in a towel. How safe and happy I'd felt.

I let out a sigh. No chance of feeling that supported and cared for anymore. I was on my own, trying to make a living by my wits. And working on not getting too stuck in my ways. I honestly believed that I had become more of a *whatever* sort of person. Even the situation with Ben. I wanted to just let it be and allow it to progress on its own.

It was funny with relationships. If people were too difficult, it was a problem, and if they were too easy, it was a different kind of problem. It seemed a wonder that anyone got together.

I deliberately didn't think about Amanda and her letters. It worked best when I focused on other things and let my unconscious work its magic. I steered my thoughts to the house tour. It always fascinated me to think about how my perception of things changed. I thought back to the meeting that Tizzy had brought me to and how I had judged all the people when I didn't know anything about them.

Serena Lawrence had seemed like a pleasant enough woman in her fifties in charge of running the neighborhood group. I had thought Nicole was driven and not particularly friendly. I hadn't known Roman Scrivner was the attorney starring in the TV commercials – only that he and his wife were sponsors of the tour. He'd seemed self-important from the start, and Ruth had seemed distant. And Landon Donte was just a name on the spine of a book. How things had changed.

I walked along the blocks of limestone that bordered the water as they curved toward the peninsula that stuck out in the water and was called the Point. I let my mind wander as I took in the view to the south. An industrial area pumping out smoke outlined the end of the huge lake, which some people considered to be an inland sea. As I rounded the tip of the Point, the view went from open water to the downtown skyline softened by the haze in the air.

My thoughts were stuck on Landon Donte. Could there be an explanation for which hand he'd used? Suicide did seem the most convenient explanation. Wouldn't there have been some hint, though? Nothing in his demeanor had suggested that he was in such despair. I thought about myself. As hopeless as I'd ever felt about the second Derek Streeter book, I'd never come close to wanting to end it all. But then I didn't have the literary reputation that Landon Donte had. It happened that writers lost their touch. How bad could his manuscript have been? No one would ever know. I thought of the shreds of yellow and white paper that were all that was left of his manuscript since he'd deleted what was on the computer.

As I got back to my corner, I saw the sign on the window of the coffee shop advertising that their soup of the day was cream of broccoli. My stomach rumbled, reminding me that I was hungry and their homemade soup was so good.

It was the slow time of mid-morning, and only a few of the booths were occupied. I was considering where to sit when I saw a familiar face. Familiar, but not exactly good-familiar.

Detective Jankowski met my gaze and waved me over.

'Doing one of your friendly interrogations?' I said, noting that an empty mug was on the other side of the table. I knew only too well the cop trick of questioning someone in a place like this to throw them off guard. It seemed more social than official, which was the point.

'Not that I owe you any explanations, but it was just breakfast with a colleague.' He pointed at the empty side of the booth. 'As long as you're here.'

I accepted the invitation and sat.

'Go crazy – food is on the department,' he said, pushing a menu across the table. I wondered what this was about. Was it going to be more of him treating me as a colleague as he'd done when we'd met right after Landon Donte's death? There was a much-used phrase that might express his sentiment: *If you can't beat them, join them.* After I ordered the soup, I waited to see what he was going to say.

'I could make some small talk to open things up, but why not just get to the point?' he said. 'You were there the evening Donte died. How about you tell me again what you saw and heard?'

'You still believe it was a suicide?' I said.

'That wasn't what I asked you,' the detective said. He poked his fork through the remnants of eggs on his plate. 'Everything about it says suicide,' he said. 'The note on the computer, the way he destroyed his manuscript, and the fact that he'd bolted himself in the room.'

'The first few lines looked as though they could be a suicide note, and then there seemed to be nothing, as if he'd deleted his manuscript. I don't know about you, but I scrolled down and kept scrolling, and after some blank screen, there was something left at the end of the file.' I looked at him again. 'I don't know how familiar you are with computers.' He pursed his lips in annoyance.

'I know how they work,' he said. 'Just because I use a notebook and pen for notes doesn't mean that I'm computer illiterate. Do you want to get to your point?'

The steaming bowl of soup arrived and I gathered up a spoonful and tasted it. Partly because I was really hungry and partly to show him that I wouldn't be rushed.

'The point is,' I said finally, 'it wasn't all deleted.'

'Which means what?' he said, tilting his head as he put me on the spot.

I hadn't thought about it at the time. 'That maybe whoever deleted it didn't know where it ended.'

He seemed unimpressed. 'He could have missed some pages in the heat of his emotion,' Jankowski said.

'If his motive was to make the manuscript disappear, I don't think he would have left anything. Look at how all the yellow sheets and his hard copy were shredded.'

He didn't seem particularly impressed. I didn't know if his investigation had included finding out about Landon's left-handedness. If he didn't know and I brought it up, he probably wouldn't take it well. As if I had one-upped him, which, of course, I would have. It seemed better to tread lightly.

'What about his hands?' I said. He shrugged and gave me a perplexed look. 'Well, wasn't he shot on the right side? I'm pretty sure I noticed he was left-handed.'

The detective's expression froze for a moment and then went back to its usual lack of expression. 'He could have been ambidextrous. There were powder burns on his right hand. Are you saying you think there was someone else?' He didn't sound particularly impressed. 'Then maybe you can explain how they got out of the room.'

'Maybe they went out of the window,' I said.

'We checked,' he said with a disproving shake of his head. 'The windows in that room are painted shut, and it's pretty clear they haven't been opened.' The detective looked down at his plate and pushed it away. 'I suppose you've come up with a motive.'

'One could be to do with the book he was writing. Someone didn't want it to come out.' I was improvising now and reaching somewhat. 'Because there was something in it that was personal.'

He seemed unimpressed. 'I suppose you have a whole list of suspects.'

Actually, I did. There was the romance writer who lived next door, who had said he wished Landon would die. Ona Chapin clearly had a problem with her father. I was just thinking about Roman Scrivner when the detective got my attention.

'Don't worry about giving me the list. You figure out how someone got out of the room, and then we'll talk. Until then, we're sticking with suicide. Enjoy your soup.'

# TWENTY-ONE

The walk along the lakefront and the unexpected meeting with the detective were just the distractions I needed. When I got home, I plopped in front of my computer and came up with two ideas for notes for Amanda Brooks. It was hard to consider them love letters. Love seemed to have nothing to do with what she wanted, and my ideas were closer to notes than letters.

I printed up what I had and put it in my messenger bag, along with Gena Fellows' scribbles on my notes so they'd be there when I met with Amanda and Nicole the next day.

With no appointments for that afternoon, I was free to work on my own book in progress. More like the book that was almost done.

All this talk about Donte and his worry about living up to his reputation had left me thinking about my issues. I had been stalling too long. It was time to push ahead, mark *The End*, and then send it to the publisher. I took a deep breath, pulled up the file on my computer, and started to work on the rewrite.

I got into the flow and was lost in Derek Streeter's world when my phone pinged with a text from Tizzy saying they were waiting for me. I was stunned when I looked around and realized what time it was.

I had a pleased grin on my face when I got to Tizzy's. The weather had stayed nice and they had set up sherry time on their back deck.

'You look happy,' Tizzy said as I sat in one of the wooden Adirondack chairs.

It was kind of blowing my workshop leader's position with them, but I told them about finally working on my book. They were both surprised when I admitted all the trouble I'd been having. 'I thought it was easy for you,' Theo said.

'It isn't easy for anyone,' I said. After that, I didn't want to say more, explaining that talking about it released the energy and it was better to leave it pent up, so it came out in the writing.

'Great advice,' Theo said. 'I'm not going to say anything about Cedric Von Brainiac.' He made the joke gesture of zipping up his lips, and we all laughed.

'I won't talk about my work,' I said. 'But there's nothing to stop us from talking about Landon Donte's.' I told them about my soup date with the detective and how we'd talked about Donte's deleted manuscript. 'What writer doesn't back up their work?' I said.

'That was the first thing you told the writers' group when we started. Always make another copy or save it in the cloud,' Tizzy said.

'The cloud?' I said with a laugh. 'He used his computer like a glorified typewriter, and, according to his assistant, he was paranoid. I think the cloud was merely a white puff in the sky to him.'

Tizzy downed the last few drops of the amber liquid. The bottle was on the table, and Theo picked it up with a question in his eye. 'Seconds?'

'Why not?' his wife said. 'The glass barely holds a thimble-full.' He smiled and refilled the tiny glass.

Setting up on the deck had included Theo's laptop, and he was busy searching for something. He looked up at us as he turned the screen to face us. There was a very old photograph of R.L. Lincoln's and Landon Donte's houses when they were first built. 'They were originally built for twin sisters, and, like their owners, the houses were identical. They were referred to as the Heller houses, but over time the names became identified with different owners. I was surprised to read that Donte's house had belonged to Daniel Willman. His claim to fame is that he won a Nobel Prize in Biophysics.' Theo shrugged. 'The family was rather reclusive. The wife lived part-time in Iceland. I think there was a problem with their child. I don't know if it was a girl or a boy. They were sent off to boarding school. And then one day they were gone. The name of the most famous resident seems to stick with the house. After what happened to Landon Donte, it will stay the Donte house forever.'

'Thanks,' I said and asked him to email the story to me.

The conversation turned to Theo's plan for a vegetable garden in their yard, and he started researching different kinds of tomatoes.

It was only after I left that I realized I had forgotten to mention the stolen vase. Probably because I didn't want to think about it.

'It's not my problem,' I said to Rocky the next morning as I grabbed my peacock-blue messenger bag for the two meetings. I'd already accepted that I'd have to go with Gena Fellows' editing, and Nicole was going to have to figure out the vase situation.

My thoughts were focused on Amanda Brooks as I walked down to 53rd. She had sent the letter of agreement with all the points she'd mentioned. The man she wanted the letters for was auditioning for a wife, and she was looking for an edge so he'd pick her. It all sounded so calculating and cold-blooded, but then it wasn't my place to judge. Maybe it was wishful thinking, but I wanted to believe that love conquered all – even if it was a cliché.

I patted the bag just before I went into the Starbucks, hoping that what I'd brought would please Amanda and do the job. I arrived first and arranged myself at a table in the corner where there was some level of privacy.

She was wearing a gray suit this time, and her hair was pulled back into a severe bun. I felt underdressed in my nicer jeans with a white shirt. She had an air of determination about her as she sat down and looked at the pages I'd laid out.

She laughed as she read over the first page. 'I don't know about this. *I had some extra words and I thought I'd send them to you.*' She shook her head before reading the list. '*Logistics, elocution, babble, languid, spizzerinctum*—' She looked up at me. 'Is that even a real word?'

'I promise you it is,' I said. 'It means the will to succeed, vim, energy, ambition.' I didn't say it, but it seemed like something she had lots of. 'I know that seems kind of silly, but I thought it would make him smile. I brought along another option,' I said and took out another note that I'd written. 'From what you said about him, I thought he might be intrigued by the offer of fun.'

*I have an idea. Let's take a day and run away from every-
thing about work and do something just for fun. We could
go bowling and, when we're done, have hot dogs at
Portillo's. And then a ride on the Ferris wheel at Navy Pier.
Ending with fireworks.*

'You made him sound very controlled and someone who does
everything with a purpose. It is hard for me to judge since I
haven't met him, but it seemed like fun and spontaneity might
be missing from his life.'

'Good perception,' she said, impressed. 'Our so-called dates
are always for an event he has to go to. They're all political
things, business things, or the opening of a museum exhibit
that his family has sponsored. I've figured out that he has a
rotation of who he takes with him as if we're interchangeable.
More than once, I've been called by someone else's name. From
what I can tell, we all have a lot in common.'

Amazingly, she didn't seem bothered by what he was doing.
Parker Andrews sounded pretty unfeeling and someone I
couldn't imagine wanting to catch. But then she seemed about
the same. It made me wonder about relationships. What did I
want? Something safe, or was I willing to take a chance on
something that could get messy and passionate, but leave me
vulnerable?

She thought it over for a moment. 'I think we should start
with the first one. It's kind of random and silly, but I like it.' She
seemed concerned. 'How do we make sure he knows it's from
me? I don't want to go to all this trouble and have one of the
others get the credit.' Her face lit with an idea. 'Timing is the
absolute factor. He needs to get it the day after we have been
out.' She pulled up the calendar on her phone. 'Tomorrow we
are scheduled to go to an opening of an exhibit at the Art Institute
followed by a reception at the garden restaurant in Millennium
Park. It has to arrive the next day.'

We discussed the various ways to get it to him, and she decided
the best way to ensure it was delivered at the right time was to
have someone drop it off at his office. I suggested a messenger
service, but she nixed it. 'Can I pay you something extra to drop
it off at his office?'

It wasn't the first time I'd done something extra for a client, and it would blow the whole thing if her note arrived at the wrong time. I agreed, and then we discussed the format. She liked the idea of it being handwritten. In anticipation, I had brought several sheets of pink stationery. She used her favorite pen to copy down the short messages.

When she got to the end, she looked up at me. 'How should I sign it?' Before I could make a suggestion, she came up with her own answer and signed it *The One.*

'This is fun,' she said, handing the sheets back to me. 'It should make me seem different from the others.' She laughed. 'The truth is, though, I'm probably not – except that I found you.'

She wrote his name on the matching envelope I'd brought and then dropped it into a large manilla envelope. She wrote all his information on the front. Then she did the same for the note about the fun day. 'I'll let you know when to drop off the second one.' She lifted her coffee cup. 'Here's to success.' She wiggled the third finger on her left hand. 'And a ring to seal the deal.'

The alarm on her watch went off, reminding her of her next appointment, and she left in a hurry. I had just finished putting some notes in my calendar when Nicole arrived. She had a flat expression and seemed impatient to go before she sat down.

She let out a sigh as I handed her the sheet with Gena Fellows' markings. 'I see your point. She seems to have rewritten the whole thing.' She took a breath and read it over again. 'The way you had it was fine – better than her changes – but I'd vote to go with her editing to keep the peace.'

'That's what I was thinking,' I said. It was the most expedient thing to do.

'Will you please see her in person and show her the revised copy, so she believes she got her way? It's ironic. Her husband is a big-deal professor, but she's the one who needs special care.'

And now for the other problem. I brought out the two photographs of the shelves at the Fellowses' house. 'This is from our first visit.' I pushed the picture toward her. 'And Owen took this when we went back.' Nicole picked up the second picture and held it close as she looked it over.

'How did that happen? Who?' She sounded distressed. 'We

have to take care of this and keep Gena Fellows from making a fuss about it.' She looked at me. 'Any suggestions?'

I had already been thinking about it and had come up with something I thought would solve the whole problem. 'Maybe we could do a little gaslighting. Make it seem like it never happened.' I had gone to my phone and scrolled through online offerings. It turned out the vases were a set and not even very expensive. I showed the screen to Nicole.

'I get it. When you go back to show her the copy, you can slip the missing one back on the shelf.' I nodded, and Nicole took over, ordering the set of vases and having them sent to me. It was promised the next day. 'But be sure she doesn't catch you, or it will be worse.'

Nicole was already pushing away from the table when she asked me if there was anything else. 'There's what to do about the description of Landon Donte's house. Should I make changes in light of what happened?'

She let out a frustrated groan. 'Just deal with it any way you want.' She was on her way out of the door before I could react.

I took a moment to drink my now lukewarm coffee and think over the two meetings. I was relieved that Amanda had liked both letters. The one with the list of words was nonsensical, but I liked the silliness. It was more fun to think about that than the vase situation. Why would anyone have taken it? Could it have been someone who had a compulsion to take things? Something Brad had said came to mind. Landon Donte had wanted him to lock the case with his awards because he was worried about somebody with flypaper fingers. Was there a connection?

For now, my big concern was pulling off the return of the vase. I was going to need help.

I called Tizzy and left a message that her wingperson services were needed. I'd give her details at sherry time, although it was actually more like cooking wine time and at my place before the writers' group met.

'This seems somehow naughty,' Theo said as we sat around my cleared dining-room table. 'Like being behind the scenes.' He glanced at the stack of pages from the group that were waiting to be handed back to them. 'Let's see what you said to Daryl.' He reached for the clipped-together sheets on the top of the pile.

There wasn't really any reason he shouldn't see what I'd written, but it felt wrong. I was about to say something, but Tizzy beat me to it. She hit his hand and told him to drop the papers. He did as he was told but got defensive. 'It's just one professional looking at another professional's comments.'

I was so used to thinking of Theo only as Tizzy's husband and now my student that I forgot that he taught English literature and knew about grading papers, even though my intent was different. Rather than a letter grade that implied a completed assignment, my comments were aimed at working on something to make it better.

'You'd better give me the details of my assignment,' Tizzy said with an excited glint in her dark eyes. 'The others will be here soon.'

'I hope you aren't disappointed when you hear what it's about,' I said. 'This isn't exactly a job for Mata Hari.' I laid out the details of the missing vase and the plan to make it seem as though it was never missing.

'I get it. You want to protect whoever stole it,' she said.

'I don't think it was an intentional act. The vase was only worth a few dollars. I think it was—'

'Kleptomania,' Theo said before I could get the word out. He had his phone out and was reading from the screen. 'It's a serious disorder that causes a person to have an irresistible urge to steal items that aren't needed and are of little value. Treatment with talk therapy might help, but there is no cure.'

'You think one of the people in the entourage is a klepto-maniac?' Tizzy said. 'Who was in the group that went to the Fellowses' house?'

'There was me,' I said with a chuckle. 'Nicole was there, Serena, the photographer Owen, and Ruth Scrivner.'

'Who do you think it was?' Tizzy asked.

'I don't know, but I think that Landon Donte did.'

Both their heads shot up as I explained what Brad had said about Donte being concerned about someone with flypaper fingers.

'Flypaper fingers,' Theo said with a laugh. 'A word play on

*sticky fingers*, which is a way of saying someone who has a tendency to steal things.'

The doorbell rang, its croaking sound ending the discussion as I got up to buzz the security door downstairs. It was a three-fer as Ed, Daryl, and Ben all came up to the third-floor landing together.

When I brought them back to the dining room, Ed took one look at Tizzy and Theo with their glasses of cooking wine and began to protest.

'First we have to deal with you getting cuddly with Ben, and now you're letting these two come early.' Ed looked at Daryl. 'Unfair. They're all getting more attention than us.'

'What was that about?' Ben asked. He was watching me take the wine glasses into the kitchen after the group had left and he'd done his usual return.

I explained needing Tizzy's help as my wingperson.

'Wingperson?' he said with a shrug. 'Has it gone so far now with all this gender-neutral stuff that you can't even say "wingman" anymore?'

'I'm not sure, but to be on the safe side, I'm using "person" or "them" whenever I can.'

'And how exactly do you need Tizzy's help?' he said. He'd brought up a plate of leftovers from the Chinese takeout he'd provided for the usual Tuesday dinner at his sister's.

There was vegetable egg roll and a lot of Buddha's delight. I looked over the assortment of bright green broccoli, carrot slices, mushrooms, and fried squares of tofu covered in a clear sauce that had a hint of garlic. 'There's lots left. You know how Quentin feels about vegetables,' Ben said with a laugh.

'Yeah, he only likes them if they're smothered in meat.'

'Exactly. And now Mikey is trying to be like him.' He realized we'd drifted away from his question, and he circled back to it. 'I hope you aren't planning to do anything illegal.' His tone was serious, but there was a teasing glint in his eye. 'I might have to arrest you.'

'You work in Weston. I don't think you have jurisdiction here,' I countered. The teasing and banter were much easier for me to deal with than a conversation about what was going on in our relationship. I did what I could to keep it light and away from anything personal.

'I don't think it would count as illegal since the value of the item we're dealing with is so negligible.' I reheated the plate of food and put it on a tray with some chopsticks. Ben had helped himself to a bottle of beer, and we both went back to the living room and settled on the couch.

'A kleptomaniac now,' he said, shaking his head. He waited until I had a mouthful of food, knowing that it would keep me quiet, and changed the subject. 'You can't keep avoiding it by talking about other things. We need to talk about where we stand.' I swallowed fast, wanting to stop him before he continued. It was already too serious.

'Isn't the girl supposed to be the one who wants the "about us" conversation?'

'Except when it's you,' he said, letting out a sigh. He put up his hands in capitulation. 'Never mind. Forget I brought it up.'

I was clearing things up in the kitchen after he left. He hadn't stayed long since he had an early shift in the morning. The whole evening had left me feeling tired, but too wired to go to sleep. I put on the kettle and took out the chamomile teabags, plopping one in a mug. I carried the floral-smelling tea back to the living room and pulled out a square I was working on that had an elaborate motif in the middle. Sometimes I needed something simple to work on, but tonight I wanted something that would capture my attention.

I was so focused that my tension began to melt and then my mind started to wander. I found myself thinking about Nicole. What if she was the kleptomaniac? I remembered how she'd been caught going upstairs at Donte's house. On a whim, I set aside the crochet work and pulled out my phone. I searched on Facebook and found a listing, but the page was restricted to friends. Not that it was likely that she would have included kleptomaniac in the description of herself anyway.

# TWENTY-TWO

The package with the set of vases arrived the next morning. I checked them against the photo I had of the ones that belonged to the Fellowses. As soon as I was sure they matched, I called Gena. She seemed pleased I was offering her a chance to approve the revised copy, and we set up a time for me to bring it over on Friday. The time worked for Tizzy, and I put the copy and vase together so they would be ready to go. I placed them next to the manilla envelope that had the note I'd written for Amanda. I opened the large envelope and took out the smaller pink one and read over the note. No surprise that her handwriting was precise and clear. I packed it all up again, setting it next to things I had to take to the Fellowses'. It wouldn't be there long since her date with Parker Andrews was that night and I was to deliver the letter the next day.

I had accepted her description of their relationship without any proof. I believed her, but I would have preferred to have some empirical backup. But she was in such a hurry to make her move. I hoped I wasn't making a mistake.

Rocky jumped into my lap, wanting some attention. 'Have I been ignoring you?' I said to the black-and-white cat. I stroked his head, and he began to purr. I was glad to see that he was into the moment instead of holding a grudge for any past neglect. My phone chimed announcing the arrival of a text. I took a breath and counted to five before I casually picked it up off my desk and looked over at the screen. I glanced down at the cat in my lap. 'See, I'm not a slave to it. I don't jump for every ping.' Rocky pressed against my hand as if to remind me I'd been petting him. I went back to stroking him while I dealt with the phone with my other hand. I smiled when I saw it was from Ben, wanting to take me out on a real date that night. I texted back, teasing him that it was really last-minute, and he replied saying that only counted if it was a Saturday night, not a Wednesday.

He won, and I agreed. I actually liked the spontaneity of it.

I was leaning over the banister as he came up the stairs. He slipped past his sister's door with extra stealth and looked up at me with a naughty smile.

He put his fingers to his lips, and we didn't say a word until I'd closed the door to my place. 'When I said a date, I meant just the two of us – no toddlers or feeding my sister. There were no SOSs from her, so I'm assuming everything is OK. I thought it would be nice for us to go somewhere.' He was dressed in date attire – gray slacks and a dress shirt with a sport coat.

I nodded enthusiastically. While I might not want to talk about our situation, I liked spending time with Ben. He saw the light was on in my office. 'What are you working on?'

I hadn't mentioned Amanda to him or the group, but now that he'd asked, I was anxious to get his opinion of the crazy list of words. 'Would that make you want to pick me out of a bevy of women?'

He read the list over again, and his lips curved into a crooked grin. 'It would certainly make me curious, but I'm just a simple cop who is hardly a smooth operator. A guy with a bevy of babes sounds like a harder nut to crack. I'd need to know a little more about him.' I gave Ben the basics that he was rich and connected. 'But what about his personality and his connection to the woman who hired you? Didn't you say that you always checked out the situation to make sure no one was a stalker or had evil intent?'

I showed him the letter of agreement that she'd drawn up. 'She wanted to keep me away from him so there would be no chance that he found out what she was doing.'

'And you are comfortable with that?' Ben asked.

'The letter probably lets me off the hook legally, but the whole situation is strange to me. She wants this guy, but she doesn't love him.'

'The way you describe him auditioning for a wife, it sounds like he's in the same place.'

'I can't dither about it. I have to deliver it tomorrow,' I said.

I explained she wanted it to arrive right after they'd spent the evening together so he would know it was from her without putting her name on it.

'What do you want to do?' he asked.

'What I'd like to do is see them together. Make sure that she was telling me the truth before he gets the note.'

'Do you know where they are?' he asked. I told him about the art opening. 'But by now I'm sure they're at the reception.'

'OK, then, let's go.' He looked at the leggings and T-shirt I was wearing. 'You might want to spruce up a little.'

It didn't take me long to change into my one good black dress. It worked for anything. I added some silver jewelry and a jean jacket. Finally, I let my hair down and put the red scrunchy on my wrist. It was one that I'd crocheted and it looked almost like a colorful bracelet. We left, slipping down the stairs and swallowing our laughter until we were outside. I had climbed into his black Wrangler, and we were on the Outer Drive, as DuSable Lake Shore Drive was commonly called, when I realized there was a problem. 'It's a private affair,' I said.

'There are benefits to the badge,' he said. 'Don't worry, I'll get us in.'

We parked and went looking for the reception. The area around the restaurant set in the downtown park was roped off and a security detail was manning the entrance. I stood behind Ben as he talked to the person controlling who was allowed in. I couldn't hear the words, just the tone, but it sounded like friendly banter. And then we were on our way in.

'What did you say?' I asked as we neared the entrance of the restaurant.

'I told them I'd promised to take you here for dinner and had no idea it was closed for a reception. I asked if they could do me a favor, professional to professional, and let us in, so I could live up to my word to you.'

'Very creative,' I said. The lights were low inside. There was a buffet and tables set up around the large space. 'I just want to see them together, and then we can go.'

'While you're on recon, I'm going to grab some snacks to keep me going until we eat,' he said, and we separated. People were milling around, and I prowled through the crowd, trying to look at people without being too obvious. I spotted Amanda at the end of the buffet table. She was holding two plates of food and surveying the area. I slipped behind a couple so she wouldn't see me. They started to move, and I took a step back, feeling my foot step on something just as a pair of hands grabbed my arms to stop me.

'Hey, there, that's my foot,' a man's voice said. I instinctively turned to apologize and cringed when I recognized Parker Andrews from the pictures I'd seen online. Our eyes met for a moment, and then I looked away, repeating my apology while I moved to the side. I stayed hidden while watching Amanda's progress with the two plates. She set them on a table and then scanned the crowd. She waved, and when I tracked who it was aimed at, I saw Parker nod back at her as he began to thread through the crowd. He was stopped continuously by people who seemed to know him. He was mannerly and polite as he acknowledged each person, but even at a distance, I picked up the flatness of his gaze. It reconfirmed what I'd thought: he was someone who needed some fun. When he reached the table Amanda had commandeered for them, he touched her arm and seemed to be thanking her. There wasn't a lot of warmth between them, but certainly no animosity either.

'Mission accomplished,' I said to Ben when I found him in the corner sipping a beer and eating some appetizers. He held out the plate and pointed to several pieces of a sushi roll. 'Freshly made and all vegetarian,' he said, nodding toward a bar set up with a sushi chef. It looked interesting, but I was more concerned with getting out of there. 'I don't want Amanda to see me.'

'Well?' Ben said as we walked to where the Wrangler was parked. 'Are you going to give me details?'

'I'm satisfied that what she told me about their relationship is true. I also saw that she is taking care of him. She got his food and found them a table while he worked his way through the crowd. He seemed comfortable with the situation and her. Thank you,' I said, looking up at Ben with a relieved smile. 'Now I can get him her note without any worries.'

'I'm glad I could be of service,' Ben said. 'Enough about them – now it's time for us.'

The brief stay at the reception was enough fanciness for both of us, and we went to Lou Malnati's and shared one of the thick-crust pizzas. Ben came back to my place for dessert.

The next morning, I dressed the way I thought a delivery person would in jeans and a hooded sweatshirt. I left my hair loose but had the red scrunchy on my wrist in case I changed my mind. I considered a baseball cap, but it seemed too much, so I went hatless.

No peacock-blue messenger bag this time – just a purse and the big envelope. 'Wish me luck,' I said to Rocky as I went to the door. There was no reason for me to feel nervous. I was just going to drop the envelope off at the reception desk. But it was still an unknown. I took the Metra train downtown and walked to LaSalle Street and the financial district. The imposing stone canyon formed by the tall buildings didn't make me feel any more relaxed. As I looked for the address, I passed a walking tour and overheard the tour guide say this area was the most filmed in the city and he mentioned *Batman* and *Transformers*.

I passed through a revolving door and walked into a shiny granite-tiled lobby. I already knew Andrews' office was on the twenty-fifth floor and went directly to the bank of elevators. There was still a fold-up seat left from the days when the elevators had operators. Now it was all on me to press a button. I had the car to myself as it whooshed up to the high floor.

There was no problem finding the office. A frosted glass door marked off half the floor and had *The Andrews Group* in prominent letters.

I paused just long enough to take a deep breath and then went inside. Something happened when I went through the glass doors, and suddenly I was totally calm, I'd become just another messenger dropping something off.

There was a small area with a few seats and then a massive counter with *The Andrews Group* in big letters on the white wall behind it. The receptionist had a beefy build, and his suit jacket seemed to strain over his broad shoulders. He looked more security than greeting committee. 'Delivery for Parker Andrews,' I said, holding out the large yellowish envelope.

He had me lay it on the counter and picked up a phone to

notify someone of the arrival. I started to back away, but he ordered me to stop and pushed a clipboard across his desk. 'You have to sign in.'

'For a delivery?' I said. 'I'm not going in.'

'For walking in the door,' he said and pushed it toward me again. I don't know what came over me, but my mind went blank, and all I could think of was Minnie Mouse. I wrote it down, hoping it was illegible and that I'd be out of there before he tried to read it. A dark-haired man in a conservative suit came out of a sliding door and took the envelope. I was already turning to go. I just wanted to get out of there. I was almost at the door when the receptionist ordered me to stop. 'Aren't you forgetting something?' he said, eyeing me.

I didn't know what he meant, so I shrugged. 'Are you demanding I say thank you?'

'What?' he said, perplexed. 'I'm not the manners police.' He looked over his desk toward my hands. 'Don't you want me to sign something that it was received? What service do you work for?'

'There's no need to sign anything,' I said, backing away quickly. When he looked down at the sign-in sheet, I knew I was in trouble and doubled my speed to the door.

'Hey, come back here. Let's see some ID, Minnie.'

I rushed to the elevator and pushed the down button. There were four elevators and they all seemed to be on the lower floors. I thought about taking the stairs down a floor, but I worried the door would lock behind me and I'd be trapped in the stairwell to the bottom of the twenty-five stories.

I looked back at the door to the office and was relieved that it wasn't opening. Still, I didn't stop holding my breath until the elevator arrived and I was on my way down. I got to the ground floor and took a deep breath of relief and was about to enter the revolving door that led to the street when I felt a hand grip my shoulder.

'Not so fast, Minnie. Mr Andrews would like to talk to you,' the receptionist/security guard said. There was nothing I could do but comply. I understood how he'd managed to nab me when he led me to a private elevator that went directly to the office. Once there, he had me sit down. I was already thinking about what I would do. I'd babble that I had just started working for a delivery service and then start crying. Tears always threw people off, and I expected they'd want to get me out of there. I'd apologize profusely but be steadfast in having no knowledge of the content of the message or who had sent it.

The younger man in the suit came out and brought me back through the sliding door. There was a desk and another seating area, but we went past it. He rapped a short knock on a door, and a man's voice said to come in.

Parker Andrews was seated behind a massive old desk. The computer on top of it seemed out of place with the old-fashioned design. He was wearing a dark suit, a blue dress shirt, and a cream-colored tie. His dark hair was neatly trimmed on the sides with a little fluff of longer hair on the top. His expression was stern as he studied my face.

'What's this about?' he said, holding the pink letter up. I was about to play dumb and go into the crying routine when he looked at me more closely. His eye stopped on the red scrunchy on my wrist. 'You. The clothes are different, but I've seen that bracelet before. You're the one from last night who was going to step on my toes.'

I was too stunned to speak and put my hand over my face, trying to will myself invisible.

'I don't know what your game is, but you'd better explain.'

'It may take a little time,' I said, almost choking on my dry mouth. 'Do you suppose I could have a glass of water?'

He offered me a chair and told the assistant to get me the water. The adrenaline rush had left me feeling dizzy. 'I'm sorry. If you could give me a moment, the water should help.' And I mentioned that being nabbed by the receptionist had left me feeling a little faint.

'Oh, no. You can't faint,' Parker Andrews said almost as a command. 'Take some deep breaths.' The water arrived and he handed me a heavy crystal glass. I took a few sips and set it down. 'How about you start by showing some ID from the delivery company.'

'I would if I had it,' I said.

'Then what about your ID.' I handed him my driver's license, and he looked it over before making a copy of it.

'OK, Veronica, what's going on?' He seemed to be getting impatient. I was in a corner, and the only way to go was with the truth – to a point. I began by telling him what I did for a living. 'I'm a writer for hire. Right now, I'm working on a project putting together descriptions of houses for a tour in Hyde Park. One of the homeowners died. Maybe you've heard of him – Landon Donte, the writer.'

He nodded. 'He was part of a lecture series we sponsored at UChicago. But what does that have to do with this?' he held up the sheet of pink paper again.

'I write all different sorts of things – descriptions of menu items, bios, and sometimes more romantic things.' He was peering at me now. 'Sometimes people have a hard time expressing their feelings for someone they care about, and I help them find the right words.'

'You mean you write something for them *as them*,' he said. His expression softened slightly.

'Yes. That's correct. I write the letters for the person, as the person.'

'Like a Cyrano de Bergerac thing,' he said.

'Not exactly. He wrote them for someone, but to someone he was in love with. I never get involved with my clients that way.'

'So are you saying this counts as a love letter?' I wondered if it was a comment on the quality, but he was smiling as if he was amused.

'Every situation is different. I have to tailor it to what my client wants and what would appeal to their love interest.'

'And you're saying that someone hired you to write this for me?'

'Yes,' I said, choking on the word. 'You should be flattered someone went to so much trouble.' I was stalling because I knew the next question was going to be who had hired me. I couldn't tell him without blowing the gig. I decided the best thing to do was to pivot away from the question. 'Your case was a challenge. I understand that you are led by your head rather than your heart when it comes to your social life.' My mouth felt as if it was stuffed with cotton balls, and I had to take a water break even if it allowed him to take over the conversation and demand who sent it. But it appeared that he was curious about what I was saying and waited while I set the glass back down. 'I understand

that you are considering several people as a relationship partner.'
I thought that sounded better than auditioning for a wife. 'One
of them wanted an advantage.'

'And she came up with this list-of-words idea?' he said.

'She approved it, but it was my idea. She wanted something
that would make you curious. I know it's kind of silly.' I put up
my hands and shrugged.

He looked at the letter again. 'Whose idea was it to sign it
"The One"?'

I didn't know how to answer and took a moment to drink
more water.

'Never mind,' Parker said, leaning a little closer. 'Now, the
obvious question: who hired you?'

'I can't tell you that,' I said, feeling a little panicky. I had to
give him something, so I gave him a hint. 'All I can say is that
timing was a factor.'

He leaned back in his chair, and his lips curved in a triumphant smile. 'I've got it: it was Amanda Brooks, my date last
night.'

'I was going to ask you not to tell her what happened, but I
guess it's all blown anyway. But look at it this way: she cares
enough about you to have hired me.'

'I don't know,' he said. 'How can I give her credit when the
letter was your idea?'

I let out a frustrated breath. 'Now that you know everything,
I can't control what you do with the information. I can't stop
you from telling her what you know.' I shrugged and let out my
breath. 'It'll be the end of the gig for me.' I stood up. 'I've got
to go. I have that house-tour copy to work on.'

The man who'd taken me into the inner office escorted me
back to the bank of elevators and went as far as to push the down
button before walking away.

As soon as I got home, I put on the kettle for some chamomile
tea. I took the cup to the living room and dug out a really
simple square I'd been working on. It was just a matter of time
before the shoe dropped. Yes, that was two clichés, but I didn't
care.

This was my worst nightmare when it came to writing love

letters. I had made it worse for Amanda. I heard my landline ring and was going to ignore it, but since the handset was on the coffee table in front of me, I looked at the caller ID on the screen. Just when I thought it couldn't get worse, it did. The call ID said *Andrews Group*. What now? There was no use running away from whatever it was. I picked up the phone and clicked the green button to accept my fate.

I'm afraid my hello came out how I felt: a mess.

'Is this Veronica Blackstone?' Parker Andrews said after identifying himself. I managed to mutter a yes. 'You sounded different. Are you all right?'

I tried to pull myself together. It wasn't my way to play the damsel in distress. 'I'm fine,' I said, trying to project some confidence. 'What can I do for you?'

'I thought I should tell you that I won't tell Amanda what I know. I get that you are trying to make a living and I won't step in the way of that.'

'Really?' I said, surprised and relieved.

'And if it means anything, I liked the list of words, particularly *spizzerinctum*.' And then he hung up.

With a sigh of relief, I finally sent Amanda a text that the delivery had been made, but with no details.

# TWENTY-THREE

It was Friday morning and time to go back to the Fellowses' house with the changed copy and the vase. I was totally focused on how I was going to handle it. I didn't want to think about anything else, but Amanda Brooks called just as I was finishing my coffee. As soon as I saw her name on the screen, I held my breath. Parker Andrews had said he wouldn't tell her, but he was under no obligation and could have changed his mind. I took a deep breath and prepared for anything as I answered the phone.

I said a tentative hello and hoped she wouldn't want details of the delivery. But my worry was for naught. She skipped the greeting and got right down to business. 'It worked,' she said. 'You're a genius. He sent me flowers and said how much he'd enjoyed our evening. You have to get him the second letter, right away. Today,' she said. She reminded me that I already had her handwritten version of the message.

'Are you sure you don't want to wait?' I said, thinking of my trip to see the Fellowses, but she was adamant.

'I want to blast my way out of his damn rotation. It's always one date, and then he has to go through the whole group before he gets back to me again.'

'How many women are we talking about?' I asked, suddenly wondering what she was up against.

'Four. I know who all of them are, and if we weren't vying to be "the one," we'd probably be friends. But I don't want to talk about them. The second letter is important because it shows how I'm concerned for his well-being. I want him to know I will take care of things for him. Coddle him. Tell me you'll take the letter today.'

Actually, I was grateful I still had the gig after what had happened. 'I won't be able to do it until this afternoon,' I said finally.

'Thank you, thank you,' she gushed. 'I might have to make

you one of my bridesmaids.' I sat back and looked at the phone when I got off. Maybe it had worked. Could it be that what I'd said about the trouble she'd gone to had made an impression on Parker?

The feeling of success was short-lived. Nicole called a few minutes later and wanted to know if the vase had arrived and when I was going to take it to the Fellowses' house. 'We need to take care of this ASAP,' she said. 'I can't have her going public with it.'

I tried to calm her by saying the vase had arrived and that I had it under control. I told her I was going over there shortly, without mentioning that Tizzy was helping me, out of concern that Nicole would object. She didn't ask for the plan but wanted reassurance that it would seem as if the vase was never gone.

I made it sound like a sure thing, but I didn't feel that confident. Would we be able to pull it off? And what if Gena Fellows went on and on about how much better her version of the copy was and I snapped? I groaned a little as I slid the revised copy for the Fellowses' house description, incorporating Gena's changes, into my bag. I made sure to bring along the copy she had made her notes on so that she would see that I had made all her changes. I dropped the vase in last, wondering if we'd be able to execute our gaslighting maneuver.

'Your version is so much better,' Tizzy said. We'd met on the street, and I'd showed her the revised copy and the original. 'But under the circumstances, you are doing the right thing.' Then she asked me for the plan with the vase. I couldn't let Tizzy do the dirty work, since if she was caught, it could jeopardize her job at the university, so I gave her the job of distracting Gena.

'This is certainly more exciting than the spreadsheet I was working on,' Tizzy said as we approached the Fellowses' house. 'Too bad I can't tell Alex about it. Perhaps I could do it with no names.' There was the hint of a question in her voice, hoping that I'd say she could share it with her boss.

'Sorry, but this is absolutely top secret,' I said with a conspiratorial smile. 'We have to keep it under wraps that there's a kleptomaniac in our midst.'

Gena Fellows answered the door with a superior air. Her gaze rested on Tizzy. 'And you are?' she said in a less-than-hospitable tone.

'She's one of the Friends of Hyde Park and she's been given the title of quality control.' I was making it up as I went along, but I seemed to have latched on to something that worked. Tizzy picked up and explained that she worked at the university, which seemed to please our hostess.

'I'm sure you saw how my changes made the piece sparkle,' the woman said. She was overdressed in designer casual wear again. 'I trust you saw the before and after.'

Tizzy gave me a nod, and I pulled out the revised copy and my original, handing them to her. 'That's why the group sent me. Even though Veronica is a professional, there's always room for improvement.'

We went into the massive living room, and I waited until Gena indicated where she was going to sit. Tizzy took a seat next to her, and I played the part of the dejected writer and chose a seat away from them, near the shelves where the four remaining vases were displayed.

Tizzy complimented Gena on everything from her outfit to the slipcovers, and Gena was so mesmerized by the positive attention that she practically forgot I was there. Tizzy moved on to giving a glowing out-loud read of the copy with all of Gena's changes. It was time for me to make my move.

I had considered simply adding the vase to the group, but it seemed too hard to pull off. There needed to be a reason why the vase had appeared to be missing. I looked at the gray floral-print chair adjacent to where I was sitting. I checked that the two women were wrapped up in admiring Gena's prose, took the small vase, and gave it a roll until it disappeared under the chair. Now I was going to have to manage the discovery.

'I'm a professional writer myself,' Gena said. 'I was working with Landon Donte. His publisher probably would have hired me to finish his manuscript if he hadn't destroyed it.'

I forgot about getting the vase to appear and focused totally on what the professor's wife was saying. I got up and moved to sit near them. 'What do you know about his manuscript? Did you see it?' I asked.

'Not exactly, but he talked about it. He said something about mixing his literary talents with popular fiction,' Gena said. I remembered that when she talked about having a mentor before, she'd mentioned offering something in return.

'Landon didn't seem like someone who would be taking on a student,' I said. 'How did you manage that?'

'He recognized my talent,' she said with an arrogant expression. 'What else?' Gena was enjoying being the center of attention. 'We had a simpatico relationship from the start.' She smiled as she relived the memory. 'There was an event at the university, and he was having a problem with his smartphone. I could see that he was frustrated and didn't want to admit that the device had gotten the better of him. I offered to help him with it in a way that he could save face. We got talking, and I mentioned I was a writer and was working on a short story about a computer that took over a woman's life. He sparked on the idea and was interested in my knowledge of computers. He invited me over and offered to have a look at my story.' She fluttered her eyes at the thought.

I wondered how true that was and how much was wishful thinking on her part. I'd already figured out that she was looking to make herself seem important, separate from being Arden Fellows' wife. Not that I would blame her. Nothing thrives well in a shadow. The connection with Landon made her feel valued in a way that being Mrs Arden Fellows obviously couldn't.

'What happened with your story?' I asked.

'Landon said I had talent, but he didn't think a short story was the best form for me and encouraged me to build it into a novel. We'd get together every now and then. He'd look over what I'd written, and I'd help him manage something with his computer.' She smiled at a memory. 'He liked to give the impression that he wanted to use his computer as though it was a glorified typewriter, but technology mystified him. He wouldn't let his assistant or anyone help him. I think it was a guy thing – he thought it made him look weak. But somehow he was OK with me helping him. It was just basic stuff. I showed him how to do email, and I set up his computer so it went right to his work in progress.' She shook her head in disbelief. 'He made a hard copy of his work every day. I tried to get him to use the cloud, but he was paranoid that someone would hack into it. He didn't trust flash drives either. He had some crazy notion that someone would get hold of it and steal his work. The only thing he trusted for sure was having the yellow sheets he worked from and a printed copy of his day's work.'

I was starting to get impatient since it seemed that all she wanted to talk about was how she had been working so closely with Landon. 'Then you never got him to create a backup copy?' I asked.

'No, but the last time I saw him, he told me he'd figured out something on his own. He wouldn't give me any details, saying it was imperative he keep it private,' she said.

'And . . .' I said, trying to encourage her to get to the point.

'That was all he said. I'm not even sure it was true.' Her expression suddenly faded. 'I can't believe he did what he did. I had no idea he was so despondent.' Then she caught herself. 'But you're here to discuss *my* work.' She let out an exasperated sound as she read over the sheet in her hand. 'You missed one of my changes.'

Tizzy took over and said she'd make sure that I incorporated the last change. I realized we were running out of time for the vase reveal. I glanced back at the chair that was hiding the vase and tried to think of something, and then the obvious popped into my mind and I reached up for my ear. 'Not again,' I said in a calculated wail. 'It's my earring.' I got up and went back to the other chair as if looking for the missing silver hoop which I had managed to slip off. 'Maybe it fell under the chair,' I said and pushed the overstuffed chair back revealing the vase.

'What's this?' I exclaimed, and Gena came over to check what I'd seen. 'Isn't that the vase you said someone in our group took?'

She seemed confused. 'How did it get there? The cleaning crew was here and moved everything when they vacuumed. There is no way that they could have missed this.' She seemed frustrated that her missing vase was back. Did she suspect that I'd engineered it? But there was nowhere for her to go with it

'All's well that ends well,' I said, and Tizzy rolled her eyes at the cliché as we got ready to leave.

'Fait accompli,' Tizzy said, using the French phrase that meant mission accomplished, when we walked out on to the sidewalk.

'And we got a little extra,' I said. 'If Landon was telling the truth, there could be a backup copy of his manuscript.' I slung the messenger bag on my shoulder. 'I'm just going to have to figure out what he did and how I can check it out.'

# TWENTY-FOUR

Tizzy had tried to get me to walk back to the campus with her and get some coffee, but I begged off, saying I wanted to be sure to make Gena's change that I'd missed. I was trying to act like a good sport about it, but having to go with all her changes was grating on me. It helped that Tizzy was sympathetic. I felt bad not telling her the real reason I had to get home, but I didn't want to talk about the work I was doing for Amanda or the problems I'd had.

I didn't feel the need to dress like a messenger this time. The black turtleneck I'd worn to meet Gena had been fine for the morning but was too hot as it turned afternoon. I switched it out for a short-sleeved knit shirt with a scoop neck, which was too light. I felt like Goldilocks when I added the jean jacket and it was just right. I debated up or down for my hair and decided to leave it loose, putting the red scrunchy in the jacket pocket in case I changed my mind. It was crazy, but I actually felt an energy change when I pulled my hair off my face.

Hand-delivering the note seemed like a wasted effort now that Parker knew the whole story with the letters, but I had agreed to do it. At least this time, I thought, it would be easy and quick. I was relaxed enough to enjoy the train ride downtown and the view of the lake. Today it appeared flat and calm. Some puffy clouds hung over it, casting shadows on the water. I was already checking the train schedule, figuring when I could catch one back to Hyde Park.

I rode the elevator to the twenty-fifth floor and went to the office door. I had preceded my visit by calling the office to say that I was dropping off something, so the security receptionist would not put me through the same hell again.

He was sitting at the front desk and looked up as I came in. There was a slight lift of his eyebrows as he recognized me. 'So you're, back, Minnie,' he said.

I held up the large envelope. 'Can I just leave it this time?' I said, starting to lay it on the counter.

'Nope,' he said, pushing the clipboard toward me. 'You still have to sign in.' I wrote my real name this time and then offered him the envelope, but he was already on the phone. The sliding door opened, and the man I'd seen before beckoned me to follow him.

It was the same routine. He knocked at the door to Parker's office, and we were told to enter.

'Do you need a glass of water?' the man asked.

'I'm good,' I said. I put the envelope on Parker's desk.

The man who'd brought me in left, and Parker pointed to the chair in front of his desk. 'Sit.' It came across as a soft command, and I pulled out the chair. I wasn't sure if it was the room and being under scrutiny, but I suddenly felt warm and took off the jean jacket while he opened the large envelope.

'I don't have to stay here for that,' I said, starting to get up, but he gestured for me to stay put. It didn't take him long to read the letter, even though this one was longer than the first.

He looked up at me and read the note out loud.

> *I have an idea. Let's take a day and run away from every-thing about work and do something just for fun. We could go bowling and, when we're done, have hot dogs at Portillo's. And then a ride on the Ferris wheel at Navy Pier. Ending with fireworks.*

'Her idea or yours?' he asked. I worried about what was coming next. I wasn't used to being there when love letters were read by the recipient. Was he going to tell me the letter was a flop?

'Amanda made you sound as if your whole life was work or work-related,' I said. 'She wants you to know that she can take care of your needs.' I remembered seeing how she'd acted at the reception, getting the food for him and finding them a table. She'd used the word 'coddle.' 'That she knows what you need maybe more than you do.' I paused and wondered if I should ask for the water as my mouth had turned cottony again. 'It seemed to me that a dose of pointless fun might be appealing. Bowling seemed like a good choice.' I wondered if I should add that it didn't require any advance planning. They could just show up at a bowling alley and rent shoes and a ball. I decided there was no need and said nothing more.

There was silence, and I rushed to fill it. 'The point was to intrigue you and tickle your imagination,' I said.

'Did she say that – *tickle my imagination?*' He seemed disbelieving.

'Not exactly – maybe I was the one who said that.' I wanted to escape and was instinctively pushing the chair back as I tried to get up. 'I'm sorry if you don't like the plan, but don't blame Amanda. She has the best intentions. She agreed, but it was my idea.'

'Do I look like a guy who would find bowling fun?' he said, giving a flourish toward his dark suit and caramel-colored silk tie.

'The point was that it was supposed to be different from your usual entertainment,' I said, feeling like a bug on a pin.

Then he smiled. 'Maybe you have something. All the so-called entertainment I have is somehow business-related – like that reception the other night. I was representing the family and had to be classy all the way. We're big donors.'

'Amanda wanted the letters to intrigue you and, with this one, show you that she wants to look after your happiness.' I hoped that was enough to get him to let me go. This wasn't part of my job description, but because he knew everything about Amanda hiring me, I had to do whatever I could to sell him on her.

For a busy person, he seemed to have a lot of time to devote to giving me a hard time. I didn't like being in this position and I'd had enough. 'If the letter doesn't please you, ignore it. I think you understand Amanda's motive. Do with it what you will. Now, I'm out of here.' I walked to the door and left without looking back.

I was spent from being grilled by Parker and had to stop for coffee before I took the train home. I sent a text to Amanda saying I'd delivered the letter. I assumed that Parker would ignore the letter, and the best Amanda could hope for was to stay in his bevy of hopefuls. I thought about the women and about him and how strange it felt to me. But how people fell in and out of love was confusing, too. Maybe the unemotional approach was a better idea.

Whatever, it was done for now.

Sara opened her door as I went past and waved me in. 'Could you sit with Mikey while I take a shower?' Somehow the little boy had got peanut butter in her hair. It was a relief to have a simple problem to deal with, and I told Mikey I'd read him a story.

By the time I went upstairs to my place, I had let go of the whole situation with Parker and Amanda. I did a few chores, and then it was time to go to Tizzy's. It had been quite a week, and I was glad to go there and celebrate that it was Friday. It was a relief to be with a couple who had been together for a long time and who still cared about each other and enjoyed each other's company. It would have been nice to talk about my dealings with Amanda and Parker, but it was way too complicated.

Theo picked up the stemmed barware and offered me my usual dose of the fragrance, followed by the offer of a sip.

I took a deep inhale of the scent I liked so much, but I declined, remembering the taste.

'Tizzy told me about your adventure this morning,' he said. 'You two have all the fun.'

Tizzy took a sip of her sherry. 'You wouldn't have wanted to be there. Gena Fellows is so needy; it's exhausting to deal with her.' She turned to me. 'Sorry I had to trash you.'

'It was all in the line of duty. She really opened up to you,' I said.

'Did you learn anything interesting?' he asked.

I had to take a moment to remember the morning, since the whole episode with Parker Andrews had blotted it out. 'We found out she knew Landon Donte,' I said. 'And they had some sort of mutual help agreement, though I think he was the one who got the most benefit,' I said. 'He gave her encouragement about her writing, and she helped him with his computer.'

'What about the vase?' he asked.

'Veronica handled it.' Tizzy laughed. 'If you could have seen the look on Gena's face when Veronica moved the chair to reveal the vase. She thought something was up, but what could she do?'

'It sure was a lot of fuss about such a little thing,' Theo said.

'The vase was hardly a big deal, but its disappearance was. Nicole was frantic for me to make it go away,' I said.

'I hope you're not upset that I got you involved in all this,' Tizzy said.

'Of course not,' I said to Tizzy. 'You meant well and you know I always need the work. So what if I had to swallow my pride and let Gena think that her writing was better than mine? The group is paying me a generous amount.'

'You can thank Roman Scrivner for that.' She started to sing the jingle from his TV commercial.

'You know that he's just the front guy,' Theo said. 'All those testimonials from happy clients don't tell the whole story. He has a bunch of attorneys working for him who do the real work. He's made himself into a personality. Speaking of personalities . . .' Theo pointed the remote at the black screen hanging over the fireplace. As the screen came to life, Theo continued. 'There's an interview with Landon Donte on the PBS station.'

Typical of the PBS style of production, there was just Landon and the interviewer sitting in a couple of chairs with a table between them and emptiness behind them. The image froze and changed to the host talking directly to the camera.

'Because of his recent death, we have decided to replay the interview we had with the illustrious writer, who had a reputation for delving into the truth of the human soul. He's a great loss to the literary world.'

I noticed there was no mention of the manner of his death, just that there was going to be a memorial service for him.

'I wonder if it's by invitation,' Tizzy said. Theo shushed us, and the interview began.

As the interview continued, something about Landon's expression irritated me. He seemed so full of himself and his own importance. He must have missed the lesson on humility. He was talking about where he got his ideas.

'I don't have to look further than the people I come in contact with all the time. And I certainly don't have to make anything up.'

'Aren't you worried that the real people might recognize themselves in your characterizations?' the host said.

Landon let out a self-satisfied chuckle. 'I have a few background characters that are pretty close to real people, but I bury the identity very well, by changing their physical description.'

He chuckled again. 'I'm like a fiction journalist. I take the truth and make it into stories,' he said.

'I understand your neighbor is the bestselling novelist R.L. Lincoln?' the host said. 'Do you discuss writing over the back fence?' The way Landon's expression changed, it was as if a bomb had gone off.

'To begin with, our houses are next to each other, so there is no back fence as you call it. And what he calls writing is not in the same universe as mine.'

'So you aren't friends?' the host asked.

'Hardly.' Then Landon caught himself. 'We have very different views on the human condition.'

'Landon Donte has the prestige, but R.L. Lincoln sells more books,' Theo said. 'I've had discussions about the value of popular fiction in the advanced class I teach. Literary books are supposed to elevate your understanding while popular fiction is for entertainment.'

'Speaking of popular fiction, or what I hope will be,' Tizzy said, 'I rewrote that short story I brought in a few weeks ago. I hate to ask you this, but could you look at it before I bring it to the group?'

'I offered to read it,' Theo said, 'but . . . well, we're not good with each other's work.'

'We've had a few screaming matches,' Tizzy said. 'It's too personal.' I was surprised that there was that much discord between them, but I also understood.

'I didn't mean to hurt your feelings,' Theo said. 'But I thought that whole section was extraneous.' Tizzy sucked in her breath, and I sensed the argument was about to begin again.

'Truce,' I said, holding up my hands. I told her to email it to me, and then I changed the subject back to Landon's house and what changes I should make.

'Wouldn't that be up to Ona Chapin? She's his only heir. It's all hers now.'

# TWENTY-FIVE

On Saturday morning, I was back at my computer. I saw that Tizzy had sent the story, but before I looked at it, I made the change that Gena had pointed out I'd missed. I marked the Fellowses' house description as completed.

It occurred to me that the other homeowner who might be super picky was Roman Scrivner. Since he and Ruth were sponsors of the event, they got two write-ups. The first was about them and their generosity, and the second focused on their home.

I changed my original description and called him a *much-admired attorney known for his heartfelt commercials*, rather than *a familiar face from numerous commercials*. I jazzed up the description of Ruth by saying she had taken an active part in the arrangements for the tour, even though she'd seemed more like a ghostly presence hanging in the corner than a real participant. I gave them credit as a couple for all their philanthropy, particularly in the neighborhood, without mentioning that I thought it was more about building an image than true caring.

I looked over my description of the exterior of the house and questioned some of the details. The glass house was so extraordinary that it had been difficult to take everything in. Nicole had looked over what I'd written and given her OK, but as I'd discovered with Gena Fellows, that didn't necessarily mean much. I did not want to show Roman copy that had glaring errors.

My phone pinged and there was a text in all caps from Sara asking me to come downstairs.

'I thought I was doing better,' she said when she opened the door and pulled me inside. She looked pasty-faced and her hair was sticking up in all the wrong places. 'The morning sickness feels like all-day sickness. I hate to ask you, but could you take Mikey out for a while?'

There was no way I would have said no, but it was actually good timing. On the way to the playground, we could cruise by the Scrivners' house and I could give the exterior another look. I grabbed my things and loaded the little boy up in his stroller. Mikey was happy just to ride and didn't mind the detour.

It was still jarring to see the three-story glass house that seemed as if it had been dropped there from space. The way that apartment buildings loomed around the house made me wonder what Helmut Peterman had been thinking. I also wondered if Roman Scrivner liked the house or if owning it was just another way to draw attention to himself. He'd certainly reacted when someone called it the Zender house and almost bellowed that it was now known as the Scrivner house. Someone had called Donte's house by some other name, and he'd reacted badly to that, too.

I looked over the house, checking details, and made some notes about the frosted glass around the front door and that there was a balcony that went around the front and side of the middle floor. Mikey might not have cared about our destination, but he didn't like being in a parked stroller and started kicking his feet, trying to make it move.

I cheated a little bit and looked at my phone while Mikey was busy in the sandbox. When I checked my email, I saw a new one from Tizzy. She had gone to look at her story again and somehow deleted it. Would I make sure to send the attachment back to her after I looked at it?

Computers were great until something went wrong. I thought of problems I'd had with disappearing files. I sent a reply, telling Tizzy not to worry. Mikey came up and wanted a ride on the swings, and I was back to active duty. When I brought him home, he was ready for a nap. Sara hugged me in thanks.

A nap sounded appealing, but I pushed myself to go back to my computer. I added the few things I'd noticed about the Scrivner house to their file.

I moved on to Tizzy's story and I understood what she and Theo had argued about. I wrote a note with a suggestion of how to change it, and then made sure to send the story back to her.

It left me inspired to work on the Derek Streeter book, and I opened the file and read through where I'd left off. But instead of feeling inspired to start typing, my thoughts went back to the whole situation with Landon Donte. What would I do if I thought the second Derek Streeter book would tank while I was still writing it? I might worry at the time, but I would wait until it actually flopped before I'd get upset or think about never writing again. I had to believe that Landon was similar. And he was so full of himself and his talent that I was sure he wouldn't believe the book was going to flop anyway. That, coupled with his appearing to be shot with his non-dominant hand, made me believe it was murder.

Detective Jankowski had ignored what I'd said and thrown down the gauntlet: unless I could show how there was someone else in the room, there was nothing to talk about. I tried to get into Derek Streeter's head to see what he'd say about the situation. The bad news was that all I could imagine was Derek saying it wasn't his case. The good news was that it led me into the flow of working on the manuscript. Hours went by, and the afternoon became evening and then night, all without my notice. Ben was working, and there was no plan for sherry since Tizzy and Theo were going to the opera. Finally, at around eight, I ran out of steam.

I floated back to the kitchen on a cloud of achievement. Something had clicked, and I knew now for sure I would finish the rewrite.

I gave Rocky a treat of special cat food and made myself a vegetable stirfry with a spicy curry sauce. It didn't take chamomile tea and crochet to send me to sleep.

On Sunday, I got a call from Serena Lawrence. Nicole had dropped out of organizing the house tour due to family issues and would not be accompanying Owen and me as we showed our work to the other three homeowners.

'It's really OK,' I said. 'She didn't go with us to the Malins' or the Fellowses'.'

'She should have,' Serena said. 'With all that's gone on, it's best that you have a chaperone from the Friends of Hyde Park group.' She didn't give any details, but I wondered if it had anything to do with Tizzy's and my visit to Gena Fellows and the reappearing vase. There was no room for discussion, and Serena said she would meet us outside R.L. Lincoln's house at the appointed time the next day.

I had decided it was a good idea to look over the copy I'd written about the romance writer's house again before I showed it to him. I had mentioned the background story of the houses being identical and how Lincoln's had kept the original design, making the point about how things that are old end up being new again. The layout of Lincoln's place was actually more modern than Donte's. The trick was having the communal space flow together. I had included something about his writing and even said that some people viewed his books as a portable vacation. It all seemed acceptable to me, and I hoped he would feel the same.

I met Serena and Owen as planned the next day.

This time Lincoln answered the door himself and said he didn't have an assistant for the moment. 'Ona has enough to deal with. The house and all his book royalties go to her. It's changed the dynamic,' he said. 'I didn't know that Ona was Donte's daughter when I hired her. She used her mother's maiden name and didn't share the information. I knew she was a little hostile to him, but I thought it had to do with some disparaging remarks he might have made about my work when they straightened mixed-up mail, which happened quite often.' He smiled as he described Donte receiving a box of his author copies. 'It was as if he was horrified at being connected with anything with a happy ending. Eventually, she told me, and it gave me a secret pleasure that she was getting back at her father by working for me. You probably figured that we have a personal relationship, too.' He looked over at the other house. 'Maybe we can build something that joins them together.' He added a chuckle to show he was joking. 'I hate to say this, but there is a much better feeling with him gone. It was like he was shooting bad vibes here.'

We stopped inside the entrance hall. I showed him a printout of what I'd written, and Owen held out the photos.

'You really didn't need to do all this,' he said, giving the stack of papers a cursory look. 'I would have been fine with whatever you decided.' I felt a surge of relief and almost hugged him.

He looked at Serena. 'What happened to the other woman? The one who seemed in charge?'

'You mean Nicole?' I said, giving a brief description of her.

'I'm not very good with names,' he said with a sheepish smile, 'But I'm sure that's who I meant.'

Serena explained that Nicole had to step down because of family responsibilities.

'I guess she finally got her wish,' he said. When it was clear we didn't know what he was talking about, he continued, 'A month or so ago, I saw her looking at Donte's house a couple of times. I even asked her if she was looking for somebody. She just wanted to know who lived there and said something about wanting to see inside.' He shrugged. 'I figured she was one of Donte's groupies.' He smiled at the word.

I noticed that Serena flinched and I remembered her story about being the inspiration, or so she had believed, for a background character who appeared in a number of his books. There had also been something about a relationship they'd had. I didn't know if she was bothered that 'groupie' might refer to her or that there might be others like her.

Serena pulled herself together and, even though Lincoln had given his approval, she wanted to show him how the copy and photographs would look in the booklet. He shrugged and offered his dining-room table.

As Owen and I laid out the sheets on the table, she looked through the open doorway that led to Lincoln's workroom. 'It's interesting that you and Landon chose the same spot for your writing rooms. Did you ever think of walling it off, as he did?' she asked. Something in the way she said it seemed to put Landon Donte on a pedestal, as if whatever he did was superior. The romance writer clearly wasn't happy with the comment.

'I like the feeling of openness. I don't care if people walk in when I'm working, and I don't have to have things just so. Not like Donte who wanted to hide away in a cave.'

I thought of my morning walk with Mikey and the stop outside the Scrivners' house and how it was still known by another name. I remembered I'd heard something like that about Landon Donte's house. 'Wasn't Donte's house known by someone else's name?' I said.

'Yes, and I heard he had a fit.' Lincoln laughed. 'People still call my place the Heller house because of the twin it was built for. I don't care.'

Serena seemed to have gotten stuck on what Lincoln had said about Nicole. She asked him how many times he'd seen her there.

'Two or three times. I don't remember exactly. Just that it was more than once.'

'That could explain why Donte's house was the first one she mentioned when she told our group about the idea of adding houses to the garden tour.'

Lincoln looked at me. 'You wrote a mystery,' he said, smiling when he saw me blush at the recognition. 'What do you think the clues say?'

I was embarrassed by the attention and quickly threw together some ideas. 'My impression of her from the start was that she had an agenda connected to the tour. There must have been something about Donte's house.' I started to say that she was new to the neighborhood, but remembered a comment she'd made that hinted she might have lived there before. When I mentioned it to Serena, she shrugged.

'She never said anything to me about any history with the neighborhood. She was so insistent about wanting to add the houses to the garden tour that I let her talk me into it. After what Mr Lincoln just said about her hanging around Landon Donte's house, it seems that it was all about her getting access to it, or him. She must have satisfied whatever she was after.' Serena let out a sigh. 'I'll take charge from here on.'

With that, Lincoln walked us all to the door.

The three of us stopped on the sidewalk outside and discussed showing our work to the Scrivners for their approval. Serena would be there for that, but when it came to dealing with Ona Chapin about Donte's house, she left it up to me and Owen. They were both in a hurry to leave after that. I took a last look at the copy I'd shown R.L. Lincoln. He'd been so easy about giving his approval that I realized I had forgotten to show him the bio I'd written. There was no reason to make a production out of it by having Serena accompany me, and I went back to his front door.

'You again,' he said with a smile. I announced what I needed and offered to have him look over what I'd written right there, but he invited me in.

'I was just about to have a glass of lemonade. Join me,' he said. I accepted the offer, and he invited me to sit in the living room while he got the drinks.

I had a good view of his workroom. I agreed with him about having an open space, rather than the cave-like room Donte had made his into. I didn't like to shut the door to a room, let alone bolt it. He set the two glasses down on the coffee table and took a chair across from me. I handed him the page that was about him.

He smiled as he read it over. He scribbled a few things on the page and handed it back. 'There are just a few corrections. Thanks for making me sound so great.'

He didn't seem in any hurry for me to leave, and we got to making conversation. I mentioned that I was planning to show what I had written about Donte and his house to Ona Chapin for her approval. I saw the way his eyes softened when I mentioned her name, and it was pretty clear he was far more than her former employer.

'Donte never got over that she came to work for me. I know I treated her a whole lot better than he did. There was definitely bad blood between them.'

'Did Landon replace her with Brad?' I asked.

'There was someone before Brad, and then there was Landon's student.'

'You mean Gena Fellows?' I said.

'So you know about her. Actually, she approached me first,' Lincoln said. 'I was doing a book signing at 57th Street Books, and she told me she was a writer, too, and that she was working on a book. She just needed some help with a few tweaks and getting it to a publisher. The big payoff she offered was that she'd dedicate the book to me if I helped her.'

'And you passed,' I said.

He laughed. 'I know trouble when I see it. Somehow she hooked up with Landon. Knowing both of them, I imagine whatever help he gave her was minimal, and she offered something he wanted in return. Probably more immediate than dedicating her book to him.' I heard him let out his breath in an annoyed way. 'I'm just tired of everybody talking about Landon Donte. From the time I moved in, I tried to be neighborly since we were both writers, but he was rude and condescending. He even tried to say that I was attempting to associate my work with his to make it seem, as he put it, "more worthwhile." I know one should not speak ill of the dead, but he was not a nice man.'

'Did you ever consider that his death might not have been suicide?' I said.

'I know your mind probably works that way since you wrote a mystery, but do you really want to go there?' His voice dropped as he continued. 'And if I were you, I'd keep any doubts about the suicide to yourself, in case you're right. The killer might not like having someone stir things up.'

His tone sounded friendly enough, but his last sentence still gave me the chills.

# TWENTY-SIX

And then it was Tuesday again. I began the day by contacting Ona and first offering my condolences, for which she thanked me in a somber tone. I wasn't sure if it was genuine or if she thought it was expected. I explained the situation with the copy and needing someone to sign off on it. I suspected it wasn't a surprise and that R.L. Lincoln, or Robert as she called him, had told her what I was doing.

'I would be glad to help you,' she said. 'If we could put it off for a few days, though, since I would like Brad to look at it, too.'

'That's fine. I will deal with the Scrivners first,' I said. I made an executive decision and decided that including Owen would only complicate things. I would handle it myself. We agreed on a day and time.

With everything taken care of, I spent the rest of the afternoon with Derek Streeter. It was a great relief to be working on the second book now that I felt the end was in sight. I had removed the hole in the plot and was now making sure the pieces fit together and rewriting places where they didn't.

I got in the flow again and was glad when a ping on my phone brought me back to reality. It was almost time for the writers' group, and I was still in the leggings and T-shirt I'd thrown on when I got up.

To keep the workshop from getting in a rut, I had planned an outing for a change. Instead of going over the pages they'd brought in, we would go out to a restaurant where they could do a writers' version of sketching. The idea was to capture people or situations around us to sharpen their observation skills. There was food and social time, too.

I changed into a more professional-looking top and had just finished adding some makeup when the doorbell went off. The group was going to meet at my place and then walk over together. I assumed it was an early arrival and buzzed the downstairs security door without checking.

I went out on the landing, hoping to catch whoever it was and save them all the stairs. I looked down, expecting to see Ed in his track pants or Daryl in one of her wild get-ups, but all I saw, until he looked up, was someone in a dark suit. Parker Andrews?

I got out a weak hello, and he gave me a wave as he continued his way up. When he got to the third-floor landing, we were face to face. Or almost, because he was taller than me.

'You dropped this on your last visit,' he said, taking my red scrunchy out of his pocket. I looked at it for a moment and then remembered I had stuffed it in my jacket pocket and it must have fallen out when I took the jacket off.

'Thank you, but it's hardly worthy of all the trouble of coming here,' I said, taking the crochet-covered elastic band.

'It looks like it's handmade,' he said.

'Actually, it is. I made it myself.'

'There you go,' he said with a smile. 'I was on my way to an event at the Museum of Science and Industry, and it was just a few blocks out of the way. There's a celebration of a new exhibit we financed. It's pretty cool, like walking inside a terrarium,' he said. 'I practically grew up at that museum.' He looked at me. 'You probably did, too.'

'Yes. Every kid around here practically lived at the museum. The exhibit you're talking about sounds great. I'll have to check it out.' There was an awkward moment when I wondered if I should just thank him again and send him on his way, but he was looking at the open door and he had gone to a lot of trouble.

'Do you want to come in?' I asked.

'For a few minutes. It's bad form to get to an event too early.' He followed me inside and stopped in the entrance hall and glanced around. 'Amanda is meeting me there. You'll be relieved to know that she doesn't have the slightest idea that I know what she did. By the way, we had that day with the bowling you offered in the second letter.' He stopped and chuckled. 'You were right about me needing something fun and spontaneous.' He made a face. 'But it turned out that Amanda wasn't exactly thrilled with renting bowling shoes or bowling. She thought the place smelled like stale beer. She almost threw up on the Ferris wheel. She tried not to let on how she felt, but it was pretty obvious.'

The frosted French doors to my office were wide open and the light was on next to my computer. 'So, that's where the magic happens,' he said, looking into my office. Rocky wandered out to see what was going on, and Parker looked down at the big black-and-white cat. Then he glanced toward the long hall that led to the back of the apartment. 'I like these old places.'

I wondered if I should offer him something to drink, give him a tour . . . I was trying to think of how I'd describe his manner. He wasn't arrogant – the wealthy guy looking down at my surroundings. It was more that he seemed curious in a friendly way.

'I suppose there's a Mr Blackstone somewhere,' he said, looking down the hall again. 'Someone who writes love letters must be a master of her own love life.'

'One has nothing to do with the other,' I said.

'Oh,' he said. 'Does that mean you haven't found your happily-ever-after?'

'I'm not sure that exists,' I said, deflecting the question. 'You of all people should know that, since you seem to view marriage as more of a business arrangement.'

'That's what marriage used to be. The whole idea of it based on love is relatively new and doesn't seem to work out that well. What is it – something like fifty percent of marriages end in divorce? And I tried the emotion-based thing when I was young, and it was a total flop. I have no desire for all that upheaval in my life now.'

'Then it seems that you have it figured out,' I said. 'How is it going with Amanda? Is she going to make it into the finals?'

'No guarantees,' he said, then he looked at me directly. 'How is she paying you? By the letter?' He stopped and took on a knowing expression. 'She offered you some sort of bonus arrangement, didn't she?'

I felt cornered, and he knew everything else, so I told him what she had offered me. 'I admire her ingenuity, and she does fit what I'm looking for in a wife. I did move her up in the rotation schedule.' He checked to see if I understood what he meant.

'She said something about you going through the list or something.' I tried to keep my voice neutral even though it all sounded so cold to me.

'I'm sorry I can't guarantee you'll get the big payoff, but maybe you can do some work for us. My aunt is always saying that we should have a family biography written.'

'I do more than love letters,' I said. Now that it seemed like a professional visit, I took him into my office and showed him what I was working on for the house tour and told him how I was overcoming all the kinks in the road with Landon Donte's suicide and a kleptomaniac on the loose. When he saw the picture of the Scrivners, his face lit up, and he recited part of the commercial jingle. 'You do know that Amanda works for him?'

'I didn't,' I said, surprised. 'All she told me was that she was an attorney.' There was nothing else to say about it, and I was about to segue into promoting my abilities by mentioning that I was working on the second Derek Streeter book when he held out a copy of the first book. 'I thought you might sign it,' he said.

'You've got a copy of my book,' I said, looking at the familiar cover.

'I collect first editions,' he said with a smile.

I signed the book and handed it back to him. He opened it and read the inscription. I had just written *Best Wishes* and my name. 'I didn't want to say anything more in case Amanda sees it,' I explained. 'Though if things work out, maybe you'll laugh about my part in it all.'

He stuck the book in his suit pocket and glanced down at some hard copies of photographs from the house tour. 'Those are the ones we're not going to use.' Parker picked up the sheet with Landon Donte in his workroom. I remembered the moment – how he'd posed, leaning against the desk, with one thumb stuck in his pocket. 'It's called the half-cowboy pose,' I said. 'He looks so confident in the picture. It's hard to believe he was hiding a black pit of emotion.' I explained being there when it happened.

'You do lead an interesting life,' he said.

The doorbell went off again. This time I checked with the intercom. It was Tizzy and Theo, and I told them I'd meet them downstairs. I explained the writers' group to Parker and where we were going for the event I'd planned for them. I grabbed the jean jacket and my purse and the messenger bag. I thanked him for the hair tie and used it to pull my hair off my face.

We walked down the stairs together. Tizzy and Theo were waiting just inside the security door in the inner vestibule. Parker was walking ahead of me, and I hoped they wouldn't think we were together, but as he went through the glass door, he glanced back at me. 'We'll be in touch.'

Tizzy and Theo both looked at me with a question in their eyes. 'Who's he?' they asked in unison.

'It's a long story,' I said. Which I didn't have time to tell them, thanks to the arrival of Ed and Daryl. We were out on the front porch of the building when Ben came up the stone stairs. He was carrying a bag of takeout food for his sister and said he'd meet us at the restaurant.

This time I'd chosen an Italian restaurant that faced the strip of Jackson Park that ran parallel to 56th Street and ended at the lake. Through the trees, I had a clear view of the Museum of Science and Industry with its domes and stone-draped female figures that served as columns. Normally, at this time of night, it was closed up and dark, but because of the event that Parker was attending, there were lights and a flow of cars passing along the front.

I imagined him meeting Amanda Brooks and wondered if there was a buffet and if she was getting his food.

The restaurant was crowded, and we had to wait for a table. The Malins were on the way out when we were led to our table. If they saw me, they didn't let on.

We'd already ordered our food, and I was handing out the pages with the prompts for the character sketches when Ben finally arrived. We kept up with the charade that he was just another member of the writers' workshop, and he sat down next to Ed.

They socialized while they ate and then got down to writing. I glanced around the restaurant, and my gaze stopped on a couple sitting in the window. When the woman looked in my direction, our gazes met for an instant. It was Nicole and, I assumed, her husband. She turned away quickly as I thought about going over to her table and asking her about her fascination with Landon Donte and his house. *As if she would tell me anything*, I thought, ditching the idea. I was sure that she'd seen me by the way she purposely didn't look in my direction when they got up to leave.

When it came time for the bill, the server said that it had been taken care of by someone wanting to remain anonymous. 'I'm OK with that,' Ed said, holding up his water glass in a toast to our benefactor. I had planned for them to read their word sketches, but it had gotten late and the restaurant was closing, so I collected them in, and we put it off until our next session.

As we were heading to the door, the host came up to me and handed me a folded piece of paper. It said: *For the woman with the red hair tie.* I unfolded it, feeling nervous anticipation, which only got amped up when I read the message: *Beware of unexpected consequences.*

Ben saw me reading and asked what it was. I showed it to him. 'It sounds like someone wants you to bud out.'

# TWENTY-SEVEN

B en told the group he was going up to check on his sister when we all got to my building. The rest of the group dispersed, and Ben and I went upstairs. It was really a ruse to make sure all was safe at my place after the strange note.

'All appears well,' he said when we walked in. 'Who do you think it's from? And who picked up the check?' he asked.

I told him about seeing Nicole at the restaurant and what R.L. Lincoln had said about her hanging outside Landon Donte's house. 'Then Serena told me that it was the first house she mentioned when she pitched adding houses to the garden tour. Our photographer showed me a photo of her on the stairs at Donte's house. And now she's dropped being involved with the whole thing. We had a conversation about her the other day. Maybe someone repeated what was said.'

'But why would she pick up the check?' Ben asked.

'I don't think she did,' I said. I hesitated. I hadn't told him anything about Amanda and having to deal with Parker. I finally told him the whole story. 'I think he's the one who did it, if you consider the timing – I just saw him, and he knew about the group and where we were headed.' Ben's expression darkened, but before he could start interrogating me about what Parker was doing at my place, I quickly added that he seemed pleased by the letters and it was probably a thank-you tip from him.

Ben didn't seem happy with my answer, and I was sure if he had a choice, he'd tell me not to do the love letters, but we didn't have time to discuss it as he had a late shift. 'Maybe you should just complete your work on the house tour and not worry what that Nicole person was up to.' He gave me a goodbye hug, saying he wished he could stay. And then he was gone.

I felt at loose ends and looked through what everyone had written. When I got to Ben's, I read it twice. There was a description of our server and a woman who had admired the case of desserts and then . . .

> *Her brown hair is caught up in a red thing that leaves a few tendrils hanging down. I envy the strands of hair as they caress her face. Her eyes sparkle with intelligence and insight as she glances over our group. I can't wait for her to look at me.*

No way was that going to be read to the group.

Amanda Brooks called the next morning. I wanted to bring up that she worked for Roman Scrivner's law firm, but then it would be awkward trying to explain how I knew. Instead, I tried to get her to talk about who she worked for, but all she would say was that it was less than desirable and would change once she was married.

All she really wanted to talk about was her relationship with Parker. I had to play stupid as she went on about their evening at the museum. 'It's working,' she said enthusiastically. 'He has definitely separated me from the herd.' She explained again how he had a group of women he was seeing and that he spread out how often he saw each one. 'It was always once every couple of weeks or so, and now suddenly it's been more than once in a week. It's like a game – he talks about the letters without coming out and saying that he knows they're from me, just that he's been getting them and is intrigued by the writer. Me!' she said with a laugh.

'That's great,' I said, with a sense of relief that he'd kept his word and not let on that he knew what she was doing.

'Can you come up with something more? But no bowling,' she said. 'I think he had fun, but I didn't. Rented shoes, a heavy ball that who knows whose fingers have been in – ugh. I don't want to entice him with things I don't want to do.'

'Why don't you tell me what you would like?' I said.

'I think my advantage is that I am good at taking care of him, and he seems to like it. It should be something that shows off my skill.'

'Can you cook?' I asked, and she laughed.

'No, and that's not the image I want to project anyway,' she said.

'Do you love him?' The words were out of my mouth before I had a chance to think if it was a valid question.

She made a surprised sound. 'Do you mean does my heart go pitty-pat when I see him?'

'I just wondered since your aim is to marry him.'

'Love is for amateurs who let their emotions get the better of them,' she said. 'I'm looking at this from a rational point of view. He is looking for a companion to have a home and children with. I like being with him, and he seems to like being with me.' And then she started with the same thing he'd said about marriage as a business arrangement.

It sounded cold to me and a little sad, but it was not my place to judge. I knew from talking to him that he was in the same place. I asked her what her dream date with him would be.

'I think he liked that I took charge with the suggestion of a fun day. So why waste time with suggestions of boat cruises or going barefoot on the beach? I was thinking we cut right to it. Something about me being the one and having Sunday brunch with his family to cement the deal. I don't want to waste time. Strike while the iron is hot. And I want it to be this Sunday.'

When I suggested getting together and having her put it in her handwriting, she nixed it. 'I don't have time. You can read me what you have over the phone and print it up on the pink paper. And drop it off at his office, like before. He made the point that having the notes arrive by messenger was part of the intrigue.' Just before she hung up, she said, 'Remember, the first bonus is on us getting engaged. I'd love to give you a check on Monday.'

At least I knew both of them this time. I took a yellow pad and went into the living room to work on the wording. She was right that there was no reason to be subtle. He was auditioning for a wife, and she wanted him to pick her. They both seemed to know what they were getting and they seemed to want the same thing.

*We both know that I am the One. We want the same thing. Companionship, a home, and family without turbulence.*

*You know that I can see to your needs and keep everything*
*running smoothly. I'm ready to step in for richer or poorer,*
*sickness and health. To be each other's companion for*
*now and the future. I would love to have Sunday brunch*
*with you and your family, with mimosas and eggs Benedict*
*in a beautiful setting where we can start to make the*
*plans.*

I sat back and read it over a few times. I jokingly thought of
adding that she'd cut up his food and make sure his mimosa was
made with fresh-squeezed juice, but, of course, I didn't.

It seemed to be what she'd said she wanted. It was direct. If
he invited her for brunch, the audition was over and she got the
part. I didn't want to think about the alternative.

I called her, and she had me read it three times. I heard her
hesitating, and I knew why. If he didn't invite her to brunch, then
it was over. I heard her swallow a few times, and then she told
me to go ahead with it.

Once she decided, she wanted me to deliver it that day, but
I had already arranged to bring the copy and photos to the
Scrivners, and I wasn't about to change my plan. I mentioned
the name to see her reaction. There was none. I wondered what
that meant.

I was most concerned about pleasing the Scrivners. Owen was,
too. Not only were they the backers of the tour and responsible
for the generous amount we were being paid, but there was the
promise of future work with them. Just to be sure, Owen and I
met to give everything another check, realizing that Nicole's
approval had probably just been cursory.

We worked at my dining-room table, going through his photographs and making sure we'd picked the right ones. I let him
read over what I'd written. I'd gone heavy on the architectural
importance of the house and how it harmonized inside and outside.
I didn't mention that it seemed very exposed with the surrounding
apartment buildings hovering over it. We rethought some of the
photographs and chose ones that didn't show what surrounded
the house.

'He's all about seeming classy and a humanitarian,' Owen said with a snort. 'You have to wonder how far a guy like that would go to protect his image.'

'As far as he has to,' I said, gathering everything up.

Owen and I shared a good-luck fist bump as we approached the Scrivners' house. Serena was walking ahead and missed it all. It was pretty clear she had stepped in because she felt she had to and wasn't very happy about it.

'Welcome,' Roman Scrivner said, looking from face to face before asking where Nicole was, since she'd been the one he'd been dealing with. Serena made an excuse for her that made it sound as though she was temporarily absent from the planning of the tour. As he led us inside, he said it was Ruth's day at the spa, so she wouldn't be joining us. We followed him up the floating staircase, which made me a little dizzy and brought us into the main area. It might be an architectural wonder and have the contemporary arrangement of all the common spaces flowing together instead of being divided into rooms, but it was whatever the opposite of cozy was. Peterman's furniture designs were about style with no concern for comfort. The couches and chairs were platforms made out of cement with a layer of cushions on top. Roman had made a point of saying that the platforms were the originals and only the cushions had been redone according to the designer's exact specifications. Peterman must have been a control freak because the 'furniture' was attached to the floor and couldn't be rearranged. The colors didn't help – mustard and a caramel brown.

Roman directed us to sit and picked a spot for himself that was in the middle. Owen and I began to lay out our work on the low glass coffee table in the center of the seating arrangement. Serena chose one of the concrete seats where she could gaze out of the wall of windows, making it seem she was just there for effect. Roman had an eye like a hawk and picked up on it and commanded her attention.

'I'd like to hear your input on the photographs and the copy,' he said to the tall, graceful woman. 'We all know this house is the star attraction. I believe it will be the real draw of the tour since it's never been open to the public before. Just look at this place.' He gestured with his hand. I did see his point. The interior certainly stood out from all the other houses.

We laid out the copy and photographs as we'd envisioned them being in the booklet. Roman waved Serena closer and the two of them leaned over the coffee table.

Owen was hanging close to Roman, wincing as the celebrity attorney started rearranging everything. I gladly stayed out of it as my presence wasn't really needed. I took the opportunity to ask about using the bathroom. Roman directed me to the ground floor; what he called the powder room was off to the side where we'd come in.

As I went down the floating staircase, I thought about how funny that he'd called it a powder room. The term came from the 1920s when the mention of women using the bathroom for bodily functions was considered improper. My guess was that calling it the powder room implied she was off to powder her nose. Did any women still wear face powder?

As Roman had said, the half-bath was near the stairs. The design was utilitarian with a toilet, pedestal sink, and towel rack. A mirror hung over the sink, and I imagined a woman dressed in 1950s attire, checking her makeup in the mirror. It was all part of this idea I had that something was left of all the people and events that had happened in a location. It was even more personal in my apartment when I would see swirls of past memories as I sat in the living room.

I snapped back to the present and. after drying my hands, thought of taking the opportunity to get a look at the ground floor. While Roman seemed anxious to show the place off, he'd kept the group to the one main area. Were there secrets hidden down here? The bathroom was set in a walled-off island that blocked the view of the rest of the ground floor. I opened another nearby door and saw that it was a large closet that seemed intended for coats and boots. There was even a bench to accommodate someone changing out of their outerwear.

I could hear the conversation coming down from the upper floor and figured nobody would miss me if I took a little longer. I ventured around the walled-off island and found an open space. It was smaller than the upstairs one and, I noted, completely different. I immediately understood why Roman hadn't shown it off. The floor above might have been kept to the architect's design, but this area had been turned into a den with comfortable furniture that could be moved around and a big-screen TV hanging on the rear of the island that held the bathroom and closet. The floor-to-ceiling glass was covered with drapes that let in light but blocked the view.

A glossy black counter with cabinets above and below had a bar sink and built-in refrigerator. I was curious about the storage space and opened one of the upper cabinets. The row of rolls of paper towels across the front seemed like sentinels and I pushed two of them aside to see how deep the cabinet was. I was surprised at how far it went back. It seemed like a bad arrangement, putting everything stored in the back out of reach, until I saw that the bottom pulled out like a tray.

Curiosity had taken over, and I gave the shelf a tug. It moved toward me. I pushed aside the paper towel sentinels to see what else was being kept there. I expected it to be backup supplies of napkins and toilet paper, but what I found surprised and confused me. It took a moment for me to recognize the metal holders as the things found commonly on tables in restaurants. The salt and pepper shakers were still in several of them, along with stacks of sugar and sweetener packets. I noted a laminated placard stuck into the holder on the top of one that described the desserts at the coffee shop on my corner. There were some random objects next to them, including a covered ceramic dish that had a sun face. When I lifted the top, I saw that it had some jewelry in it. And then my eye landed on something familiar. I felt a chill as I saw a tiny silver vase that looked just like the one that had disappeared from the Fellowses' house. I was reaching for it when I sensed footsteps. I pushed the lower portion back and rushed to close the cabinet.

'There you are,' Roman said. 'You were gone so long I was afraid you got trapped in the powder room.' He sounded concerned. 'It's happened before. One of the shortcomings of being on the historic preservation registers is that we can't just make changes in the place. Peterman designed the door handles, and they have a habit of falling off. No problem if you're on the outside, but if you're on the inside, you're trapped. I certainly wouldn't want that to happen to you,' he said, peering at me. Then his gaze went to the cabinet, which I hadn't managed to close completely. 'But it seems you moved on from the powder room.'

I had to think fast. 'The roll of toilet paper in the powder room was near the end and I was looking for a replacement,' I said.

Even I was impressed with my quick thinking. 'It's considerate of you to be concerned,' he said. He came up next to me and opened a lower cabinet displaying rolls of toilet paper. He glanced up toward the one I'd been checking out. 'That one just has paper towels,' he said. 'But I'm sure you know that.' He stared at me and waited until I'd nodded.

'Anything else you saw is strictly private. If it were to get out, I would know who to blame and there could be consequences.' There was a definite threat to his tone.

'You mean the changes from the Peterman design,' I said, glancing around at the contemporary bar area and soft seating. 'Don't worry. Your secret is safe with me.' I gave him a knowing smile as if we were co-conspirators and that his threat was meant in a joking way. I hoped it would distract him from what I'd come to realize. Ruth was the kleptomaniac.

He seemed uneasy and pointed toward the stairs. 'We should join the others.'

Serena was leaning over the coffee table, shuffling papers. She looked up as I retook my uncomfortable seat. 'Roman has made some suggestions,' Serena said. 'You need to extend the section about them at the beginning. As sponsors of the tour, they should be spotlighted more. Rather than mentioning he's familiar from the television commercials, it should be more about his law firm and how they look out for the underdog. And more about their contributions to the neighborhood. Roman thought you could write something about Ruth's hands-on approach.'

I wondered if Serena knew the double meaning of what she'd just said. It appeared that Ruth had had her hands on a lot of stuff, and it was all in that cabinet. For a man so concerned with his image, having a wife who was a kleptomaniac had to be a problem.

I pushed it to the back of my mind and focused on the copy for the booklet. Roman took up when Serena stopped talking. 'Ruth puts herself out there,' he said. 'Just as she took part in the interviews for the tour, she has been a part of other events that we've sponsored, like the soup and sandwich kitchen. She's ladled out soup a number of times. I'd like to have you play up the good things she's done,' he said, looking at me before turning back to the rest of them.

I nodded in agreement but was wondering how many ladles were there after she left.

'There's something else,' he said. 'I'm afraid that because of Landon Donte's death, his house has become the center of attention. If we are considering the actual house and the inhabitants, this place should be the centerpiece of the tour. The house is on the historic registry and the design is unique. Not to brag, but I am a bit of a celebrity.' He stopped and considered for a moment. 'I thought about it some more and now I believe it might be best to eliminate it from the tour altogether. It's connected with his suicide.'

'I think there's a question,' I said.

Serena shook her head. 'We all know that you wrote a mystery and are probably looking for plots in everything, but since you are representing our group, please don't start spreading stories that someone murdered Landon. The situation is bad enough as it is without making it into a crime story.'

'The man shot himself in a room that he'd bolted shut,' Roman said.

I probably should have let it go, but I couldn't resist bringing up the obstacle I'd noted that stood in the way of it being certain it was suicide. 'From what I saw, it appeared that Landon had used his right hand.' I paused as I looked over the group. I got Owen to pull up the photograph and showed it to them. 'As you can see from this, Landon was left-handed.'

'But what about the police?' Serena said.

'They are calling it an apparent suicide,' I said.

'And that's what they will leave it at,' Roman said. 'We were all there when it happened and we know he was in the room alone.'

'Do we?' I asked.

'Don't tell me that you're going to try to stir things up,' Roman said.

'He's right,' Serena said. 'Leave it be.' It sounded like a command.

'Don't worry, I'm not going to bring it up to the detective on the case. I was just thinking over what we know as opposed to what we think we know.' I switched around, trying to find a less painful spot on the hard furniture. 'I never saw Landon during the dinner. Did any of you?'

Roman started to say yes, but Serena cut him off and said that he was probably thinking of the exchange between Landon and his daughter at R.L. Lincoln's house before we all moved on to Landon's. 'Brad told us that he was in his workroom and would be with us shortly. He could have already been dead,' the president of the neighborhood group said.

'Somebody said they heard a gunshot,' Roman said. 'I can't say *I* heard it, though.'

'We're not here to discuss what happened to Landon Donte. It's not our concern.' Serena looked to Roman. 'Your house will be the star of the tour without a doubt. But the point of us doing the event is to raise money and, well, not to be ghoulish, there are probably people who wouldn't have bought tickets to the tour, but will do so now that the house is infamous.'

I could tell that Roman didn't want to agree, but I saw Serena's point. I gathered up the papers that I'd brought and put them along with the notes I'd taken about changes I needed to make in my messenger bag. I was lagging behind as we went down the floating staircase, and Roman caught up with me.

'I'm not going to beat around the bush. You should focus on this project and your career. Play ball and forget what you saw, and there could be a lot of work coming your way.' I was too stunned by the directness of his offer to even bother noticing the cliché.

# TWENTY-EIGHT

I had a lot on my mind when I went home. But one thing I knew for certain was that there was a limit to what I could share with Tizzy and Theo. But I also couldn't say nothing. Tizzy helped me get the job and had been the one to help me cover up the stolen vase. Rather than trying to pick and choose what I could and couldn't say, I avoided the whole thing by not going for sherry time.

It was just as well because that meant I could go straight to my computer and work on the changes Roman wanted without looking at the clock. The piece I ended up with wasn't long in terms of words, but it took a long time to do it. I had to go over notes and do some research. The problem with doing research is that I always got distracted from my original destination and spent too much time indulging my curiosity. Did I need to know how common Roman was as a first name? I also found out more than I needed to know about the Altschuler Brewery family. There was nothing I could use in writing about Ruth. Actually, there was almost nothing about her. My impression was that she was the runt of the litter.

When I worked like this, I had no sense of time. I was stunned when I looked away from the screen, glanced toward the angled window in my office, and saw that the sliver of sky visible above the brick wall of the next building was a dark blue.

I stretched to get the kinks out and tried to will my mind back to the present. It was Wednesday night and past the traditional dinner hour. My phone chimed with a text from Ben. He was at a barbecue place picking up food for his sister in payback for the countless meals she'd made for him. Sara was feeling poorly again, and her husband worked crazy hours at the twenty-four-hour pharmacy.

Their dinner was all ribs and brisket, but he said he'd gotten a selection of side dishes for me. The list of coleslaw, corn pudding, hush puppies, and macaroni and cheese was heavy on the carbs but sounded delicious.

I texted back that I was hungry and waiting. As I sat back in the chair, I wondered if I should be upset that Ben had sprung the food thing on me at the last minute. Assuming that I was available, with no forewarning. It seemed as if we were somewhere between where he was supposed to ask me out on a date with an acceptable amount of advance warning and where we were so connected that he could show up any time unannounced and it was OK. Having his sister as a neighbor made it more confusing, since a lot of his visits were after he'd seen her.

I made sure to save all my work and then cleared everything up. The whole place was in the dark, and I went through turning on the lights. I was still dressed in what I'd worn to meet Roman, so I changed out of my professional outfit of slacks and a white shirt and pulled on a pair of leggings and an oversized red T-shirt. I'd pulled my hair back with the red crocheted hair tie, but it had come loose and fell to the floor as I pulled the shirt down. It reminded me that I had to do the letter for Amanda and deliver it the next day. Without delay, since she was hoping it would lead to an invitation for brunch that Sunday.

Ben arrived with the food for us, and we laid out all the containers on the coffee table and just passed them back and forth as we shared them. He went to brush a tendril of hair off my face, and I thought of the piece he'd written. When I told him it might be awkward if he read it to the group, he started teasing me. 'You thought that was about you?' he said in an incredulous voice. 'As soon as I tell them it was the hot woman at the next table, I'm sure it will be fine.' He took a forkful of the macaroni. 'But maybe you're right.' He passed me the hush puppies and turned thoughtful.

'My sister is floating the idea of asking you to be the new kid's godmother. That would make you a permanent part of the family,' he said.

At first, I was flattered by the idea, but then my mind flew to what ifs. If I had thought it would be a problem having Ben in the workshop if things fell apart between us, it would be a total disaster if I was Baby Wright's godmother. I'd never been a godmother, but I assumed part of the duties would be attending birthday parties. What would that be like if Ben and I had ended whatever this was? I pictured a birthday cake with three candles. By then I'd really fit the bill of spinster, a single woman with a really old cat. Ben would be there, too. Would he bring a date? I knew from having encountered his ex-wife that he was attracted to obvious women who wore clothes that left little to be revealed when they took them off. I was getting carried away with the image, and along with having clawlike fingernails painted magenta, I aged his supposed date and made her look hard and a little desperate.

'What are you thinking about? You have the oddest look on your face,' Ben said. 'I didn't think being asked to be a godmother would be so upsetting.'

I wondered about sharing my mental image with him. But I worried that it would just lead to the discussion about us that he kept trying to have and I kept running away from.

'It wasn't about that,' I lied. 'I was thinking back to meeting Roman Scrivner.'

Ben shook his head with disgust. 'I hate those commercials. Do people really believe that line he says? "You're hurt. I'll help fight against evil insurance companies."'

'I wasn't thinking about the TV jingles,' I said. 'He sort of made me an offer I can't refuse.'

That got Ben's interest, and he forgot about the personal stuff and wanted to hear the details. I didn't have to worry about him spreading stories around the neighborhood that could be traced back to me, so I let loose and told him all about my exchange with Roman.

'He caught you snooping,' Ben said, shaking his head with disapproval. 'You really shouldn't do that.'

'I'm supposed to be describing the house,' I said, feeling the need to defend myself. Then I caved. 'It was a stretch, I guess.'

We both agreed that Roman's offer/threat was connected with me keeping quiet about his wife being a kleptomaniac.

'I didn't think of it until now, but I bet Doctor Malin knows about kleptomaniacs. She's a psychologist,' I added by way of explanation. Something toggled in my memory from the visit to the Malins' house. Hadn't she grabbed Ruth's hand and then something had fallen on the ground? 'I'd like to talk to her. I could arrange to show her the copy for their house and then bring it up.'

Ben seemed glad to let the subject go and move on to something more fun.

I contacted Christine Malin on Thursday morning. She seemed to have lost interest in the house tour and tried to push anything related to it back on to her husband. I had to tell her that there seemed to be too much about the elevator. 'Jerry is a little obsessive,' she said. 'I can see you for a few minutes between patients tomorrow, but you'll have to come to my downtown office.' I had the feeling that she wanted to make it as difficult as possible for me. But the joke was on her since I was going downtown anyway, to deliver Amanda's letter.

'That would be fine,' I said in a cheerful voice. The noise at the other end of the phone made it sound as though she was disappointed by my response.

After that, I pushed everything aside and worked on the Derek Streeter book. When I finally stopped, I sat back, took a deep breath, and let it out. I was in the home stretch.

Working on my book had left me with a good feeling, and the next morning I was ready to deal with Amanda's letter and Dr Malin. I dressed in one of my professional outfits of black slacks and a black top, using the infamous red scrunchy to hold back my hair. The air felt languid, a reminder that it was almost summer. But you couldn't assume anything about Chicago weather. The warmth could change to chill with a shift of the wind. I took the jean jacket just in case.

Tizzy had texted me just as I was leaving, making sure that I was coming for sherry later and to offer an update. I checked on Sara on my way out, and she and Mikey were doing OK for the moment.

I let my mind wander on the ride. It felt as though things were beginning to wind down. I patted the peacock-blue messenger bag on the seat next to me. The letter inside was probably the last one I'd have to write for Amanda. It put Parker on the spot. The next step might be writing something up about their engagement. Unless . . . I didn't even want to think about the letter failing. I also didn't want to be there when he read it.

The weather had changed by the time I came out of the train station. It was cloudy with a chill wind, and I put on the jacket. I walked to the financial district quickly. I wanted to drop off the letter and move on to the meeting with Christine Malin.

I walked into the Andrews Group office with a purposeful air. The security person/receptionist looked at me when I came in and he smiled.

'Can I just leave it this time? I'm in a hurry,' I said, pen in my hand, ready to sign in. He pushed the clipboard to me and I scribbled my name. I started to hand him the manilla envelope.

'No,' he said, reaching for the phone.

The assistant arrived a moment later and beckoned me to follow him. 'Mr Andrews insists that you deliver anything in person.'

I knew what came next and followed him through the sliding door. 'You could just take it to him,' I said in a last-ditch effort. 'All this seems like a waste of your time.' I was thinking of my time as well, since I had to get to Dr Malin when she was between patients, and if I missed an opportunity, I'd have to wait a whole hour for the next one.

We went into Parker's office. He looked up from behind his desk with an amused smile.

'Let's see what Amanda has to say for herself.' He held out his hand, and I passed the manilla envelope to him. I was too busy feeling tense to notice that he pulled out a stack of sheets instead of a pink envelope. 'It's a long one this time.' He was reading over them before I realized I'd given him the wrong manilla envelope.

'Sorry,' I said, reaching for them. 'That's for another client.'

He didn't hand the pages back but instead continued to read them over. 'Are these for the house tour you mentioned?'

'It's become much more than a tour of houses; it's more about the people who live in them, particularly Roman Scrivner since he's the sponsor.'

He nodded. 'That jingle of his is stuck in my head.' When I gave him a perplexed look, he explained. 'You hear it over and over if you're an insomniac.'

'Are you saying that you are?' I asked. He nodded.

'I wake up in the middle of the night with my mind spin-ning.' I debated whether I should offer a suggestion for help. *Why not?*

'I'm not a doctor or anything,' I said, 'but when I feel that way, I find that chamomile tea helps. I crochet, too, but I don't suppose that's something you'd want to try.'

'You're right. I don't think hooking is for me,' he said with a friendly smile. 'But I'll try the tea.'

'I'm surprised that you know crochet is connected to hooks,' I said, and his smile broadened.

'My nanny was an avid crocheter. I still have the old granny square blanket she made for me to prove it.' He wrote a note about the tea and looked up. 'And now for the real reason you're here.' He held out his hand for the correct envelope.

I felt my heart rate go up as I handed it to him. He extracted the pink envelope and took out the sheet. As he read it over, I saw the words in my mind.

*We both know that I am the One. We want the same thing. Companionship, a home and family without turbulence. You know that I can see to your needs and keep everything running smoothly. I'm ready to step in for richer or poorer, sickness and health. To be each other's companion for now and the future. I would love to have Sunday brunch with you and your family with mimosas and eggs Benedict in a beautiful setting where we can start to make the plans.*

He read it over several times before setting it on the desk and looking over at me.

'Hmm, no more silliness about words or going off for a "fun" day. This is pretty direct. She wants brunch with the family to make plans.' He glanced down at the paper and back up at me. 'I'm curious how that worked. Did she tell you what she wants and then leave it to you to put it into words?'

I'd hoped to avoid this. 'I'm just the letter writer, not her advocate,' I said. 'She did tell me what she believes are her selling points, which are seeing what you need and then taking care of it. I think it's called coddling.' He didn't say anything and I tried to explain by giving an example. 'The way she got your food at that reception and found a table.'

'That's what she thinks I want?' he said. 'I didn't really pay attention at the reception. I never eat at those events. It's about making an appearance and talking to people.'

I felt the need to stand up for her. 'I think she meant it as a way to show you that she's the kind of person who knows how to take care of things like a house and family,' I said. 'You did tell me that was what you wanted. You made it sound as though you wanted an arrangement based on mutual need, rather than based on emotion – which you both seem to feel is pretty iffy. You know . . . that it doesn't last,' I said.

'I did say that, didn't I?' He let out a sigh. 'I certainly like Amanda. She's intelligent and clever enough to have hired you. She has managed to make herself stand out from the others.' He nodded as if agreeing with himself.

'It's not my place to say it, but it sounds like the two of you are in the same place when it comes to marriage. That it's a rational arrangement.' He looked up at me.

'But I'm guessing that's not what you would do,' he said.

'That's irrelevant,' I said. 'This is just about what the two of you want.' My smartwatch vibrated, and when I glanced at the square screen, it reminded me of my meeting with Dr Malin. I pushed back the chair. 'I'm not a matchmaker. I just put people's feelings into words.'

He noticed that I seemed in a hurry and seemed disconcerted. He was used to being the one who ended a meeting. 'I have to get somewhere,' I said, standing. I patted the back of my hair checking that the scrunchy was still in place. 'And thank you for picking up the tab for my group. It was very generous.'

He gave me a blank look and I continued. 'The other night when you dropped off my hair tie. You were going to the museum for an event, and I mentioned my writers' group having dinner at an Italian restaurant.'

'So, you figured it was me.' he said. 'I like doing random things like that.'

'The note was confusing,' I said, thinking how it had seemed sort of threatening.

'Note?' he said with a perplexed look. 'Not from me.'

# TWENTY-NINE

I almost sprinted to get to the building where Dr Malin had her office. It was on the ground floor of a two-story building off Michigan Avenue. I walked into the reception area just as a woman walked out. I assumed she was the patient as she had a defeated look about her, and her gaze was locked on the ground.

A youngish man was behind the reception desk and looked up as I approached. I quickly told him that I had arranged to see Dr Malin between appointments, not wanting to waste time.

He contacted her, and a moment later she opened the inner door and motioned me in. She led the way down the hallway of doors to one that was open.

The interior had a window on an enclosed courtyard which had a fountain bubbling water and an orderly Zen look. The office itself was two chairs facing each other with a small table in between. A box of tissues sat on the small table next to the patient's chair, while the therapist's chair was slightly elevated and had a larger side table with a pad of paper and a pen.

She sat down quickly in the larger chair and motioned for me to take the other one. I commented on the soothing atmosphere, and she explained that was the point.

I brought out the house description that I had tweaked after seeing her husband and handed it to her. 'I don't really see why you went to all the trouble to bring this to me,' she said in a crisp tone. It was interesting to note that her manner when I'd met her at her home was no different from now in her office. She came across as cold and brittle, and yet Jerry seemed to adore her. Who could figure relationships? I thought back to Parker and Amanda. What was that tired phrase about different strokes for different folks?

'There's nothing like meeting in person,' I said. 'It's my first choice whenever I can.' I glanced around the room. 'I'm sure it's far more beneficial to your patients to see them in here than on a computer screen.'

'You're right, but computer appointments do work for people with certain problems.'

'You mean like someone who is a kleptomaniac,' I said. 'Then no worries that they leave with something?'

'What makes you bring up kleptomania?' she said, looking at me with new interest. 'Is that your problem?'

'No,' I said with a smile, holding up my hands to show they were empty. 'It's someone I know.'

'You can have them make an appointment,' she said.

'Then you've had patients with the problem before?' I asked. 'Maybe somebody from the neighborhood?'

She stiffened. 'I would never say anything about my patients. It's unethical and illegal. People come here and lay themselves open, feeling confident that whatever they say will be totally secret.'

'Then you don't show any reaction to what they tell you?' I asked.

'It would be no help to them if I got all huggy and dabbed at their tears. It's my job to help them work their way out of their problems,' she said.

'Even people with kleptomania?' I asked.

'You seem to be obsessed with that issue. Maybe it's not really a friend,' she offered in her usual crisp tone.

I realized I was digging myself into a hole. There was simply no way I could bring up her grabbing Ruth's hand and something tumbling to the floor. The only option was to talk about the description of her house.

'Leave all the information about the elevator,' she said. 'It is Jerry's thing. I'm surprised he didn't tell you how he's been offering help to the neighborhood. He thinks everyone should have one now that they have become so affordable.'

I asked her what sort of work Jerry did, and she reminded me that he was a structural engineer. 'And looking after me,' she said with the hint of a smile. It was the first time there was any warmth in her voice.

The cell phone on the table next to her pinged, and she picked it up.

'My next appointment is here,' she said, standing. As I made my way to the door, she said if my 'friend' wanted help, she was here for them.

I caught the Metra train home at two twenty. As the train started to move, I sent Amanda a text that the letter had been delivered. I left it at that, realizing that Parker hadn't committed to the brunch. I wondered if I should have tried to talk her out of being so direct. My thoughts moved on to the visit with Christine Malin. It hadn't been very useful except to hear that Jerry was spreading the word about elevators. And she now thought that I was a kleptomaniac!

I'd forgotten all about Parker's denial about the note. If not him, then who? The thought was interrupted as I looked out of the window and saw the train was at my stop. I ran through the car and got out of the door just as it was closing.

When I got home, Rocky was waiting by the door and offered a few meows before leading the way to the kitchen. I felt guilty when I saw that his bowl was almost empty. I filled it with dry food, which he attacked hungrily. 'You and me both,' I said as I felt my stomach rumble. I'd just had coffee before I left, too intent on my meetings to think about food.

'When in doubt, peanut butter wins out,' I said, amused at my rhyme. I toasted the bread before I slathered on the peanut butter and cherry jam. I cut the sandwich into little triangles and took it into my office. The note for Parker was still on the screen, and again I thought maybe it had been too soon to be so direct.

There was nothing I could do about it now, so I closed the file and opened the one dedicated to the house tour. I went to the section on the Malins. Christine had pointed out a missing word, which I fixed. And then the Theo in me took over, and I started researching house design. It had never occurred to me that room placement was affected by health issues. It turned out that while calling a bathroom a powder room seemed to have come from the 1920s, the concept of a half-bathroom was related to the 1918 pandemic. In those days, coal and ice were delivered to homes, and the delivery people came inside after they'd been to other houses. The half-bathroom was meant as a place for delivery people, and probably guests, too, to wash their hands and use the facilities, keeping their germs away from the residents.

I lost track of time again. The ping of my phone brought me

back to the present and a text from Ben saying he was out front.
It took me a moment to see the dark sky and remember that I
had committed to doing my plus-one duty. This time it was the
birthday party of one of his fellow cops. I looked down at what
I was wearing and realized the work outfit I'd worn for the meetings wouldn't do.

I called his cell and announced there'd be a delay and invited
him up. There was a discussion about getting past his sister's
apartment without being discovered. Mikey seemed to have developed a super sense of knowing when his uncle was nearby.
'There's no way to escape if the kid sees me,' Ben said. 'He'll
have a meltdown if I don't go in and give him piggyback rides
up and down the hall.'

'You're too much fun for your own good,' I said. 'There must
have been something in cop school about how to move around
without being detected by a three-year-old,' I teased.

He agreed to take his chances and come up. I watched from
the third-floor landing, trying not to laugh as he did a cartoonish
maneuver past the apartment door.

'Home free,' he whispered with a grin as he reached the top
floor. 'I happen to know that Quentin's home, so he can take
care of whatever.' He looked at my bare feet and slightly
disheveled work outfit.

'I had some appointments and then I worked all afternoon,' I
said with a shrug once we were inside my place.

'Anything interesting?' he asked. Then he glanced at his watch.
'You can tell me about it in the car. Being fashionably late is
one thing, but arriving when the party's over is bad form.'

He helped himself to a beer while I changed. Then we
repeated the tiptoe move down the stairs, barely making it out
of the vestibule on the ground floor before having a fit of
laughter.

'That was just the dose of fun I needed,' I said as he opened
the door of the Wrangler for me.

'That bad, huh? You can tell me about it now,' he said as he
pulled out on to the street.

I began with the delivery of the letter and how awkward it
had been since the message was so direct.

'You should have made her use a messenger service,' he said.

'That isn't the way my business works. I do what the client requests. She paid me extra to hand-deliver the letters.'

'Maybe you should rethink how you do things,' he said in an authoritative tone I didn't care for. I wasn't used to anyone telling me what I should do, and I didn't like it.

'At least it's done with,' he said, seeming unaware that I'd bristled at what he'd said. I offered a vague yes. It was true. The letters were done, and who knew if there would actually be anything else? To change the subject, I brought up that Amanda worked for Roman Scrivner's law firm.

It didn't help, and Ben went off on how tacky it was for an attorney to advertise like that. 'It's all about the image he wants to project as someone who cares. Sponsoring the tour you're working on is just about making him look good, too. He seems oh-so friendly in the commercial, but I bet it's a different story if you do anything to cross him.'

I certainly wasn't going to bring up my snooping at the Scrivners' after that comment, and I abruptly changed the subject to Landon Donte and how many people seemed to have had issues with him.

'You mean you've come up with a bunch of people who could be suspects if he hadn't killed himself?' Ben asked, and I nodded. 'We've still a way to go before the party. So feel free to share.'

'I don't know about suspects. Gena Fellows claims to have had a student–teacher relationship with him, but I'm not so sure what it really was. Her husband might not have approved. Roman Scrivner seems to be worried about being upstaged by Landon Donte, and, as you said, who knows how Roman would react if someone got in his way? But if he was murdered, I think it might have been something in his manuscript. It was deleted, after all. Even if Landon was that despondent, would he get rid of it?' I thought back to when I'd seen what was left on the computer and the shredded pages in the trash can. One thing stood out. 'If Landon was the one deleting it, would he have missed a few sentences at the end? If only there was a copy somewhere,' I said wistfully.

'I don't think missing a few sentences means anything. If he was that despondent, he might have been careless,' Ben said.

'So careless that he forgot which hand to use,' I said. The conversation ended as he pulled the Wrangler in front of the bar. Sounds of music filtered out through an open door.

'Time to forget about murder and put on your dancing shoes.' Ben gave my hand a squeeze and cut the engine.

# THIRTY

I t had been a fun evening, and I'd pushed away my concerns about Ben telling me how to run my business. Maybe I was just too accustomed to being independent. That probably didn't work when you were in a relationship. I'd have to figure out a middle ground. In the meantime, I had to go grocery shopping early as I had plans later in the day. I had been trying not to check my phone every few minutes for a text from Amanda. I was waiting for confirmation that Parker had asked her out for brunch. I stuck the phone in my pocket so I had two hands to maneuver the cart with bags of groceries up the stairs. As I rolled it across the second-floor landing, Sara opened her door.

'These came for you while you were out,' she said, holding out a floral arrangement of white flowers. They were pretty, but the arrangement seemed like something for a funeral. 'Aren't you going to see who they're from?' There was a small white envelope stuck between the blooms.

'Probably a client. A thank-you gesture,' I said, avoiding the envelope. My first thought was that they were from Parker, and I didn't want to get caught up in explanations. I was trying to think of a graceful way to leave when Mikey appeared and demanded Sara's attention. I thanked her for taking them in and added them to the grocery cart before continuing upstairs.

As soon as I was in my place, I pushed through the blooms, took out the envelope, and looked at the message: *Think carefully before you disclose anything. Your future could depend upon it.*

There was no name, but I didn't think they were from Parker. My first thought was Roman Scrivner and that it was a threat. The fragrance of the flowers had been nice at first, but the jasmine and gardenia scents became overwhelming, and I set the whole thing out on the front balcony.

Despite my comment, Roman must have realized that I'd seen more than the changes he'd made to the den and that I knew they were things that Ruth had pilfered. Roman wanted to be known as a philanthropist and custodian of an architectural treasure. If it came out that Ruth was a kleptomaniac, that's all anybody would think about. Just as Christine Malin had done, they would want to check Ruth's hands and bag before she left any gathering or even a restaurant. I stopped on that thought, as it sunk in for the first time what it meant. Ruth was one of Christine's patients. Roman, no doubt, wasn't concerned about her disclosing anything since legally and ethically she couldn't.

There wasn't any way for me to tell Roman that I had no intention of talking about Ruth's problem, so I did the next best thing. As soon as I'd put the groceries away, I went back to the copy about the Scrivners and their house. I pumped up the adjectives in the section about their generosity in sponsoring the tour. I added to the information about Ruth, making her sound like the grand lady in charge of putting the tour together.

I went over what I'd written about their house. I surprised even myself with the phrases I came up with to use – like *a dazzling example of an architectural genius's work.* I would make sure to get a final OK from him.

I knew Roman was worried about Donte's house getting more attention than his. I looked at what I'd written about the writer's house and wondered if I should try to downplay it as I made adjustments that took into consideration what had happened to Landon. I read over what I'd written after the first visit there.

*The Victorian-style wood-frame house belongs to Landon Donte, author of* The Lament of Larry Latham, The Presumption of August, *and other highly regarded literary works. Originally an identical twin to the house of popular novelist R.L. Lincoln, it is now more like a distant relative. He has customized the lower floor to create a writer's cave where he conjures up the plots and characters of his prize-winning prose.*

*The dining room has a display of his many awards along with the angled windows that let in light but look away from the nearby structures. The eat-in kitchen has an old-fashioned farmhouse feel where the writer can enjoy his breakfast while gazing out at the mulberry tree in the*

*backyard. The conservatory that was added to the back of
the house gives a year-round feeling of summer.*

I wasn't sure how I could change it. And what could I say about
his workroom – that it was his last stop on this side of the veil?

I decided to leave it be until I talked to Ona. I had arranged
to meet with her that afternoon to go over what I'd written. I'd
only met her a few times and, even then, only in passing. All I
really knew was that she was Landon Donte's daughter and R.L.
Lincoln's companion. I wasn't sure how else to describe her
relationship with the popular author. There was something else
I knew about her now. As Landon's only child, she was now heir
to everything he left.

I was always apprehensive about showing my work for someone's approval. Because they were paying for it, clients did
nothing to soften their criticism, and it sometimes bordered on
cruel and demeaning. So far, the only homeowner who had been
that way was Gena Fellows, and I understood it was all about
making herself seem more important. I had no idea how Ona
would be and could only hope for the best.

When it was time to go, I debated whether to take the messenger
bag or just carry the sheets in a manilla file. I decided the
peacock-blue messenger bag looked more professional.

I looked at the familiar house as I opened the gate. From the
outside, everything looked the same, and there was no hint of
what had happened. I admired the profusion of tulips and daffodils
blooming next to the stairs as I went up to the porch. Ona opened
the door as I was still ringing the doorbell.

'Come in, come in,' she said, ushering me inside. I was embarrassed to admit that I hadn't considered her as one of the main
players and had glossed over her before. Now that she'd moved
center stage, I viewed her with more interest. I guessed she was
in her late twenties. I noted hints of her father in her expression.
I had no idea if her light brown hair came from him or her
mother, since Landon's hair was white. There was a fragility
about her that I guessed came from her current circumstances.

'Where shall we do this?' she said more to herself than to me.
It seemed obvious that she felt uncomfortable. She seemed
relieved when I took over and suggested the living room.

She sat down facing away from the door to her father's work-room, and I sat down opposite her. The door had been repaired and was open, giving me a partial view into the room.

'I guess we should start,' I said, taking the few pages out of my blue bag. I heard her swallow rather loudly.

'This is all so strange.' She looked around the room and touched the arm of the chair she was sitting in. 'It's all mine, but it doesn't feel like it.'

I nodded with comprehension. 'I understand,' I said. I explained that I'd inherited my condo after my father died. 'I was living there, but it still took a while to accept that it belonged to me. I'd hear my father's voice telling me I was going to ruin the kettle if I didn't turn it off before all the water boiled away.' I smiled. 'I still hear it in my head, but it's a lot softer now.'

Her eyes had appeared flat but came to life at my comments, and she smiled. 'It's so nice to have someone understand. Brad feels strange, too. I have kept him on, but I think we both feel as though he's still working for my father.'

I had put the sheets of paper on the small table next to where she was sitting, but she hadn't even glanced at them. I sensed that she was more interested in talking now that I'd become a bit of a kindred spirit.

'I used to live here,' she said with a sigh. 'But my father never treated me like his daughter. I was always more like a helper. He had a very inflated view of himself and his importance. Everything was always about him and his work. He couldn't be disturbed when he was "conferring with his muse," as he put it. He'd fuss about any noise,' she said. 'That was before he made the changes and everything echoed through the house.' She let out a heavy sigh. 'I didn't expect him to do what he did.' She glanced up at me to see if I understood. 'He was very upset that his last book was considered a disappointment by the critics. He didn't think me worthy to discuss his work with, but I thought he was confident that the book he was working on was going to make up for the last one.'

'Do you know what it was about?' I asked.

'He was never one to talk about what he was working on – just about himself and his talent. But even that mostly ended when I went to work for Robert.' I flinched at the name, then remembered that she called R.L. Lincoln by his first name. 'My father viewed me as a traitor. No matter how much he put down what Robert wrote, he was jealous of him. It wasn't just the book sales, but how prolific he was.' She looked around the living room as she took a deep breath and ran her hand along the cushion on the couch in a manner that suggested she was claiming ownership and she was pleased with it. I understood that as well. I'd done the same move on the leather couch more than once.

When I'd first arrived, her demeanor had been tense, but as we'd talked, she'd let out some deep breaths and her shoulders had eased. 'It's nice to have someone to talk to who understands,' she said, confirming my impression. 'It's been a lot for me to deal with. But I am lucky that my father didn't marry again. Then all of this would have gone to her.'

'So he didn't have a will?'

'He had a trust. When he got the last divorce, her name was taken off of it, so there was just me.'

'You had no interest in being a writer?' I asked.

Her eyes moved and her mouth twisted as if she was having an unpleasant thought. 'I did for a while. But when I showed my work to my father . . .' She stopped, and her expression turned resolute. 'According to him, being the daughter of such an illustrious talent came with expectations, which I didn't measure up to. I believe his words were that the story that I showed him was predictable and had no depth.'

'That must have stung,' I said, feeling for her.

'More than you know. That's why I changed my name.' Her phone rang, and when she looked at the screen, she said she needed to take the call. 'Feel free to look around,' she said. The way she gestured with her hand, it was clear she meant somewhere else in the house.

I stopped in the entrance hall. I'd seen the first floor a number of times, but never the upstairs. She didn't seem to mind if I wandered. The staircase was massive and felt so much more secure than the floating one in the Scrivners' house. As I neared the top, I thought back to the elevator in the Malins' house and how welcome that would be in a house like this.

The second floor was just a hall with doors off it. At the front was a small bedroom that I guessed was meant as a nursery. The bedroom next to it must have been Landon's. It had the same windowed outcropping that the living room directly below it had. The walls were painted a dark green, and it wasn't very appealing. I continued down the hall and opened the door on the other side of the hall. This room was over the dining room and had the same angled window. The furnishings were spare, and the room appeared unused.

'My old room,' Ona said, coming up behind me. She walked past me and went inside. I followed her and watched as she checked out the interior. It was furnished with a bed and dresser, but all the personal stuff was gone. 'You should have seen it when my father got the house. It was all pink wallpaper and thick carpeting. It must have belonged to the daughter of the family who lived here before us.' She glanced around the bare room. 'We found a box of old dolls when we moved in, and a broken chest of drawers. The story was that the girl whose room it had been had a mental breakdown and went off to a boarding school. It made me feel uncomfortable, as if she'd left behind some of her troubled vibe.'

I opened the closet door and was surprised at the dark expanse. The bar to hang clothes on was toward the front, and it was hard to tell how far the narrow space continued. Ona put her hand on my arm. 'I heard scratching coming from back there when we first moved in. It creeped me out, and I never wanted to look back there.' She swallowed hard. 'And I still don't.'

I asked her if she'd talked to her father's publisher about the book he was working on.

'That's history now,' she said. He deleted the manuscript and shredded all the hard copies.'

'And there's no backup copy anywhere?' I said.

'My father, the genius, didn't trust computers and insisted the only backup he needed was the printout he did every day.' She looked up at me. 'I'm glad it's gone. The genius's work is done forever.' She caught herself. 'I'm sorry if that sounds cold, but you didn't know him as I did. He didn't care about those he hurt.'

She led the way back downstairs. 'We should get to why you came,' she said. 'I'm sure you probably have more important things to do than listen to me go on about my father.'

We returned to the living room and took the same seats as before. I handed her the page and said that I realized it needed to be reconsidered after what had happened. 'Since the place is yours now, feel free to make notes on how you'd like it changed.'

She sat back on the couch and had barely looked over the paper before she picked up a pencil and started to write something. It was silly, since I had offered her the opportunity to add what she wanted, but it still made me uncomfortable to watch while she edited my work. She didn't even look up as I wandered through the open door into Landon's workroom. All the traces of blood were gone. The walls of bookshelves and the thick carpet on the floor made the room seem insulated from the rest of the house and the outside world, which no doubt had been the writer's plan.

Ona didn't seem concerned about my nosing around, so I stepped behind the desk and looked at the desk chair. It was unsettling to realize that was where Landon had been sitting. The view toward the windows was blocked by drapes on the other side of the room. It really did feel like a cave. The wastebasket had been emptied, and there was no chance of any shreds being put back together like a puzzle to display his final work. The computer was dark, and when I touched a key, the screen didn't instantly turn on as it had when I'd been in there before. Ona seemed occupied in the other room, and I pressed the power button. I had low expectations, since there was always a password that needed to be entered, and I had no idea what Landon's would have been. But to my surprise, it went directly to his word-processing program and his farewell note. Then I remembered that Gena had said something about setting it up so that it went straight to his work.

I read it over again.

*You have to wonder why people do what they do. Or say what they say. I'd heard it all over the years of tending bar at the neighborhood hangout where everyone from university students to locals gathered. People drank too much and then talked too much. Did they think I didn't hear what they said?*

There was nothing for a few lines and then: *This is drivel. I have run out of ideas. I'm done.*

I wondered about his choice of words. Would somebody with such an exalted opinion of himself call his work 'drivel'? I would have thought he would say something more along the lines of it wouldn't be appreciated or understood. I scrolled down the page which was blank, where he'd deleted his writing. The next page had a page number which must have been typed in rather than formatted. And then a few lines appeared. I had to wonder about all that was missing.

I thought of myself and how I backed up my work with flash drives and saved it on the cloud. But there was another way, I thought, remembering how Tizzy had sent me her story. Sometimes when I was feeling concerned about losing my work, I'd done it, too. Something Gena said she'd done for Landon made me wonder.

I glanced at the toolbar on the top of the screen and saw an icon for mail. After what everybody had said about Landon's computer skills, I expected nothing when I clicked on it, so I was surprised to see a menu showing a list of emails.

I took another glance toward the living room, where Ona seemed to be finishing up with her notes. I needed to act fast. I scrolled through the list of emails and came to one with an attachment. I began to get excited when I saw that it was from Landon to himself. Could it be that he'd taken what Gena had taught him and figured out how to keep a copy of his manuscript? Since he'd seemed a little paranoid, he wouldn't necessarily have shared what he did with anyone. I was considering whether to open the attachment when I heard Ona fumbling with the papers. She'd made it clear she wanted the manuscript gone. She'd delete it for sure if she saw what I was doing. Feeling my heartbeat kick up, I forwarded the email with the attachment to myself and shut everything down. I was pushing away from the desk when she came in. Her gaze stopped on me, and she had a troubled expression. 'Find anything interesting?'

'No, nothing,' I said quickly as what I'd found sunk in. 'Let me see what you've done.'

She'd barely handed me the pages with her scribbles when the doorbell rang. 'It's the caterer to set up for Sunday,' she said.

'What's happening on Sunday?' I asked.

'The memorial service for my father. And the reception for invited guests. You're welcome to come.'

A woman stuck her head in the living room and held up an urn-size coffee pot and asked where they should set up. Ona apologized to me and said she needed to deal with them. I was glad to have an excuse to make a quick exit. I promised to do the best I could to incorporate the changes she'd suggested and then rushed home, anxious to check my email.

# THIRTY-ONE

I went directly to my computer, dropping my bag and jacket on the floor. The email I'd forwarded was at the top of my inbox. I took a deep breath and clicked on the attachment, hoping it would be open on my computer.

I watched the screen as my word-processing program opened and then popped up a message about having to adjust to my version. I held my breath, afraid it was going to show up in something unreadable. At last, the file opened and the screen filled with readable type.

I recognized the first paragraph from what I'd seen on Landon's computer, but there were no lines about drivel, and when I scrolled down, the copy continued on and on. I wanted to give myself a high five. I had managed to get hold of probably the latest version of his manuscript.

I got a cup of coffee and sat in front of the screen reading through it. It was still in a rough state, but I got the gist of it. As someone had said, he'd attempted to mix his literary style with a popular fiction sort of plot. It was about a bartender at a popular hangout in a university neighborhood. He felt that he was treated like a nobody, just there to serve up drinks. He concocted some plan for blackmail and revenge. It wasn't the plot that interested me as much as the characters. A regular at the bar was described as a romance novelist who wrote about relationships, but couldn't manage her own and tried to pick up very young men. Landon had described a female character as *needy and unpleasant as she clawed her way to the center of attention.* She was married to a much-beloved chemistry professor who had a dark side. There was a psychologist who was disgusted with his patients and after a few drinks gave out juicy details about them. He regularly talked about the kleptomaniac married to the well-known TV newscaster who always left a session with a souvenir. I flinched when I read the description of Lorelai. She was the daughter of a famous archaeologist who was trying to follow in her father's footsteps but couldn't measure up to his brilliance.

When I'd seen it on Landon's computer, there had been a partial sentence at the end. I'd read: *eyes changed after a few beers. Her mild exterior melted, exposing the hot hungry tigress on the prowl.* Now that I saw the whole thing, all I could do was shake my head. It read: *The graceful woman with the azure eyes changed after a few beers. The mild exterior melted, exposing the hot hungry tigress on the prowl.* I shuddered, wondering how many people Serena had told she was the basis for the graceful woman with the azure eyes who kept appearing in his books. I also wondered if there was a whole other side to Serena that nobody knew about.

Landon had attempted to disguise the characters, but if I could figure out who the real people were, others could, too. I sat back and let it all soak in. Reputations and lives could be ruined by what he'd written. I could think of a number of people who would want that manuscript to disappear, and Landon with it.

While I was still taking it all in and thinking back to when I'd seen the supposed suicide note on his computer, an image of the trash can with shreds of paper came into my mind's eye. I had glossed over it at the time, but that was before I thought about how many pages there were. The pile of shreds couldn't possibly have been a couple of hundred sheets. I knew from my own experience of shredding paper that it took a while. Whoever did it must have run out of time and stashed the rest of the intact pages somewhere else.

My mind was swirling, and I was glad when the ping on my phone brought me back to the present. I hoped it was a confirmation from Amanda, but it was from Tizzy, reminding me of sherry time. I felt a moment of relief, thinking I would have someone to talk it all over with, but then I had second thoughts about what exactly I could share. If someone had managed to fake the suicide, they thought the manuscript was gone. Talking about it could put Tizzy, Theo, and me in jeopardy. I couldn't say a word until I figured it all out.

I decided to keep the conversation to my visit with Ona, and I'd even brought along her notes on what I'd written.

Theo had everything set up when I arrived, and Tizzy greeted me with a hug.

'I feel as if it's been forever since we talked,' Tizzy said. 'What have you been up to?'

I laughed and said it had only been a couple of days, and then was vague about what I'd been doing. I didn't even want to mention that I'd gone to the Scrivners' for fear I'd slip and mention something about the cabinet with all the things Ruth had taken. Tizzy knew there was a kleptomaniac but not who, and it seemed best for all to leave it that way. I told them about my visit with Ona.

'That's terrible,' Theo said when I repeated what Landon had said to his daughter.

'The saddest part is that I don't think it's even true.' I brought out the sheet with her scribbles. 'I read over the changes she suggested. I can't use a lot of them since they seem to be her personal feelings about the place, but they seem well written.'

They encouraged me to read them out loud.

*As soon as Landon's wife left, he started to make plans to redo the house to please himself. Without telling his daughter, whom he treated more as an employee than as his only offspring, he met with a contractor and an engineer about the changes he wanted, which completely altered the energy of the place. It was no longer going to be a house for a family, but made to please his fancy. Since he never consulted his daughter for her opinion about the changes, when the construction began, she moved out.*

'We talked for a while, and as soon as she realized I was a kindred spirit, she opened up about how strange she felt inheriting the house.'

'Is she going to live there?' Tizzy asked.

'She didn't say.' Her question reminded me of seeing her old bedroom and the closet. 'She didn't seem particularly attached to the room. There are other bedrooms. I can't imagine she'd want to stay in Landon's old room. There was another one. Maybe it would feel like a fresh start.'

We reached a lull in the conversation after that, and Theo

brought out his manuscript and started talking about Cedric Von Brainiac. 'I'm changing what he's looking for,' Theo said, pushing his horn-rimmed glasses back up. 'I think it should be a forgotten treasure. What if it had been left by the Wizard of Knowledge in the secret world, and then Cedric went looking for it?' Theo's eyes were darting back and forth as he went on, thinking out loud about what the character he'd created would do. Out of nowhere, he seemed to have conjured up a hard copy of his work and he held it out, showing me a drawing he'd made of the entrance to Cedric's secret world of adventure. He was very proud of the drawing, and I didn't want to break the news that publishers tended to hire illustrators for the pictures.

'Veronica is here as our friend, not writing coach,' Tizzy said.

'OK, then, she can take them with her,' Theo said, passing his manuscript to me. 'They count as my pages for next Tuesday.' Then he excused himself, muttering something about an idea he'd had.

'Don't mind him,' Tizzy said, rolling her eyes. 'He gets lost in his work.' He'd left his martini barely touched, and she went to take a sip. She made a face and replaced it. 'I'll stick with sherry. I'm not so sure it was a good idea for me to suggest he join the group,' she said. 'He used to be so anxious to do research for my time travel book, and now all we talk about is Cedric.'

She finished up her glass, and I got ready to go, pleased that I hadn't said anything I shouldn't. The only tidbit that I shared was that Ona didn't believe her father would kill himself.

'That and three dollars will get you a cup of coffee,' Tizzy said with her eyes alight, teasing me with the updated version of a cliché. It was hard to imagine coffee ever being a dime. Just then my phone pinged with a text from Amanda. Sunday was on!

I was keyed up when I got home. I had felt a slight sense of relief when I saw the text from Amanda, but I got tense all over again as I thought about Landon's manuscript. I was more convinced than ever that it was murder. But what could I do about it and where were the pages that hadn't been shredded? I didn't feel comfortable telling Detective Jankowski about it, since he might take the view that I'd stolen the manuscript, whereas I thought of it as borrowed.

I tried to distract myself by cooking a proper meal and attempted to lose myself in making spaghetti with marinara sauce made from scratch. There would be leftovers to keep me going for days. I added a salad and set a place for myself at the dining-room table. But as soon as I sat down, my mind went back to the manuscript, and I barely tasted the meal. I was done in a few minutes and dropped my plate in the sink.

Maybe work would calm me, and at least I'd have something to show for my time.

Rocky followed me into my office and jumped into the burgundy wing chair and promptly fell asleep. I started with the pages I had from my visit with Dr Malin. I made the few corrections and then wondered about the truth of the part Landon had put in his manuscript about a therapist who talked too much. But more than that, what it would do to her reputation and career if the book came out? At the very least, local people would be likely to figure out the character was connected to her. Just as they'd figure out the used-car guy was Roman Scrivner. I assumed I wasn't the only one that Serena had told about being the basis for the character with the azure eyes. I doubted she wanted to be known as a woman on the prowl at a bar. These thoughts were not helping, and I took out the sheets with Ona's notes. I could only imagine how hurtful it would be if she saw the character her father had based on her. Or maybe she had already seen it. When I'd finished with the piece on Landon's house, I pushed away from the computer. I still felt jumpy and uneasy.

I started thinking about the other characters Landon had created that might cause upset. For some reason, Nicole came to mind, even though it didn't seem she had any connection to Landon. I checked around online about her and found little until I went back to her Facebook page. It was private but gave away just enough for me to see that she indeed had a connection to Landon's house. None of these thoughts were helping.

I finally turned to my old standby of chamomile tea and crochet. The combo did some good, even if the square I made was a fright and would have to be redone. At least I was calmed enough to fall asleep, though I had a crazy salad of dreams. Everything was disjointed and hardly made sense. Parker gave Amanda a ring, but it turned out to be a plastic number, the sort you'd find in a cereal box. And then Ruth Scrivner took it. Roman was chasing her through R.L. Lincoln's house and then Landon Donte's. Out of nowhere, there was a flutter of papers, and Cedric Von Brainiac was scooping them up with a butterfly net. Then he got in an elevator and disappeared.

I awoke with the sheet twisted around me, barely feeling rested. I leaned back into the pillow and closed my eyes, considering more sleep. Immediately, I slipped into that twilight space between waking and sleep where images float by. Cedric Von Brainiac, based on the drawing Theo had done, giving him a red cape and his initials across his chest, flew by and then came back. He seemed to be looking at me and shaking his head. What was he trying to tell me? On impulse, I got up and found the pages Theo had given me and read them over. Something popped out and I had an aha moment. Was that what the dream was trying to tell me? I had to find a way to check it out.

# THIRTY-TWO

I made my Sunday breakfast and had the print edition of the newspaper, but I couldn't focus on either. I sat at the dining-room table, staring into space, thinking about the upcoming memorial service and reception. I'd already decided to skip the service and was working on how I could look around unnoticed during the reception.

The day was warm and humid with no sun. I dressed in a midi-length black dress and ballet flats which seemed appropriate attire and also good for blending in the background. The memorial service was being held at the Cultural Center downtown, and I waited for the appropriate time to go to the reception.

The Scrivners were just going in the gate as I arrived. Roman held the gate for me and Ruth acknowledged me with a nod. I wondered if she was aware that I knew her secret. Brad was dressed in a suit and standing inside the yard, directing everyone to follow the stone path around the side of the house and go directly into the garden room.

Roman held my arm as if he was guiding me toward the uneven surface, but he leaned close and whispered, 'I hope you enjoyed the flowers and the message.'

He only took a moment longer and then stepped closer to his wife and grabbed her hand. Was it affection or was he trying to keep her sticky fingers occupied?

A crowd was already in the garden room, and there was a din of conversations. I separated from the Scrivners and surveyed the crowd for familiar faces. Serena Lawrence was telling a woman that Landon had always included her as a character in his books. 'So sad that you won't know how he portrayed you in this one,' the woman said.

The Fellowses were talking to another couple. As I drifted by, I heard Gena speaking in a somber tone, explaining that Landon had taught her how to write.

Jerry Malin was standing with his wife. She drained the glass of wine in her hand and pushed the empty on him, gesturing that she wanted a refill. I arrived at the catering table just as he did. I asked for a glass of sparkling water, and he asked for a splash of wine and the rest water. He saw me watching. 'It's what Christine asked for. She's not much of a drinker, but likes to appear sociable,' he said.

Just then I saw that Nicole had come. 'I'm sure she wants one more look at the place,' I said.

'She had a connection to Landon Donte?' Jerry said, and I nodded.

'I think she used to live here,' I said. I saw Nicole weaving her way to the door that led to the kitchen, and I went off to follow her.

The kitchen seemed quiet after the din in the garden room. Nicole went directly into the dining room. I let her get a head start since I had a pretty good idea where she was going. I slipped up the stairs to the second floor and Ona's old bedroom. Nicole was looking into the closet when I got to the doorway.

'This used to be your house,' I said. I didn't go into how I'd figured it out. It wasn't the most complicated detective work. Although I hadn't gotten access to her Facebook page, I saw that she listed herself as Nicole Willman Wentworth. I'd heard someone call Donte's house the Willman house. I'd remembered something else. 'You left abruptly and went to boarding school.'

She seemed shocked that I knew, but also a little relieved. 'It wasn't a boarding school. It was more like a mental hospital. My parents tricked me and told me that I was going to a spa. I left with a week's worth of clothes. The doors were locked, and I stayed there for a year. By then, they'd sold this house and moved to Princeton. They'd discarded most of the stuff from my room and all I had left was a box of what they thought I'd want to keep.' She looked around the room. 'From the moment I moved here with my husband and kids, I wanted to get inside this place. There was something I hoped was still here. When my other attempts failed, I got the idea of the tour, knowing it would give me access.' She shook her head with regret. 'But something always got in the way. Somebody always caught me when I tried to get up here.' She glared at me. 'Like you did now.'

She sucked in her breath. 'This is my last chance.' She pushed away and went into the closet. I followed her as she used the flashlight on her phone to illuminate the space behind the bar to hang clothes. There was a shelf at the back and a small metal door. I thought of Ona and the scratching sounds she'd heard, which is why she'd never ventured to the back of the closet. Nicole's breath caught as she looked inside.

'It's still here,' she said in a whisper. She held something to her lips and kissed it, and then we went back into the room. 'It's all I have left of Aidan.' She showed me a locket that was engraved *Forever Together Through All Time*. Inside there was a picture of a teenage boy. 'He's why I fell apart. He was my everything and he overdosed. My parents didn't even give me a chance to get my things.' Tears had begun to stream down her face.

'So this has nothing to do with Landon Donte?' I said.

'Only that he wouldn't let me get it when I knocked at the door.'

'Why did you drop running the tour?' I asked.

'I told the truth. I have two kids, and I couldn't manage it anymore. I gave up on getting the locket until I heard about the memorial service.' She looked at me. 'Are you going to turn me in?'

'For what?' I said. We walked back to the stairs together and hurried back to the garden room.

'Thank you,' she said, surprising me with a hug.

'You could do something for me.'

She didn't even ask why I wanted to know, but she reconfirmed what I'd thought. More had been done to Landon's workroom than adding the bookcases behind his desk.

Everyone was doing their coming and going through the door that led directly outside, and no one noticed as I went back to the kitchen. I hoped my footsteps weren't too loud as I circled through the dining room, entrance hall, and into the living room. The door to Landon's workroom was open. The carpeting on the floor masked my footsteps, and I stopped in the middle of the room. Nicole had given me exact information about how the room had looked when she lived there. Like other rooms in the house, this room used to have an angled wall, which I could see was now squared off. I looked at the bookcase at the back of the wall and thought of Theo's drawing.

He'd changed the entrance to Cedric's world to a sliding book-case. I'd heard that Landon was paranoid and let it be known that he kept a gun in the drawer for protection. Could he have built in a secret passage to use as a hiding place if someone invaded the house? He certainly wouldn't have shared that information.

I dropped my small purse on the chair as I stepped closer to examine the bookcase and found an almost imperceptible split in the vertical support of the shelves. Theo described Cedric pulling some books out to open the bookcase, and I tried doing the same with Landon's, with no luck. I checked the desk drawers for a button or lever, but there was nothing. I was about to close the drawer when I saw a small back thing that looked like a remote control for a garage door.

I pressed all the buttons and thought it hadn't worked. But that was just because the mechanism was so silent. A small portion of the bookcase slid open, exposing a dark area behind. OK, then, I'd solved the problem of the locked room.

I peeked in the dark opening to see where it led. I was about to back out when I sensed someone behind me. Before I could turn to see who it was, I was shoved forward and the bookcase silently closed.

My gut reaction was to try to push open what had closed behind me, but it wouldn't budge. I looked around the pitch darkness. I waited for my eyes to adjust, but they didn't. There was probably a light somewhere, but after spending a few moments running my hands against the wall, I realized it didn't matter if there was one. I couldn't find it anyway.

When I stretched my arms out, my hands touched the walls, giving me an idea of the size. It felt hot and airless, and I began to hyperventilate, feeling as if I couldn't get enough air.

The reality was that whoever had pushed me intended for me to be stuck in there. No one would come looking because no one beyond Landon and whoever had faked the suicide knew about the secret space. It seemed to be getting hotter, and I wondered how long it would be before the air ran out. Maybe years later someone would decide to remodel, and they'd find my skeleton and wonder how I got there.

I started to worry about Rocky. Who would feed him? What

would Ben think? My mind was a jumble of disconnected panicked thoughts. I needed to calm myself and get rational. Hating to use up the oxygen, I took a couple of deep breaths and my panic subsided, but I knew it was just temporary. OK, it was a secret passage, so it had to go somewhere. There had to be an exit. I regretted having left my purse by the desk. If only I had my phone. I felt something underfoot as I made my way down the wall until I found the end. I felt around the wall. There was a sliver of separation in the wall to make it seem like a door. I tried to push or slide it open, but it did nothing, and I figured there had to be something like the remote to open it. I checked the walls and floor, and there was nothing. 'Open up, you stupid door,' I said. Of course, nothing happened. I was at an impasse, and my main goal became to keep myself calm so I could think straight. There had to be an answer. There was always an answer. I did what I could to center myself and let my mind go free. And then some pieces began to fall together, and I had an idea. To succeed, my plan depended on a number of things I wasn't sure of; on the other hand, I couldn't think of anything else. I took a moment before I went forward. If it didn't work, I knew I'd be devastated.

Who knew that a college class I'd barely gotten through might someday be my savior? I took a deep breath and took my shot, and then I closed my eyes and waited.

The sudden light blinded me for a moment as I saw the way ahead open. I didn't waste any time and rushed through it. I was in the kitchen. When I looked back, the exit had closed and I saw it was connected to a shelving unit with cookbooks and some kitchen supplies. I took a moment to savor my freedom and suck in a lot of air. Then I marched back to the garden room, knowing someone was going to be surprised to see me.

# THIRTY-THREE

'You weren't expecting to see me,' I said, looking over the assembled group. Most of them gave me a blank look in return. Only one showed a reaction. Jerry Malin swallowed hard and started backing away toward the door. But as he tried to go out, he bumped into Detective Jankowski who was on his way in.

'Stop him,' I yelled.

Jankowski's cop training had kept his reflexes hair-trigger sharp, and despite his usual tired appearance, he linked arms with Jerry and brought him back into the room.

Christine Malin's gaze went from her husband to me. 'What's going on? Unhand my husband.'

Detective Jankowski glared at me. 'Ms Blackstone, please explain.'

By now the whole room had gone quiet, and all the attention was on us.

'I saw the manuscript,' I said to Jerry.

'No, you didn't,' he countered. 'I got rid of it.' Then he seemed to realize what he said. 'I mean, I heard it was deleted and the hard copy shredded. Landon was disgusted with his work and wanted it to disappear. That's why he shot himself.'

'Landon wasn't very good with computers, but it turned out he sent a daily email to himself with the manuscript attached,' I said. 'And you didn't have time to shred all the pages; I tripped over the rest of them.'

'What is this all about?' Christine Malin said, looking at her husband.'

'I did it to protect you,' he said. 'The psychologist in his book did things . . .' Jerry looked around at the crowd. 'I did it for all of you. Landon was desperate and barely disguised the characters from the real people they were based on.' His eye had stopped on Roman Scrivner. 'Landon didn't care whom he hurt. He figured that no one would sue him because it would confirm who he had based the characters on. You should look at me as a hero.'

'You went there to give him advice on adding an elevator,' I said. 'Your wife said you were offering advice to people in the neighborhood about adding one. I heard Landon had the help of an engineer when he did the remodel that included the secret passage. That was you, too, wasn't it?'

Jerry Malin sagged and seemed distraught. 'I accidentally hit a key on his computer when I was considering a spot for an elevator. Landon had gotten a phone call, and I snuck a look at his manuscript.'

'Stop talking, Jerry,' Christine Malin commanded.

'Secret passage?' Roman Scrivner said, and others echoed his words. I led the way to Landon's workroom with the crowd following behind.

I pulled open the drawer and used the remote to open the door in the bookcase. 'Someone trapped me in there,' I said, looking back at Jerry. Detective Jankowski had his arm in a death grip. 'When I was stuck inside, I remembered that Ona had said her father used a contractor and engineer with the remodel. Jerry Malin is a structural engineer and had mentioned Landon had considered an elevator like the one the Malins had. When Jerry had shown off his to me, he made a point of explaining that it had voice-activated controls and how he had wanted to make sure it didn't start moving based on idle conversation.' I directed my attention to Detective Jankowski. 'Just like cops do with commands for canine units.'

'That's a little different,' the detective said. 'That's so suspects can't give the dogs commands.' He shrugged. 'But I suppose the intent is the same.'

'I remembered that Jerry had used French. I took French in college.' I didn't bring up my lackluster performance. 'And I knew the word for open was *ouvrir*.'

'I did it for all of you,' Jerry Malin said. 'He trashed you and you and you.' His gaze went from Roman Scrivner to Ruth to Gena Fellows. 'And even you.' He looked at Serena Lawrence.

'Shut up, Jerry,' Christine Malin snapped, just as the detective took out a pair of handcuffs.

\* \* \*

When the mobile command unit showed up again, Detective Jankowski brought Jerry and me inside. They went into a small room at the back to talk, and I was left to watch what went on between them. Jerry, knowing full well his rights, fell apart, and his story poured out. He and Christine had met Landon at one of his local book signings. There had been some socializing after the event. Jerry and Christine had introduced themselves. Landon had been interested in what both of them did, and they got together afterwards. Looking back, Jerry realized that Landon had used both of them. Jerry had put together the design for the secret passage and even did some of the work himself to make sure the exit from his workroom stayed secret. Landon had liked talking to Christine about the motivation of his characters. Jerry hadn't worried until he noticed that, after a few glasses of wine, she started talking about her patients, giving away enough information that Landon recognized who some of them were.

'I confronted him after I saw the bit of his manuscript and said that it was too obvious that he'd made Christine one of his characters. He tried to blow me off and said nobody would know who she was. Maybe not in the larger world, but in the neighborhood, people would figure out it was her. Her reputation would be shot. She'd lose all her patients and worse. I tried to talk to him about it, but he shrugged it off and said he couldn't take her character out because it was the whole basis of his blackmail plot.'

Detective Jankowski said something to the effect that he understood how Jerry felt, wanting to protect his wife. I knew it was a cop trick to try to get Jerry to say more. And it worked.

'I had to make that manuscript disappear,' Jerry said. He let out a breath. 'I'd make it look like Landon killed himself. Everyone knew that he was worried about the manuscript he was working on because his last book hadn't done that well.' Jerry stopped and seemed to be considering whether to continue. He took another breath and then laid out the whole plan.

Brad had said that he was locked in his workroom when we all got there for the progressive dinner. Everyone was milling around, and no one noticed when I went into the kitchen. I used what Landon had looked upon as the exit from the secret passage as an entrance. He was deep in writing something on those yellow pads when I came in. I had him in a chokehold before he even realized I was there. It only took a few moments before he passed out. I got the gun from the drawer and put his hand around it and used his finger to pull the trigger. I typed the note and deleted the manuscript. I ran out of time when I was shredding the pages. I left the rest in the passage, along with my jacket since there was some blood on it.' Jerry slumped back in the chair as if he'd released a huge weight from his chest. 'I came out in the kitchen and joined the others as they went to check on Landon.'

His mouth twisted in anger. 'I tried to keep Veronica Blackstone out of it when I heard she was saying that Landon was left-handed.' His shoulders dropped. 'How did I miss that?'

Watching on the small screen, I understood now that it was Jerry Malin who left the note for me at the Italian restaurant. Another cop who was listening with me made a note about the jacket left in the passage. I chided myself for letting that get past me. Now I remembered that Jerry had been wearing a sport jacket when they arrived and then later only a black dress shirt.

The afternoon was fading into evening when I was finally released from the RV that served as the mobile unit. The news vans were already circling, but I managed to slip out through the alley and avoid them. It was a relief to be outside and doing something normal like walking home. My mind was still spinning from everything that had happened, and it was barely connecting that it was Sunday evening.

Detective Jankowski had gone above and beyond and managed to clear my purse as evidence and given it back to me. As he handed it back to me, he mumbled, 'Good job.'

I was grateful to have my phone and keys. I'd already texted Ben and given him the barest of details of what had happened. He was on his way over to hear the whole story. I needed to let myself decompress and, instead of going directly home, took a walk around the campus. There were just a few people walking dogs. I sat on the bridge over Botany Pond and let everything settle in my mind. It was a lot to take in.

When I finally felt more settled, I walked back home and was relieved when my building came into sight. I had just started up the stone stairs when I heard someone call my name.

'Parker!' I said, surprised as he joined me on the step.

'I didn't have your phone number but remembered where you lived from before. I wanted to apologize. I know you were probably depending on the bonus that Amanda promised you if your letters ended in a proposal.' He stopped and leaned against the building. 'I couldn't do it. She started to cut up my eggs Benedict, and I knew I couldn't propose. It was nice being cared for – to a point. I ended it with her.' He let out his breath. 'I'm sorry and I'd like to make it up to you.'

'You don't have to,' I said. 'The letters didn't work. It happens.'

'It's not your fault. The letters were great, and they did intrigue me about the writer.' He looked at me directly. 'My family was all there for the brunch, so after everything went south, I brought up the idea of having that biography written that I mentioned to you before. They're all onboard.'

I was more than stunned and gave him my card. 'We'll be in touch,' he said and then noticed that I seemed rather frazzled.

I gave him a quick rundown, and his eyebrows shot up in surprise. 'You certainly have an interesting life,' he said before going down to the sidewalk.

I hadn't noticed that Ben's Wrangler pull to the curb. He was out of the car and staring at Parker as he walked away.

'Who's he?' Ben said, giving him a cop stare.

'Parker Andrews,' I said as we went upstairs.

'What's he doing here?' Ben went all alpha male. 'I thought he was the one getting the letters.'

'That didn't exactly work out, but I think he's going to be a client for a long-term project,' I said.

Ben was walking behind me, and I couldn't see his face, but the sound he made in reaction to what I said sounded like a growl.

My landline was ringing before I got the door open. I had been too preoccupied to pay attention to my phone, but now I started to hear the pings. Ben offered to deal with the phone calls, but I said I would do it myself. The media was going crazy, looking for comments. I could understand how it was pretty sensational having the suicide of a famous writer become a murder because of something he'd written. Then throw in a secret passage and the resurfacing of the supposed deleted manuscript.

Ben got us a pizza and seemed uneasy as I dealt with all the calls and texts. 'Now that you're going to be working with that rich guy, I feel like we should really have that talk about where we stand.'

I must have looked a little crazed because a moment later he apologized. 'This probably isn't the time to have that talk. Huh.'

I put up my hands, one of which was holding the cordless handset that had just started to ring again. 'You have that right. It's been quite a day.'

# THIRTY-FOUR

t took a little over a week for things to settle down.

Jerry Malin was charged with first-degree murder with the possibility of more charges based on what he'd done to me. The only upside for him was that he had succeeded in protecting his wife and everyone else Landon had used in the book. Ona kept me in the loop and told me she and the publisher had decided to bury the manuscript. Not only were they worried about lawsuits, but also it wasn't very good. Sad, but true that Landon seemed to have lost his mojo.

Even though she was off the hook, Christine Malin decided to shut down her practice and get a research position where her patients were all rats.

I'm sure Roman Scrivner was relieved by what happened with the manuscript, but he was still concerned that I knew about Ruth. He called me and asked for my continued discretion and told me that he'd hired a shadow for Ruth who would keep her problem in check.

I was glad that Serena never saw what Landon had written about the woman with azure eyes. She realized they were going to have to redo the house tour since the Malins' house was now out, and Gena Fellows had insisted they take their house out as well after the vase incident. Nicole had resumed her position in charge of the tour and was looking for other houses to include.

I made sure to tell Theo it was his character Cedric Von Brainiac who'd given me the idea of the secret passage. Theo loved that he'd been part of the solution.

I hadn't known what to do about Amanda. She finally contacted me and told me what I already knew. She was disappointed, but also relieved. When she really thought about it, she found Parker boring. I didn't tell her that I was going to be working for him. She'd already signed up for a singles retreat and felt hopeful about meeting someone.

And then it was Tuesday and time for the writers' group to

meet. I was glad for something ordinary after all the excitement. I buzzed the security door when the doorbell made its croaking sound and opened my front door to welcome everyone.

Ed and Daryl came up with Tizzy and Theo. I knew Ben was going to be late because he was on dinner duty again. The bell rang again for our newest member, Gena Fellows. She had begged me to join, and I hoped I wasn't going to regret it.

Ben came in just as they were all gathered around my dining-room table, and I was ready to make my announcement. 'I wanted to let you all know that I finished the Derek Streeter book and sent it in.' I let it sit for a moment before I continued, 'I heard from my editor today and they love it.'

They gave me a round of applause. Only Ben held back. I knew he was upset that I hadn't told him about finishing it or sending it off. There were some things I just kept to myself.

We finally got down to reading, and it went surprisingly well. Ben did the charade of leaving and I left the door on the latch. I knew it was going to be more than dinner. That talk he kept bringing up.

I couldn't put it off anymore. And maybe I didn't want to. He was going to have to understand that I was my own person.

Ben arrived with a platter of hummus, pita bread, and salads. He set it on the coffee table with the aluminum foil still over it.

'Talk first, eat later,' he said. I could see that he was as uncomfortable as I was, though he tried to hide it behind his cop face. 'It's been kind of whatever between us,' he said in his police report voice. 'That doesn't exactly work for me. Because . . . because . . .' His cop voice melted. 'Well, because I'm pretty sure I love you.' He let out a sigh of relief, having said it.

'Oh,' I said, a little taken aback by his declaration. Now it was on me to say something. 'It's no problem when I'm writing about feelings for my clients. I can throw the L-word around with ease, but when it comes to this lay-your-feelings-on-the-table, vulnerable stuff for myself, I'm not so good.'

'And . . .' he said, waving his hand as a prompt.

'I'm pretty sure I feel the same,' I said, and he laughed.

'I think that's enough for tonight.' He pulled off the aluminum foil. 'Now, let's eat.'

# ACKNOWLEDGMENTS

I t was a pleasure working on this book with Joanne Grant and everyone at Severn House. Jessica Faust has been with me from the beginning and continues to help me navigate the publishing world.

It is fun writing about Chicago and my old neighborhood. Writing about a place makes me see it with a fresh eye. The Hyde Park Classics group on Facebook had provided lots of interesting information and photographs to remind me of the familiar streets even when I'm thousands of miles away. The Hyde Park Historical Society is a wonderful group that I am glad to be a part of. Penny Fisher Sanborn and Pam Fisher Armanino are my backup for memories. Judy and Barry Kritzberg are a connection to the past and present in our building. I never would have expected to become friends with a real-life Tizzy Baxter, but then I met Abby Bardi.

And I'm most grateful for the support of my family—Burl, Max and Jakey.